THE
SERIAL
KILLERS
CLUB

THE SERIAL KILLERS CLUB

A Novel

JEFF POVEY

WARNER BOOKS

NEW YORK   BOSTON

Warner Books

Time Warner Book Group
1271 Avenue of the Americas, New York, NY 10020
Visit our Web site at www.twbookmark.com.

Printed in the United States of America

First Edition: June 2006
10 9 8 7 6 5 4 3 2 1

Library of Congress Cataloging-in-Publication Data

Povey, Jeff.
    The serial killers club / Jeff Povey. — 1st ed.
      p. cm.
    ISBN-13: 978-0-446-57842-4
    ISBN-10: 0-446-57842-8
    1. Serial murderers—Fiction. 2. Societies and clubs—Fiction.
  3. Serial murderers—Crimes against—Fiction. I. Title.
    PS3616.O874S47   2006
    813'.6—dc22

                                       2005023747

Design by rlf design

For Jules—
you are all I will know
for truth.

On tue un homme, on est un assassin.
On tue des millions d'hommes, on est un conquérant.
On les tue tous, on est un dieu.

Kill a man, and you are an assassin.
Kill millions of men, and you are a conqueror.
Kill everyone and you are a god.

—Jean Rostand 1894–1977
  Pensées d'un biologiste
  (*Thoughts of a biologist,* 1939)

PROLOGUE:
CLUB SERIAL KILLER

I guess it's not every day you end up with a dead serial killer lying at your feet.

There I was, going about my life, when right out of the blue this lunatic is leaping out of the shadows, coming at me with a big knife, and screaming that he was going to cut my heart out. At the time I was working on a dockyard, tossing goods on and off ships, and was packing a lot more muscle than people—and serial killers—realized. I fought like a man possessed, and somehow or other he was the one who wound up with a knife sticking out of him. I guess I don't know my own strength sometimes.

I can't remember every last detail—we are talking four years ago—but after the shock had faded a little, I know I was intrigued enough to want to learn a little more about my would-be killer, and it seemed only natural to go through his wallet. What I found—apart from a few measly dollars—were news clippings detailing his killing career. He obviously liked the attention cutting people's hearts out had granted him, because each clipping was immaculately folded and pressed into a see-through vinyl credit card holder so that if he wanted to, he could open his wallet at any given time and get a little buzz from reading about himself. He also had copies of boastful messages that he had sent to the media and had signed them all

"Yours sincerely, Grandson-of-Barney." I have to admit that this sent a big tingle down my spine. Grandson's exploits had been reported on television—watched by millions, I imagine—and there I was, sharing quality time with the guy.

I figured out I would have been Grandson's sixth victim, and I think it was this realization more than anything else that proved to be an epiphany in my life. Epiphany isn't my word, by the way; I got it from federal agent Kennet Wade, this great guy I hooked up with for a time. I sort of felt privileged. I know that probably sounds crazy, but after a largely anonymous life it gave me a big rush to think I'd attracted the attention of such a notorious serial killer. To be singled out from God knows how many thousands was pretty awesome, and I think this was the true nature of my epiphany. The sheer euphoria of finally being noticed. I could have hugged Grandson there and then.

Not that I did, I hasten to add.

The last thing I found in Grandson's wallet was a clipping from the "Lonely Hearts" section of the local newspaper. It was ringed heavily and read something like "GOB, We know you're out there, so why not come in from the cold and share a pastry with us? Yours, Errol Flynn."

I couldn't believe it.

Why would Errol Flynn of all people want to write to a serial killer, and how could he do that when as far as I knew, he had been dead for close to fifty years?

I have to admit, I was intrigued. I mean, who wouldn't be? Errol Flynn is one of the finest actors ever, and here he was posting messages to me. Not that he knew it was me, but in my book it was close enough.

I truly didn't want to be investigated by the police for the killing of Grandson. Chances are, with the way my luck pans out sometimes, I would've been accused of murder and hanged on the spot. So after locking Grandson's body in a trunk and stowing it aboard a

South Africa-bound ship along with various other trunks belonging to a theatrical troupe, I sat back and monitored the papers for another message from Errol. But two weeks passed and there was nothing forthcoming. I couldn't believe it; why didn't Errol post another message? It started to get me down. I was so close to establishing what I felt would be a lasting friendship with the great man, and all of a sudden he clams up. But just as I was debating whether or not to send an angry letter to his fan club, it hit me—maybe Grandson hadn't replied to the first message, and maybe, just maybe, Errol was still waiting to hear from him! I raced to the nearest library, grabbed all the backdated evening editions I could find, and scoured the personals column to see if Grandson-of-Barney had responded. There was nothing. My heart started pounding—I still remember that very clearly—and before I could help myself I'd posted a reply on GOB's behalf: "Errol, I'd love a Danish, Barney's Boy's Boy."

I spent the next ten days going out of my mind waiting for a response, when all of a sudden there it was in timeless black and white. "BBB, Do you like Chicago? Take a flight if you want to know more. Warmest Regards, Errol."

Chicago? That was at least two thousand miles away, maybe more. I was devastated. What sort of person travels two thousand miles in the hope of making a new friend?

No one's that lonely.

No one.

I can still remember the gorgeous woman I sat beside on the Chicago-bound flight; she must've been a film actress, although despite my repeated questioning she never actually came out and admitted to it. She was beautiful, though, easily the most stunning woman I had ever set eyes upon, and as I sat there telling her my life story, I knew that my luck had changed. Being in the presence of a creature this compelling was like a message from the Great Above; she was an angel guiding me along my path, and to this day

I sincerely regret taking down her phone number wrong. The one she gave me turned out to be a fish factory on the outskirts of the city, and I guess in all the excitement I didn't hear her right.

So there I was, all of four years ago, setting foot in the Windy City for the first time, not knowing where my life was going but knowing instinctively that something good was about to happen.

There was a message waiting in the personal ads as soon as I touched down: "GOB, The Club awaits you. Bring plenty beer money. As Ever, Errol F."

I quickly posted another ad, just something like "I'm here, now what?" The reply I got threw me because this was from none other than Tony Curtis: "Gobby, Let's meet, let's eat. Tony Curtis." I hadn't been expecting someone else to be involved—let alone another movie star—and then remembered that there was mention of some club and couldn't imagine what sort of club would let me—in the guise of a world-famous serial killer—join up. Then it dawned on me—this was some sort of police operation; they were trying to entice Grandson out into the open with promises of pastries and Hollywood celebrities, just waiting to pounce the moment he showed. I felt pretty pissed off, I can tell you. Two thousand miles for this?

But the more I thought about it, the more it seemed pretty crazy to lure Grandson all the way to Chicago, where, according to his news clippings, he hadn't actually killed anyone and would therefore possibly be outside the Chicago Police Department's jurisdiction. So maybe that wasn't it after all.

I still couldn't figure it, though. Why invite a killer to a club? I'd heard about women writing to, and then eventually marrying, serial killers while they sit out their days on death row, and I wondered if maybe some sort of fan club had sprung up to honor Grandson-of-Barney. Now wouldn't that be something? I admit the idea excited me, and I kind of got carried away with it, thinking it might be fun to pose as this killer and maybe even find a future wife into the bargain. When you spend a lot of time on your own, you tend to find yourself grabbing at things without really thinking them through. And I guess I was up there grabbing with the best of them.

I posted another ad, Tony replied, and a coded small ads dialogue started up over the next month or so. I was still wary, though, trying to ask as many veiled questions as I could, and eventually discovered that there were not two but eighteen members of the Club, both male and female, which boosted me no end, and that they were very, very keen to meet me.

While this was happening, I managed to find myself some work at the city zoo of all places, cleaning out the cages and generally making the life of the imprisoned jungle cat that little bit more comfortable. This turned out to be the job I was born to do and would find hard to replace should I ever get fired—or mauled.

I also rented a small furnished apartment—a place where the landlord had taken it upon himself to bolt every piece of furniture to the floor—and started to settle into the Chicago way of life, which is pretty similar to any other type of life, only wetter.

The final ad the Club posted listed the name and address of a bar and grill that I should attend on the following Monday evening— Grillers Steak House. Everyone would be there, and I was guaranteed a fun night out or else Tony Curtis would personally pay any expenses I incurred. I like a money-back guarantee as much as the next person, and that helped swing it for me. Also, their presuming me to be a serial killer would make me a pretty formidable force if things weren't entirely to my satisfaction.

Obviously I hadn't the faintest idea as to what I was letting myself in for, but I had come this far and there was no turning back. Besides, if the Club didn't meet with my expectations, then I'd never go back. Plain and simple.

I rented a suit for the occasion—a cotton three-piece, yellowy beige—which I rounded off with a red shirt and a dark blue tie. The guy at the rental company even complimented me on my stylish arrangement.

When the taxi dropped me off it was raining heavily, and even in the short walk to the bar and grill entrance the yellowy beige turned brown, so that by the time I got inside I knew I had a color clash on my hands.

Grillers was one of those all-wooden affairs—mahogany benches running along under windows, teak paneling covering every square centimeter of wall, a worn and unpolished floor, maybe room enough for eighty diners, a large bar in the middle of the restaurant, again made from wood—it was like they'd used half the rain forest to build the place. Framed prints of English castles were nailed to the walls, the lighting was low, a little country and western music drifted from a jukebox over the heads of the few diners who were in that night.

As I stood in the doorway, peering into this wooden maw and clutching a soggy copy of the evening edition—my identifying sign— a shout went up, a big bearlike voice grabbed my attention, and as I turned to a far corner of Grillers I saw them for the first time, all eighteen of them, sitting there like an office party spilling out of control. All their faces were turned toward me, and I suddenly realized that this was it, the moment of truth. I had taken the precaution of memorizing everything I could from Grandson's clippings and hoped I'd be confident enough to pass myself off as him. I was lucky that there had been a television documentary on him (no pictures of Grandson, thank God, apart from a blurred closed-circuit TV image that could just as easily have been a Sasquatch wearing dungarees) two weeks earlier, and this television psychiatrist had given a quite brilliant profile of him—"a rodent-loving vegetarian who works irregular hours."

The owner of the bearlike voice stood up, waved a thick slab of hand, and clicked his fingers loudly, his large body rippling underneath his tight white short-sleeved shirt. "Over here. We saved you a place."

I looked down at my hand, the hand that was holding the

evening edition, and saw that I was trembling. I quickly dumped the paper onto the nearest vacant table and shoved my hands deep inside my trouser pockets. I didn't want anyone seeing that I was nervous. After taking an almighty breath, I straightened my back, stood as tall as I could, and walked toward the Club members. In my head I went over and over all the stuff I had learned about Grandson. Hates lowlifes, likes vegetables . . .

"Nice suit." I still remember someone saying that as I passed, nodding and smiling to the faces that looked up at me. I think it must have been Chuck Norris, but I couldn't say for sure.

The big guy who waved me over offered his hand to shake as he belched into my face. "I'm Tony." I offered my trembling hand and watched it disappear inside his huge fist, and as I stood there, my arm being pumped furiously, all I could think was that Tony Curtis had ballooned to enormous proportions and lost all his looks into the bargain. I could feel everyone staring at me, weighing me up, and again I tried to stand as straight and as tall as I could.

"I'm, uh–"

"Uh-uh–no names. Not real ones."

"Oh. . . ."

Tony waved his huge arm at the others sitting there. "You ain't gonna remember none of this, but from the left that's Cher, Burt Lancaster, Roger Moore, Rock Hudson, Richard Burton, Tallulah Bankhead, Chuck Norris, James Mason, Jerry Lewis, Dean Martin, Raquel Welch, Errol Flynn, William Holden, Carole Lombard, Humphrey Bogart, Stan Laurel, and Laurence Olivier. Hoo boy, didn't think I'd remember all that."

Some said hi, some just nodded; all looked pleased to see me, though. I could sense the anticipation hanging in the air. And I remember scanning the excited faces and being just a tad dismayed that the female element of the group was by and large not the kind of woman I had seen myself settling down and having children with.

"Hi. . . ." I nodded to the Club, smiling. "Glad to have made it."

Tony slapped me hard on the back. "Welcome to the Club, Gob."

"That short for Goblin?"

A woman said this, but I couldn't see which one, and a few people laughed, which made me relax a little. It already looked like being the fun night Tony had promised.

A big, powerful-looking black guy—Tony called him Stan Laurel—pushed out a seat, and it dragged along the wooden floor. Stan winked at me. "Come and sit here, little guy. You want me to get you a cushion so you can reach the table?"

Laughter erupted again, and I found myself laughing along with them. I remember theatrically slapping my thigh as I took a seat beside the hilarious Stan.

"You wanna high chair instead?"

Tony banged the table, brought things to order.

"I'm gonna let you know a few things about us first, Gob, but after that the stage is all yours." Tony sat down, swiping a lump of bread from a plate belonging to the woman he called Cher.

Despite the huge grin spreading inside me, I tried my best to look earnest and attentive as Tony spoke.

"For the uninitiated—which is you, Gob—this little Club of ours has been going some three years now. And we've got Rock and Roger to thank for that."

Tony glanced over to Rock and Roger, two handsome blond men clad in black turtlenecks. I wondered if they were twins as a small ripple of applause ran the length of the table. I was starting to relax, enjoying the overriding feeling of goodwill emanating from everyone present. I even found myself clapping along with them.

"Thanks," said Roger.

"Thank you," said Rock.

Roger and Rock took the applause like old pros, and I immediately sensed that I was going to like these guys a lot.

"If they hadn't broken into some student's pad—without realizing they had both selected the exact same victim on the exact same night—then all of this might never have happened."

I remember the word *victim* banging like the Liberty Bell against my forehead, and my whole head seemed to arc back, recoiling from the blow. I sat there, hoping that someone was going to correct Tony and make him say the word he really meant to say.

No one said a thing.

"Anyways, as they both stood there, rooted to the spot, the dumb-ass student woke up, raised the alarm, and the next thing Rock and Roger are escaping together. Rock's rental car had a flat, and Roger tells him to jump in his sedan and they drive clean across the state line."

My eyes bulged wider and wider.

"They walked into where we are seated now—this very same bar and grill. . . ." Tony again waved his thick arm as if he were showing a group of tourists around famous Hollywood landmarks. "Even the name—Grillers—was telling them something in a rhyming couplet sorta way."

I couldn't shake the roar building inside my head. It didn't come out as words, but if it had done, then it would have told me: "Get out of here! Now! Get the hell out, you stupid—"

"And they went to one of those two-man booths over there, ordered a meal and a couple of beers."

"Buds." Roger nodded at me, making sure I got every detail.

"I had the chicken, Roger had the fish," Rock added.

I was sure I was going puke.

"So they got talking and decided that they should maybe tell each other the next time they selected a victim—just in case they overlapped again."

My rented suit felt like it was tightening around me by the second, squeezing the life out of me.

"They talked a lot about why they did what they did, who they really blamed for being turned from ordinary decent people into vicious serial killers."

My cheeks puffed out at the words *serial killers,* and I had to force myself to swallow a surging torrent of bile. I looked around to see if there was anyone in the restaurant who could help me. Apart from a couple of large ladies and an elderly man seated with his grandson, there was no one. The wooden walls were closing in on me, and I felt like I was in a giant coffin and I couldn't catch my breath.

"Now this is where the real fun started, because"—Tony laughed at this, shook his head—"I still get a kick out of this—on that exact same night I happened to be sitting in the booth directly behind R and R. I had just finished my shift—and dammit if I didn't lean over the top of the divider and let them know we sure had a heckuva lot in common." Tony kept shaking his head, dabbing beads of sweat from his top lip as he did. He looked me right in the eye, and all I could do was let out a faint whimper. "Pretty soon after that, we started making it a weekly thing. And after a while we decided that we should set up a club. Just a place for serial killers to come and go, to reveal their stories, and to get off on knowing like-minded psychopaths. Hey, it's like all minority groups—there really is nowhere to meet these days."

The room spun around me like a fairground ride on full power. I couldn't see anything but this evil blur of serial killers. I gripped the edge of the table hard until my fingers ached.

"We made contact with as many killers as we could. Being a cop sure came in handy there, I can tell you. And all told we didn't make too bad a job of it."

"You did great, Tony."

"Better than great."

"I tell you—this is the best goddamn club I've ever been a member of."

Killers were looking at me, vouching their agreement with

eager, nodding heads. I looked at the members—my eyes running over each one in turn—and all I could think was, This is a joke, right? It's a setup. There's a hidden camera somewhere. Christ almighty, tell me it's a joke!

"Anyway, that's enough about us, Gobby." Tony sat down, swiped some grilled chicken from someone else's plate. "Now let's hear about you."

"Yeah—give us your story."

"Never heard a goblin talk." I could hear the voices but didn't know who they were coming from.

"You cut out hearts, right?"

"As in lonely hearts."

"Then bake them."

"How many you done?"

"He's small time—five at most."

"He's certainly small."

Tony snapped his fingers loudly, and gradually the voices faded. He then turned and looked directly at me. I whimpered again.

"We'll need a name first."

My jaw was clamped so tight, I really didn't think I could speak.

"C'mon, Gob, spit one out."

I had no idea who was speaking, but I knew I had to say something, anything.

All I can remember now was mumbling something about this actor I'd always admired. This dashing, handsome mirror image to myself.

"Douglas."

"Huh?"

"Douglas who?"

"Kirk Douglas? Michael Douglas?"

"Fairbanks. Junior. Douglas Fairbanks Jr." How I got those words out I'll never know, but it seemed to satisfy them.

Tony clapped his hands loudly. "Okay then, Dougie ... let's hear your story."

I don't know how I did it, but I somehow regurgitated stuff from the documentary on Grandson-of-Barney. I told them I usually went after lonely, loveless deadbeats, and one of them—Chuck, I think— asked if I'd ever considered suicide. I still don't know what he meant by that, but he sure got a big laugh for it.

I embellished about cutting out hearts and using them to make personalized Valentine's Day cards, got a little carried away, and somehow made the outrageous claim that a major greeting card company was interested in buying the copyright. I found that once I started talking I couldn't stop. They asked me why I did what I did, and I said it was all down to my mother. She had starved me of love from an early age. This was only half-true. My father had also starved me of any emotion other than contempt and anger. So there I was, repaying the compliment by starving other people of love—in the shape of removing their hearts.

God alone knows how I got through the evening.

And now here I am, four years later. And still a day rarely passes without my reliving that horrifying night. Four long and hard years that have seen me rise to the prominent position of Club secretary.

Just last month I managed to get a response from an ad I posted in the *Tribune*. There's a new killer out there, and we're hoping to get her to join up. The membership has been dropping off alarmingly since that fateful night—in fact, excluding myself, out of the original eighteen and the few others who joined in the interim, there are now only ten members left, and there's been a big drive on recently to try to arrest the decline. Tony is really cut up about the fall in numbers, and being chairman, he has taken it more personally than most.

I have tried to tell him that people just get bored and move on, but he won't listen to me.

"Something's not right, Dougie . . . something stinks. All these members who left. Why d'you think they went? It's a fucking great club, and those freaks leave without so much as a good-bye?"

I give Tony the same shrug I've been giving for the past few years now. "Hell if I know."

It's not the best answer.

Truth is, it's not even an honest one.

I really love the Club. *Really* love it, I mean. Okay, it wouldn't be everyone's first choice, but to me it's the only ticket in town. Trouble is, over these past four years some members worked out that maybe I wasn't who I said I was—obviously me not being a real serial killer means that Grandson-of-Barney hasn't killed anyone new since I joined the Club. I mainly told the Club that I was going through a killer's block, which is sort of like writer's block minus the typewriter. But despite what I thought was a perfectly acceptable explanation, a few of them still got a little antsy about me. Some challenged me in private, others made it pretty uncomfortable for me at Club nights. And I hate to admit this, but I had no choice but to shut them up before they outed me as a nonkiller. Eleven times in four years I've had to do this. I'm not proud of myself—not one bit—but like I say, I absolutely love the Club, and I'll do anything to keep my membership going. To be honest, I doubt there's a better night to be had anywhere in the world.

DOUBLE DECAP

"Y OU KNOW ME—I'm a family man. Very much a family man. Give me a family to behead and I'm as happy as the next guy."

Burt Lancaster gets a lot of laughs for this. He looks confident, and I know he's probably spent hours in the mirror rehearsing this routine. I have to admit, his timing is perfect, his delivery excellent, and he's playing us like a comedian would play an audience. It's going to be another in a long line of fun Club nights.

"I broke into this house and realized immediately that the husband was a DIY nut. There was barely a thing he hadn't built himself. Even the stove had that 'Made by a Moron' look."

Burt is in top form.

William Holden is sitting to my right. He offers me a cigarette, and I accept, lighting it with my silver-plated lighter. I smoke only at meetings, and this is because I have found, much to my amazement, that all serial killers—or skillers, as they like to call themselves—smoke. Don't ask me why, they just do.

"So I'm thinking, What would be a good way to behead a DIY nut?"

Burt is drawing us in, teasing us. Chuck Norris calls out: "Get him to build you a guillotine!"

Everyone laughs at this. We all love Chuck, and if given the chance to be anyone for a day, I think we'd all choose Chuck Norris.

Burt lets the joke settle, nods approvingly, and then draws us in, making us hang on his every word.

"I decide to fetch his Black and Decker Workmate from the garage. But then I catch sight of something hanging above it on the wall. It's this really well-looked-after saw . . . a real polished beauty—and I just know I have to use this . . . well, this really great tool, this truly cool tool."

I glance at William Holden, who is sitting to my left, and whisper quietly, "Writing any more novels?"

William frowns, looks down his nose at me. "I don't write novels. They're factually based works." I know this, but I just want to tease William a little. He's given the same answer a million times over to the exact same question, but it's fun and we enjoy the buddy-buddy repartee of it. Sometimes I ask him twice if I get drunk later on.

"I bought your other two novels. They're a terrific read."

Someone shushes me, I think it's Cher, and I hold up my hand, gesture an apology, and go back to listening to Burt's star turn.

"So there I am, his prize saw in one hand and his prize head in the other. I'm staring at his white-as-a-sheet wife, and all I can think to say is: 'Try going to department stores. You'll find everything you need there.' "

The Club erupts, and Burt laughs with them.

William wipes tears of laughter from his eyes, and as Burt takes a seat to a well-deserved round of applause, William edges closer to me. His voice is never more than a throaty whisper, and I have to listen hard to take in what he is saying.

"As it happens, I've got this great idea for a novel," he whispers, getting into his stride.

"Wow." I pretend to be impressed. "What's it about?"

"It's semiautobiographical. About my childhood. Well . . . it's really about my mother."

"You have a title yet?" I already can guess the title. *My Bastard Mommy.* In huge bloodred letters. They always blame their moms—*always*.

"Got a few ideas, but nothing firm. Though I want to keep it nice and simple. Something like *Where Was the Love, Bitch?*"

"Great title."

"You think?"

"If I saw that in a bookstore, I'd snap it right up."

William smiles and exhales smoke, and I see James Mason breathe in the plume and then immediately reach for his extra-nicotine nonfilter cigarettes.

William is very keen to tell me a story I've already heard a hundred times before. I half wish I'd sat somewhere else, but it's all part of the great vibe, and I let William's words wash over me like a cup of warm milk.

"It started on bath nights. I was about eight. Mom was pretty spiritual and saw the bath as a mini river Jordan. Held me under every night till I was purified. I spent my entire childhood waterlogged."

The talk of water sends me hurrying to the washroom in less than five minutes.

I find I am still giggling at Burt's hilarious story when I notice a guy looking at me as if he can't figure out what is so funny about urination. He's tall, handsome, immaculately turned out, and pretty much all-American. I try to explain.

"Just heard the funniest story ever."

The all-American nods vaguely, though his piercing eyes tend to look deep into me for a second, as if looking for something, like a computer doing a search on its hard drive. I feel a little uneasy, quickly break his look, and pretend to giggle again.

"I've got stomach cramps from laughing so much."

The all-American leaves, but on the way past me he does the weirdest thing. He puts a hand on my shoulder and squeezes it.

"Nice to meet you," is all he whispers. Then he is gone, leaving me feeling invaded. Men just don't do that to other men—touch them while they're taking a leak, I mean. That is breaking a taboo that has held since the dawn of civilization. I'm sure even cavemen knew not to touch each other during a piss.

I zip up but can't shake the imprint of the all-American's touch on my shoulder. It's almost as if he's still squeezing it.

Tony Curtis bursts in, belching and laughing to himself at the same time. "That Burt . . . man, can he tell a story. Never knew decapitation could sound so funny."

I try to get back on track. "I agree totally. It was, uh . . . it was incredible."

"He could bring on appendicitis, he's so funny. . . ."

Tony proceeds to have the longest, hardest piss in history, and while he does he glances over to me. "That Burt's an A-OK guy."

I look at Tony, and for a moment I feel like we're the oldest of buddies, and I smile. "Absolutely. Double A-OK. He should get his own TV show." I laugh as I fill the sink. I make a point of scrubbing my hands thoroughly, because Tony has killed people on account of their lack of cleanliness and good manners. Cleverly ignoring the fact that he can't talk without belching in your face.

"The Decap Show," Tony belches out, then leaves. Without washing his hands.

It's been another amazing night at the Club, and when I get home I am too wired to sleep. They really are a great bunch of guys. But more to the point, they accept me—and that is worth more than my weight in gold. I spent way too long waiting to join the human race, and I'm damn well going to make up for lost time. In fact, things are going so well for me that I'm considering running for Club president next year.

SUDDENLY

I THINK I'M BEING followed by the all-American who squeezed my shoulder in the washroom.

I have been seeing him for about four days now. Everywhere I go, he seems to go. He's not making himself discreet, either. He knows I know he's there, and this bothers me. A lot.

I've been playing it cool, just going about my mindless cage cleaning as if all I really am is a guy who has dedicated his life to wiping up after animals. I've been getting up, going to work, coming home, and making myself appear as normal as normal gets.

The all-American has been with me every step of the way, and for the life of me I can't figure it out. Who knows, maybe this is my first stalker.

I peek out between the slats in the blinds and see the guy sitting in his dark blue sedan. It is late, and I am impressed that he can sit there for so long. I stare out at him and feel a slight chill creeping up the back of my neck. This can't be good.

I snap the blinds shut and debate starting work on a tunnel. I wonder if I could dig down far enough to break into the sewage system and lose the guy that way. I could surface in another town and take it from there—I've re-created myself once, I can do it again. I walk into the bathroom and dearly wish I knew how houses were built. If I ripped up the lavatory, would there be a hole big enough for me to crawl through? Would I, in fact, want to do that? There must be all kinds of human waste down there, and I have as much dignity as the next person.

I walk into the kitchen, where there are loose floor tiles, and I remove some of them—only to be faced with a solid concrete base. I test it with my foot and realize it is probably too thick to break through. Not without the aid of a pneumatic drill, that is.

Last thing I want to do is leave the Club, but maybe if I lie low for a couple of months, I could return later—minus stalker.

I hear a rap on the back door. I look up, startled. I can see through the screen door that it's the guy who's been following me. He looks taller close up and extremely handsome. Not Chuck Norris handsome, more of a wholesome look, not unlike myself. He knows I'm in, and any debate about hiding in my bedroom and pretending I'm not there really isn't worth having. I stand there for what seems like ages. He raps on the door again. I give out a meek, "Hello?" and hate the fact that I sound nervous.

"Federal agent Kennet Wade. That's Kenneth without the 'h.' Have you got a moment?" His voice is deep and solid.

"No. Sorry. I haven't." What else am I meant to say?

"I'm with the FBI." He says this as if it's a key to opening any door he wants.

"The who?" I'm buying time, frozen there in the middle of my kitchen, ripped-up floor tiles scattered all around me.

"The Federal Bureau of Investigation."

"Oh . . . the FBI. . . ."

"That's correct. Can I come in?"

"Are you going to shoot me?" I don't know why I say this, it just comes out. Probably because I fully expect him to do so, especially when I'm seriously considering making a run for it.

My question throws him.

"Shoot you?"

"I meant to say, uh . . . arrest me. . . . Are you going to arrest me? That's what I meant to say." Christ, I'm nervous, babbling like a brook.

"Could you just let me in, please?" The word *please* surprises me. It also softens me. I hadn't expected politeness. I know it's a mistake, but I start to quite like Agent Kennet Wade.

"I'll have to see some identification before I do anything like that."

"I can only show you if you open the door."

I'm not going to fall for that one. No way. But five huge and silent seconds pass, and I crack. I open the door a tiny bit and peer out. Agent Wade leans forward, then holds up his ID. It's a nice picture, and it does him justice. I go from his photo to the real thing, and our eyes meet. His are a penetrating blue, whereas mine are a deep velvet brown. Another difference is I can't seem to get mine to blink. They just stare out, bulging, expanding, revealing every ounce of my fear and guilt.

"Can it wait till morning? I'm really tired right now."

Agent Wade gives a solemn shake of the head. This guy is very commanding and not the sort of person I find it easy to say no to.

After several more huge and stifling seconds, I open the door, step aside, and let Agent Wade in. He's wearing a very heady aftershave, and I wonder if it's anything I could afford.

I close the kitchen door behind him. I wait, gathering my confidence, and then turn to face him. He is looking at the scattered floor tiles.

"I've got mice." Agent Wade nods but doesn't really seem to care that much.

The room falls silent. I'm not sure what I'm meant to say, and Agent Wade also looks like he is having trouble finding his voice.

"So . . . what's this all about?" I try desperately to sound calm and dignified.

Agent Wade starts to say something and then stops. He smiles, more to himself than me, and then he tries again.

"This is a little hard to get across. . . ."

I study Agent Wade, and he is making me curious. I can't get a handle on him.

"How do I put this? I uh . . . well . . . I know what you do." He looks me straight in the eye when he says this. "I know what you do." He repeats it, in case I didn't get the gist of what he's saying.

"You mean cleaning out cages?"

"No. I don't mean that."

I knew he didn't, but I can't say anything now that will implicate me, especially when I notice that a calmer and more penetrating look has returned to Agent Wade's face.

"Sorry, but that's all I do. Clean out cages."

"No. That's not all that you do. Mind if I smoke?"

Agent Wade is already tapping out a filterless cigarette for himself, and all I can do is offer a mild shrug. "Sure . . . go right ahead. . . ."

Agent Wade lights his cigarette with a silver-plated lighter that isn't unlike the one I own. He exhales upward and studies me for a long moment. "I have a still from a security camera."

He fishes in his pocket, unbends the photograph, and hands it to me. And there I am, in grainy gray and white, three years younger and ramming a knife into Errol Flynn's groin. I'm standing in a darkened basement, and although it is hard to make out exactly who is doing what to whom, I know the FBI have some incredible technology at their disposal, and even if it doesn't look exactly like me, they have ways and means of altering the picture so that it does.

Errol worked as a security guard in a tenement block. He had killed nine fat guys by stabbing them repeatedly in the groin, but only after he had shaved their bodies and fastened a bra around their flabby chests. His mother had terrified him all his life, ritually beating him and locking him in their cellar for days on end. It was only when he got to fifteen that he realized his mother was really his father in drag. I for one absolutely understand why he decided to go out and start butchering guys who could pass for women. To his credit, he never made the mistake of killing a woman who looked like a man, and I, for one, salute that sort of clarity.

"It's taken three years to find you." Agent Wade looks at me, expressionless. "I've been on the case from day one. Been all over the country, covered practically every square inch of it."

I try to give Agent Wade a steely, no-nonsense look. "I never saw that photo before in my entire life." This is delivered with more than a nod toward defensive outrage—and I imagine for a moment that I'm in court. I think I'm on to a good case for the defense and decide to run with it. "Never, I tell you. Never."

" 'Course you haven't. It wasn't released. Not publicly."

I feel a swell of inner triumph, smell the sweet scent of victory. "Well, there you go, then. There's no way I could have seen that photo."

Agent Wade stands his ground, cool and determined. "Pardon me, but it's not the actual photo itself that brought me here. This is more about the content of the still. Of what it represents."

I pause as a huge hole in my defense starts to open up before my eyes. I decide the only way out of this is to ride roughshod over everything Agent Wade is saying.

"As far as I'm concerned, all that matters is whether or not I have seen that photo, and I state, hereby and categorically, that no, I have not seen this photo. Now good day to you."

Agent Wade looks at me with a faint expression of amusement. Or at least it looks like amusement. He remains where he is, not about to move, and we both know he is not going anywhere tonight. His voice remains even and rich and solid, and it is starting to grate on me.

"We've had over forty agents looking for you. I guess I lucked out. It's because I had a head start. I'd compiled my own profile on you."

Profile? On me?

"I clean out cages." I don't know why I keep repeating this. It's hardly something to boast about.

"I know that—but you clean other things as well."

Agent Wade says this in such a way as to add a secret knowing, an almost sexy undertone, trying to entice an admission from me.

The kitchen falls silent as I try hard to think of other things I clean. I look at the sink, and although it sparkles I don't truly believe I could get away with telling Agent Wade I also scrub my sink religiously, if that's what he's alluding to. I then think of offering a guided tour around my home, pointing out my fastidiously spotless world to him. These thoughts seem to careen around my head, and I can't make any sense of them. I then realize that I am having a panic attack and it is giving me a migraine.

"Would you like an Alka-Seltzer? I'm going to have one."

Agent Wade gives a small assured movie-star shake of the head.

"No one knows I've found you." These words, which should be a huge relief to me, fill me with dread. "I've spent six days agonizing over this. I wanted to call in, to tell the boys I'd got you . . ."

But he didn't. Even after six days. He didn't call for backup, and now I'm feeling very, very scared. My mouth has gone completely dry.

"When we realized what you were doing, there was a real big brouhaha. . . ."

A what? What's that? I want to ask, but I seem to have developed lockjaw.

"Most of us, despite our training, couldn't help but revert to our natural instinct for justice. We argued long and hard that you should be allowed to carry on. That you were doing the right thing for both president and country. . . . But of course we came slap bang up against the moral majority, and I for one couldn't sit in the same room as them. They tried to tell us you were evil and that you had to be stopped. At that I just got up and walked out of the building. Some of the guys came with me. We hung around in the car park, trying to cool off. We just couldn't believe an institution as great and as powerful and as well-meaning as the FBI would want you arrested and dumped on death row."

The thudding in my head is quickly outpaced by the thudding in my heart.

"Anyway, my superior came and found us. He was as cut up as we were. He was sorry, but the official line was we were going all-out to catch you. But not in an overt or public way; after all, *they didn't want copycats springing up.*" He says this with a real hateful sarcasm. "Can you believe that? They didn't want the public fighting back. I nearly handed in my badge right there and then."

And I stand there thinking, Why didn't you, you bastard? Why didn't you?

"My superior had a plan, though. He reasoned that we could at least let you squeeze in a few more kills before you were caught, and he tied red tape all over the show, buying you as much time as possible. He felt it was the least he could do."

I walk to the sink, pick up a tumbler, fill it with cold water, and then mix in an Alka-Seltzer, watching it fizz. I take a long sip before it is even a quarter dissolved.

"How long did you think it would take to finish your crusade?"

Agent Wade's words, aimed at the back of my head, somehow manage to dodge round it and hang in the air before my eyes. I pause. Crusade? What crusade?

"How long did you figure?" Agent Wade asks this gently, prodding a response from me.

"I don't understand."

Agent Wade mistakes this for modesty on my part, smiles gently. "Sure you do."

"'Fraid you've lost me."

"C'mon—it's obvious what you've been doing. Killing serial killers."

I hesitate. "I have?"

He smiles again, showing his even white teeth. "Have you ever."

In a way, I guess he's right. But it was never a crusade, more just a way of staying in the Club.

"I can give you two months."

"For what?"

"To finish your crusade."

I pause. My lips feel like they are stuck to the tumbler; I am neither drinking nor not drinking. Eventually I turn round to face Agent Wade. "You mean kill the other members?"

He smiles again. His teeth are dazzling. "You catch on quick."

"But they're my friends."

Agent Wade's smile evolves into a quick-fire laugh. "You are one funny guy."

"I'm not kidding. The Club is my life."

Agent Wade straightens, looms over me, searching my face, wondering if I'm joshing or telling the truth. "People don't tend to kill their friends."

"I had to in order to keep the other friends."

"That doesn't make sense."

"I admit it doesn't sound like it does, but in fact, from where I'm standing, it makes a lot of sense. Besides, they would've killed me if I'd let them."

Agent Wade suddenly looks tired—bored even—of the conversation. "Listen, I don't really care about your logic. You've got two months to off the rest of them."

"And what if I refuse?"

"You fry."

The words are blunt, delivered like a mallet to the head.

"But there are, uh . . . there are nine other members. I can't just start slaughtering them. They might finally figure out what I've been doing all these years. Things could turn nasty. One slip and I'm a dead man."

"They haven't rumbled you so far."

I try to fight the growing desperation in my voice. "Listen, you've got the wrong guy. I'm not a killer."

"Even though you kill people."

"It may seem like that, but no, sir, a killer is the last thing I am."

Agent Wade offers no riposte, just stands there imposingly still. I try another plea.

"Wouldn't it be easier if you just came with me to the Club one night and arrested them?" It breaks my heart to say this. I'd do anything to save the Club.

Agent Wade pauses to think this over; he glances up to the ceiling and sees I have cobwebs up there. Maybe I'm not as clean as I think.

"The thing we like—or at least the thing I like—about what

you do is the fact that the killers die anonymously. No books get written, no TV movies get made, no big news reports get splashed all over the country, there's no trial, there's no nothing. Apart from their anonymous little deaths. I see it as being kind of ironic, if I can use that word. No one ever cares about the victims, they only ever care about the killer. This way you make sure no one cares about anyone. They die, their killing sprees stop, and no one's the wiser."

I can see Agent Wade has put a lot of thought into this. He has presented his case logically and with a controlled amount of passion. He hasn't come at it like a slavering vengeance seeker; instead he is approaching it like a good and honest man with a good and honest ideal.

"There aren't going to be any arrests." This sentence drips with complete authority.

I think about asking for time to mull his offer over, but in truth I know I have no other option. He has the power to send a thousand volts through me.

I start nodding my head, slowly, as if I'm weighing the options, making up my mind, acting like I have a choice. "I'll definitely get the chair if I don't cooperate?"

"I'll pull the switch myself."

I stop nodding and in a clever show of consternation chew my lip instead. I realize I have little or no choice and thrust out my hand—as if to shake. "Two months. No problem."

Agent Wade is surprised to see my hand thrust out like this, and he shakes it instinctively. I know he feels uncomfortable with this, his grip weakening as soon as his fingers touch my hand. But I carry on pumping his hand and even start beaming at him.

"I've always admired the FBI."

THE NON-PLAN PLAN

THERE'S A CLUB meeting tonight, and I hurried home early from the zoo, showered and shaved, ate a quick TV dinner, and put on a hooded sweatshirt and jeans. But when I opened the front door to leave, I was shocked to find Agent Wade standing there waiting for me. He looked me up and down and then tutted loudly. "You can't go to the Club dressed like that."

Rather than get into an argument—I was running late anyway—I did as he requested.

I am now wearing a black sweater over a dark blue shirt and tie with dark gray slacks, and Agent Wade is waiting at the bus stop with me. We shelter from the rain under the thick plastic roof of the stop. He lights a cigarette, and as I watch him I realize I am a lot more nervous than usual. I want the bus to come early so I can escape Agent Wade's unnerving glare.

"Got a good plan?"

"I tend to make it up as I go along."

Agent Wade has a slight recoil at this. "You do?"

"It's worked so far."

"Jesus." He sighs. "You've got to have a plan. Everyone has a plan of some sort."

"I don't."

"Then make one. Now."

I feel myself getting a little defensive. "Who's the one with experience here?"

Agent Wade sighs hard. His eyes challenge me. "So which one you gonna kill?"

"I dunno yet."

"Christ."

I don't like the contemptuous look he gives me. "You're the one who dropped this on me."

"I thought you'd at least have some method—"

"Just trust me, okay?"

Agent Wade nods slightly as he breathes smoke out of his nostrils. He then runs his tongue around his teeth as he studies me. "Will the victim suffer?"

I fall silent for a moment.

Agent Wade gives me a warmish smile. "Just for the report."

"Oh . . . I hadn't realized this was going to be so official."

"That's the FBI for you."

I see the bus appear at the top of the street. It stops at a red light some hundred yards away, and I am forced to look at Agent Wade as he looms up close. He fingers my lapel, straightening it as he talks. "You're sure it's going to work? This non-plan of yours?"

I don't mean to, but I snap at Agent Wade. "I have been doing this a few years now." His presence is really making me tense.

Agent Wade tightens the knot in my tie. "Just checking."

Out of the corner of my eye, I see the traffic lights turn green; the bus changes gear and heads for my stop.

"There's really no need."

Agent Wade finishes straightening my tie, makes a small

fist, and playfully "punches" my chin, or rather pushes it a couple of times with his knuckles. "Don't mind me. I'm the new kid on the block."

The bus pulls up and Agent Wade steps away as the doors open. I glance at him, can offer only a weak nod and a half-smile. "See you later."

Agent Wade gives me a hard pat on the back as I start up the steps. "Give them hell, Dougie, give them hell."

I pay my fare, and only when the doors close behind me do I feel in any way relaxed. I take my seat as the bus pulls away, and I catch sight of Agent Wade standing to military attention and saluting me as the bus goes past. I find myself saluting back to him and don't really know why.

CAROLE
LOMBARD

HI, BETTY

I CAN HEAR SOMEONE TALKING, but I'm not really listening.

I can't believe the predicament I'm in. I can't eat I'm so disheartened, and I've smoked eight cigarettes in half an hour.

I cast my eyes around Grillers Steak House, which is more wooden than ever, as the management has covered the ceiling in beech paneling. I search out the hazy faces of the Club members, partially veiled by the incessant smoke from their cigarettes. I whisper a sad and plaintive apology to them all. I'm really sorry I have to kill all of you, but that's life, I guess.

I still can't believe that in two months' time there isn't going to be a Club anymore. That hurts more than anything. I honestly don't know how I'm going to cope afterward.

The woman sitting at the broad table directly opposite me gives a weak but hopeful smile to no one in particular, bows her head, and talks down to her plate of liver, onions, and hash browns.

"I know it's a terrible way to get famous, but I really have no real talent for anything else. If you can call murdering people a talent, that is."

I immediately realize that the nine people I have to kill is about to become ten.

Which is great. Just wonderful. Thank you, God, really appreciate it.

When the woman turned up tonight, she asked everyone to call her Betty, after Betty Grable. I can't see Betty's legs, but I don't imagine for a minute they would turn her into a Forces Sweetheart, though I do pretend to drop my napkin so I can bend down and look at them—just in case. I discover there are twenty legs crammed together under the tables, and I'm not altogether too sure which are Betty's, so I sit back up again and try my hardest to concentrate on what she is saying.

Betty looks to be in her mid-thirties but is probably younger. This isn't surprising, as skillers generally look older than they really are. I'm probably the only member who has managed to retain my youthful looks. Forty-one, but still getting asked for my ID in bars and clubs. The others say this is on account of my being shorter than the average, but I don't agree and prefer the thought that in the long run eternal youth is a far greater asset than being tall. I mean, anyone can be tall these days.

"Well . . . that just about sums me up." Betty offers a nervous little giggle. Carole Lombard sarcastically mimics her nervy titter in return, and I have to say that Betty doesn't deserve that. Betty immediately lowers her eyes and watches Tony reach over and scoop a hash brown from her plate.

A silence descends on the table, and it seems that no one has anything to say until Burt's nasally voice breaks through the stilted silence.

"First time's always the hardest." Burt is a late-thirties, round-shouldered, wiry-haired guy with a squint in his right eye. He never ceases to surprise me at these meetings, because he doesn't look like the type of person who would ever speak out in a crowd, yet he nearly always leads the way with the first remark. Burt is a junior high school teacher, so I imagine that screaming at little kids every day of his life must help his confidence no end.

Betty blushes, raises her eyes to Burt. "Thanks, uh . . ."

"Burt. Burt Lancaster."

"Thanks."

Betty and Burt share an intimate look, and I note that it helps relax her.

Cher puts a friendly hand on Betty's wrist and looks encouragingly into Betty's eyes. "Debut night is always pretty crappy."

Betty takes heart from this, and after she smiles at Cher she turns and catches my eye. I quickly offer her my own trademark look, a casual yet compelling grin. I lean as far forward as I can so she doesn't miss it, but James Mason unthinkingly reaches over and lights a table candle right in front of my eyes. I give James a serious glare, which he mistakenly reads as an offer of a drink. "Mine's a Miller Lite, and Mother'll have a St. Clements." A drink that will sit untouched all night because James's mother is a figment of his imagination. It's a total waste of money and I'm thinking of billing James.

"That was great, Betty. Just great. It's so good to have a new member," Tony Curtis says as he tries to contain a belch. He constantly speaks on the advent of a belch; thus his words forever sound trapped, and I for one always feel the need to give him a hearty slap on the back—or maybe not, considering he kills people for much less. "Anyways, as resident chairman of the Club, it is my duty to ask you to reveal to us—in as much detail as possible—what it is, exactly, that you do. Betty Grable, welcome to the Club."

The group suddenly becomes alert and interested. They lean forward, their eyes and ears ready to devour any and every morsel that comes their way. The people drowning under the dark skies outside are forgotten, the rotten food is ignored, and cigarettes are lit in hopeful anticipation of a decent story.

Betty glances at Burt for support, and there is something in his look that says, Be calm, Betty, take your time, I'm with you.

I rub my hands together under the table and feel myself rocking back and forth in my chair. Boy, do I like the stories. And I've decided to make the most of them now that there won't be any in around eight weeks' time.

Betty takes a moment, composes herself, and as I watch her I can't deny that there is something about her—something I hadn't noticed earlier because I wasn't really concentrating. It's a palpable sense of warmth, of love and kinship. She emanates a niceness that is as wholesome and American as it gets.

"You probably know me better as the 'Burner Bitch.' At least that's what the papers are calling me."

I can detect a tuneful lilt in her voice that makes me think of that English actress who played Mary Poppins. A classic film for any age group.

"I've killed six guys so far. Burned their balls right off them."

My eyes water instantly.

"My first victim was a welder—in fact, he taught me how to use a blowtorch in the first place. Because they can be pretty tricky things to master." Betty takes a big slurp of red wine, and it helps her confidence immeasurably. "I tell you, he so had it coming. He really did. Whenever I, uh—you know—slept with him—"

"Slept with him? That's a bit on the polite side, hon." Tallulah shoves her pointy, rodentlike features toward Betty, eyes screwed up, buckteeth very prominent. "Either you fuck a guy or you don't."

"We're not all like you, Miss Bankhead." This comes from the haughty Cher.

"Like any man would go near you anyway, Tallulah." The protective Burt's nasally tones make Tallulah scowl darkly, and she petulantly gives him a one-finger sign.

"You need a tattoo. All over your face."

Betty is thrown, loses her way; her confidence starts to trickle away. Tony clicks his fingers repeatedly, like a hypnotist pulling someone out of a trance—only they're not coming out of it no matter how hard he clicks. "Hey! You know the rules. No talking during story time!"

Betty regroups, gathers herself, and takes three big gulps of wine. After dabbing her mouth with a napkin, she continues.

"Anyway, uh . . . This welder . . . I'd wake up beside him and feel like killing myself. The horrible things he made me do. Then one day a light went on in my head. I got this incredible idea, this pure and clear vision. I marched straight round to this welder's workshop, picked up his blowtorch, struck a match, and . . . well, let's just say his screams could have shattered glass."

Betty takes another slurp of wine, leans forward in her seat, and I know for a fact she is now roaring drunk. With her unfocused eyes and smudged lipstick, she looks completely different from the meek, boring woman who did so little to entertain us at the start of the evening. I think this look suits her.

She turns and for some reason focuses on me in particular—her pupils dilating, her voice growing sadder by the second, everything about her now deep and emotional and inebriated. And I know instantly what she is about to say. There are tears in her eyes as she casts a faraway look at the Club members in turn. Her chin and lower lip start to tremble. "I, uh . . ." She takes a big tragic breath that I've seen a hundred times in the movies. "I guess a lot of it has to do with my childhood. . . ."

Christ, just when I was starting to enjoy myself. I switch off immediately. Not another childhood thing. If I've heard that once, I've heard it a million times. Betty's voice drifts away as I concentrate on a small prayer running around in my head.

Just once, God, I'd like to hear something original. Every time without fail they blame their moms.

I stare out the window and watch the rain crashing down on the bowed heads of passersby, and it occurs to me that life is really all about staying dry.

I then look back at the less than rapt members and wonder who I'm going to kill first.

"I admire humanity. I admire the way it survives. War after war after war, and we're all still here—surviving. Disease, floods, earthquakes—you can throw the whole lot at us and we'll get through it. That's the secret, you see, the key to everything. That in the end we survive." Carole—burly, midforties, six three, bearded, and with a severe case of halitosis—sits at the bar. The Club has long since broken up, and a few of us are now sharing more informal moments. After Betty had finished, I applauded louder than most, but only because I thought she could be quite attractive if she went to a good hairdresser, removed her large, pink-rimmed glasses, and had extensive liposuction.

Carole hadn't applauded Betty. He had remained aloof

and austere, pretending he had heard it all before. Then again, he always does this, and I'm not alone in thinking he is becoming unbearably arrogant. Legend has it that everyone had to stifle gales of laughter when Carole first joined the Club; his big gruff lumberjack voice announcing he was to be known as Carole Lombard should have triggered some real high-class mockery, but the Club had learned their lesson the last time something similar had happened. From what Tony told me, seeing Raquel Welch pick up Errol Flynn and ram him headfirst through the wooden divider between two booths made the Club respect people a little more after that. Raquel Welch proved to be one mean and angry son of a gun, and I think the Club members were relieved when he suddenly stopped coming.

Not that I want any thanks for it, but the Club really picked up after Raquel "quit."

"To survival." I raise my glass, and Carole together with Chuck Norris raise their drinks.

"Survival."

"The dying art." Chuck grins. He's my all-time favorite person at the Club. He's always got some ironic quip to make. He's also handsome in that way that makes him instantly likable. He's like a face on a poster or a billboard—that guy who is totally happy with life and all it has to offer. Especially if it's a Marlboro Light.

Carole doesn't really get Chuck's joke. He believes himself to be above humor. He is always too busy trying to intellectualize everything, as if he's in constant search of an answer to life and all its attendant glories. Practically every meeting sees him airing a new theory on why things happen like they do. His latest idea—the one that forced me to suck in my butt cheeks in case I lost all control—is that serial killers are just nature's way of telling us the world is overpopulated. I have never fought so hard to contain my laughter; it was like trying to hold a live wolverine inside my gut.

Chuck glances over at me and winks. "So? What d'you think of the new recruit?"

"Uh . . . she seemed, uh . . . okay. Very pleasant."

"Gonna ask her out?"

"Me?"

"Yeah. Didn't you see the way she was looking at you?"

"She was just glassy-eyed from being drunk."

"Only on your beauty, Dougie."

I shouldn't be amazed, but I have to admit that I am. I honestly hadn't realized.

Chuck gives me a big clap on the back. "Whatever it is, Dougie, you've got it. Hasn't he, Carole?"

Carole says nothing, just shrugs, and I can tell he's jealous. I grin at Chuck. "You'd know better than anyone."

Chuck lights up, shakes out the match, and takes a big suck on his Marlboro. I love the way he does that—it's just so cultured. "I were you, Dougie, I'd make a move on her."

"But what about those other guys she dated? Look what happened to them. . . ."

Chuck glances at Carole, and I catch a grin pass between them. "She obviously just hasn't met the right guy yet."

"Well, I'll think about it. I wouldn't want to rush into anything."

"Strike while the blowtorch is hot. That's what I say." The wryly grinning Chuck rattles his empty whiskey glass—the ice chiming against the glass—and manages to catch the eye of our regular table waitress. It was only after the second Club meeting that I learned she was deaf. In hindsight, I should have guessed she was, because to be honest, she had to be. There's no way we could reveal the things we reveal while a waitress with perfect hearing dishes out our inedible meals.

As the smiling waitress approaches, Chuck does something with his hands that she immediately responds to by weaving an intricate pattern with her own fingers. Chuck replies, and I realize that he must have taught himself sign language. I glance at Carole, and for once even he looks impressed. The signing between Chuck and the waitress becomes more intense, and then she suddenly bursts out laughing—or what passes for a deaf person's laugh—and it's obvious that Chuck's terrific wit loses nothing in translation. The waitress laughs again, and I feel a smile playing along my lips as I turn to Carole.

"I'd give my right arm to be able to sign like that."

Carole yawns long and hard, glances at his watch. Over in one corner someone puts the latest release by the group Murder Rap on the jukebox, and this seems to irritate the hell out of Carole.

"Boy, I hate that stuff."

"You're kidding. I've got the CD."

Carole gives me a hard look. "Mighta known. Music companies rely on assholes like you, Dougie. They're only in existence because you and your kind help perpetuate and prolong their garbage-producing careers. That band will be finished in a year, and some other group of pricks will be unleashed upon us."

I keep glancing at Chuck and the waitress, who seem to be enjoying a much more meaningful conversation, and look down at my fingers, wishing I could sign.

"You don't have to follow the trend, Dougie, you don't have to be a part of the crowd. But you do it all the same because you think it gives you an identity. Rather than carving out your own, you're quite happy to have yours foisted upon you."

That's a barrel-load of grievances Carole has there—I never knew he was so hung up on Murder Rap—but I feel I have to put him right on a few things. "They're a good band. Their album is number three on the billboard. You say what you like, Carole, but you really can't argue with that. They're at number three."

Carole snorts down at me, his noxious breath making me feel bilious. "You don't get it, do you, Dougie. You just don't see the big picture."

"I think I see enough of it—"

"Someone like me, Douglas . . . well, I look at the whole picture, and then I see beyond it."

"When you say you see beyond . . . how far is that, exactly? Are we talking miles or furlongs?"

Carole pauses, sighs again. My jokes are humbling him, but he won't admit it. "You are so tiresome, Douglas. Chuck has a good sense of irony, but you, well, you can't grasp anything, so you resort to infantile humor. It's all a pathetic attempt to cover for your appalling insecurities and total lack of self-knowledge."

As I sit there, I realize that I hate Carole.

He gives a tired shrug. "What the hell. I guess people like you have your place in the grand scheme of things. I mean, without you around I'd never get to feel this good about myself." Carole laughs at this like it's the greatest joke in the world, and I feel his big hand ruffling my hair as he pushes me, rocking me like I'm some big kid.

I start laughing along with him, but only because I now know who I'm going to kill first.

Later I go to the men's room, sidestep to the pay phone, and put in a call to Agent Wade.

"Hi, it's me."

"Hi you. Killed anyone yet?" There's nothing like getting to the point.

"That's why I'm calling. I've made a decision."

"And?"

"I'm going to do Carole Lombard."

There is an undeniable pause on the end of the line. "Who?"

"Carole Lombard."

Another long pause follows, and I can almost see Agent Wade sitting there trying to come to terms with the fact that the real Carole Lombard is not only still alive, but also a serial killer.

"Can't you just stick to the members?"

"He is a member."

"He?"

"I know, the guy freaks everyone out."

"Okay . . . whatever," is all he offers.

"Oh. Before I go, we got a new member tonight."

"And?"

"Well, I'm just saying, there's one more, and I was hoping maybe I could be given more time."

"That isn't going to happen."

Agent Wade's words are delivered with an undeniable finality.

I shrug in a fake casual way, not that he can see me do this. "Just asking."

I hang up.

It's time.

WELL EXECUTED

I RUN ALL THE WAY. I'm pretty fit and can run forever if I want to. I wanted to be a long-distance athlete when I was younger. I wanted to run races that were maybe a hundred miles long, or maybe one lap was a hundred miles and I'd enter for a fifty-lap race and just start running. I would love to run right around the world, but Carole's place is closer, so I go there instead.

I am soaked through to the skin by the time I arrive, and after a quick glance up to the thunderously wet sky, I get this crazy notion in my head that this is the sort of city where arsonists should come for rehab.

Carole is so big and mean looking that he doubts anyone would burglarize his tiny little apartment, so getting inside requires little in the way of skill or imagination. Fortunately for me, skillers believe themselves to be invulnerable to petty crime and think that they are so wild and scary that no one in their right mind would do something to upset them. They're as untouchable as English royalty. You should hear the outrage if any of them ever gets a parking ticket.

In Carole's case, the reality is he owns little to interest a thief, unless they're studying for a doctorate. Inside are endless rows of important-looking books. Their titles are the strong, no-nonsense, no-play-on-words type: *Psychology: The Way Forward, Psychoanalysis: The Way Back, Jungian Theory: From the Side On, Grimms' Book of Fairy Tales.* The last one is, I'm pretty convinced, the only one Carole has read and managed to grasp. His apartment, a shabby ground-floor affair, a living room, a kitchen, and a bedroom, has a strong, sour, distasteful odor. It fills the apartment, and I become so sidetracked as to how Carole can live with this stench that I start ransacking the place in an attempt to find the source of the odor. Eventually I come across a tube of denture cement in his bathroom cabinet—it sits beside a special two-headed toothbrush and a tin of soothing powder for his gums. When I unscrew the lid on the denture cement tube, I arc my head back. The stuff smells of acid, and I swear I can feel it attacking my eyes. I then grin to myself as I realize that Carole isn't so perfect that he can't fall victim to what must be one of the greatest marketing ploys of this century. By making denture cement smell this bad, the manufacturer forces you to buy at least three times the amount of denture toothpaste in order to maintain any semblance of an odor-free mouth. I'm so wrapped up in this discovery that I almost don't hear the front door open. I freeze instantly. The next few moments are, as always, a question of my trying to balance my natural terror with the need to keep a level head. I try to give myself positive things to think about while I fight down an all-consuming onrush of terror. I try hard to concentrate on quarterbacks as they prepare to unleash a forty-yard throw while eight guys, each weighing three hundred pounds, try to jump on them. I think about the coolness and clearness of thought that requires. I also sometimes ponder the men who build the last floor of a towering new skyscraper. There they are, hundreds of feet up in the air, defying high winds and the relentless impeachment of gravity. They carry on mixing cement and sticking bricks on top of one another as if they haven't a care in the world, and that to me defines the word *heroic*.

I can hear Carole moving around in his apartment, probably wondering why there's a window open and why some of his stuff has been scattered around. Like I say, skillers don't believe burglars will touch them, so he's probably working on a more lateral theory—maybe something like an animal has somehow found its way into his apartment. As I listen to him, I know I have between five and ten seconds before he finds me. This is the moment where I think, Quarterback builder, quarterback builder, and it goes round and round in my head until I get this surge of confidence and finally make up my mind that there is no turning back.

"Hello? Anyone there?" Carole walks into his living room, switches on a side light. That's good. A low light is always good. A main light tends to add a starkness, the low light adds mystery and a black-and-white B-movie nuance. The real Carole Lombard would appreciate this.

Carole whistles. "Here, puss. . . . Hey . . . puss?"

I take one last calming breath and emerge from the bathroom, holding my hands up, making out I'm defenseless, harmless. "Carole, I've been thinking . . . about what you were saying back at the Club."

Carole stands there, struck dumb, completely thrown.

"And I came to the conclusion that you are way off the mark. W-a-a-a-a-y off the mark."

"What are you doing here?" Not such a know-it-all now. "You break in here, you little shit?"

"Thing is, you've got it wrong." I persist in making my point. "Intelligence and insight hold as much weight as a gnat in a tornado. Insignificance is our only true standing in this world."

"You've got ten seconds to explain yourself, Douglas." I can see Carole is getting angry, more than a little jumpy, and he's going to react like all great pseudointellectuals in times of stress. He's going to go for me like a rabid dog.

"I just did explain myself. Perhaps you didn't quite grasp what I meant. Let me tell you in layman's terms."

It happens quickly. Carole's rage erupts. He comes at me, lurches forward. I am too fast, though, too agile, and I duck away from him, reaching for a book that lies on his coffee table, a thick and heavy tome entitled *Get Smart, Get Even, Get a Life!* I swing it round and smash Carole on the back of the head with it. I hit him so hard that his false teeth fly out and almost hit a portrait of someone who I think is Einstein, and it is this moment that freezes him long enough, possibly through the sheer embarrassment of it all, for me to take one step farther away from the electric chair.

With all things being equal, I know for certain that Carole could never be truly clever even if someone came along and beat the intelligence into him. Which is exactly what I attempt to do with an oversize copy of *Encyclopedia Britannica*. I don't enjoy this, but I do find a fallen page devoted to the African termite family, which is actually a lot more interesting than it sounds.

Afterward, when I'm removing all trace of my being in Carole's apartment, I find the false teeth. I can't help myself and pretend to have a conversation with Carole's teeth, clacking them open and shut, making like I'm on Letterman.

"So, Dougie . . . tell me about this crusade of yours."

"Well, Dave . . . it's sort of hard to explain. Isn't really my idea, truth be told."

"C'mon, don't play the demure little guy with me. You pull this off and you're going to be a hero."

"I am? How d'you figure that?"

"You're ridding the world of serial killers. There aren't going to be any left after you're done. America will sleep a little easier in her bed thanks to you."

"A hero? Me?"

"Sure thing, Dougie. They're going to write books and make movies about you, women are going to hurl themselves at your feet. You will be so famous, even I will have to get in line for an autograph."

"Jeez. Never thought of it like that."

"Let's face it. You, sir, are the next all-American hero. Or small-American hero, in your case."

"Oh my, Dave—let's pause for some big ironic laughs, shall we?"

"Sorry, Doug . . . forgive me. Blame the writers on this show. In fact, I'll fire them right this minute."

"I'll make sure I give them my autograph before they leave."

I go to Carole's body and wedge the teeth back into his mouth. Only I put them in back to front, with the teeth facing into the throat, and fight to suppress a small giggle when I imagine the coroner trying to work out if Carole was either trying to eat himself to death or was just plain stupid.

When I get back to my apartment, Agent Wade is waiting in his car outside. He is listening to heavy metal on the radio but turns it off as I approach.

"How'd it go?" is all he asks.

"Like clockwork." I can't help crowing a little. "For a non-plan, it went according to plan."

"Anyone see you?"

"You kidding? You're talking to an old pro here."

"Sounds like you made a good start."

I'm not proud of myself, but I fake a confident look for Agent Wade's sake. "I guess I did."

"Still prefer it if you had a plan."

"I really don't need one. Tonight proves that."

"All the same . . ."

Agent Wade turns the loud rock music back on. It takes me a few seconds to realize that the conversation is over. I shrug and head for my apartment.

I can't deny that the thought of being a hero is starting to appeal to me. I lie in bed wondering who I should do next, and to my surprise, I feel a growing sense of anticipation. I can feel myself basking in the warm glow of all-American-ness when I hear my bedroom door creak open.

I can hardly believe my eyes when Agent Wade walks in— smoking thoughtfully—and sits at the foot of my bed. I feel his weight make my mattress, and me, rise a few centimeters. He looks around my small bedroom, takes in the pale lilac decor, the battered oak wardrobe, the small set of pine drawers, the single bed.

Finally he looks at me.

"I don't like the non-plan plan."

I'm not sure what to say at first, try to gather my thoughts. "But it works."

"The FBI would fire me on the spot if they knew I was going in planless. It's like going into a shoot-out without your pants on."

"But you're not going in, I am."

"All the same, I'm in charge of this operation. And I say you start by mapping out a plan of action. And I want it in writing."

"Writing?"

"A thousand words minimum."

I sigh, hope he gets how annoyed I am. "I haven't got time to write reports."

Agent Wade's eyes blaze into mine. "What you'll do is what I tell you to do. Now get planning. And writing."

Agent Wade leaves my bedroom, and the warm glow I was experiencing earlier has turned cold enough to make me want to get up and switch on the heating.

WILLIAM
HOLDEN

APB: MISSING SERIAL KILLER

C AROLE LOMBARD had killed fourteen. Prized open their skulls and dined on their brains. They were all college professors, men and women who quite possibly had a lot more to offer life than he ever would. Anyone who thought that they could "ingest" intellect and not have to do correspondence courses like the rest of us is one severely stupid person. You could tell this just from listening to Carole's stories at the Club. By far and away they were the most labored and tedious I had ever heard. He was technical and deliberate, with little or no rhythm, and he definitely could not get into his characters. His rank halitosis didn't help matters, either.

I am convinced he won't be missed.

"So where's sewer mouth?" Tony looks around at me and the other nine members attending the next Club meeting. I immediately feel my heart stop. It's been three months since the previous skiller went missing, and I'd forgotten about that initial nausea-inducing wave of anxiety I always experience at the first meeting after their disappearance.

No one says anything as Tony eyes us in an imperiously calculating fashion and then speaks out of the corner of his mouth. "What time you got, Burt?"

"I make it a quarter after."

"I must be a little fast. I've got twenty after."

William Holden's soft tones make him sound like he is constantly whispering. This and his emphatically bald head complete his totally sinister appearance, and he comes across as the Identi-Kit serial killer. William has no hair whatsoever on his body, and although there's a medical term for it, I just tend to think of him as being one of nature's freaks.

"That's forty-five minutes late, ladies and gentlemen." Tony belches as he stares out at us. "I will not tolerate that kinda irregular timekeeping."

"What are you gonna do? Fine him?" Pointy-faced Tallulah Bankhead gives a thin-lipped, petulant smile. Apart from killing people, it seems the only other thing she enjoys in life is to goad people. I'm ashamed to admit that I once almost got into a fistfight with her when she kept interrupting one of my more imaginative eulogies on my killer's block.

"Or maybe make him write out a hundred times, 'I must not be late for meetings.' "

Everyone has learned to rise above Tallulah's petty taunts by now, so Tony just scowls at her and then looks over to me.

"You ride here with Carole sometimes, Dougie. He not on your bus tonight?"

"Uh . . . not that I noticed."

"Too busy leering at some chick, huh?" Chuck nudges my arm, and I give him a "well, you know me" smile. We're both pretty much the studs of the Club, and I think from the way everyone laughs along with Chuck that they all appreciate what he's implying here.

"What if Miss Lombard isn't late?" Cher leans forward, takes a hard puff on her cigarette. She speaks in a very definite and precise manner, just like the real Cher. "Maybe he isn't gonna turn up ever again."

Cher never calls anyone other than Mr. This or Miss That.

I was astonished when I first saw Cher walk into the Club, because she is the exact double of the real Cher. The absolute spitting image, same age, same height, same hair, same voice.

Tony eyes Cher curiously. "Care to emulsify on that?"

Cher holds Tony's look. "All I'm saying is that . . . well . . . maybe he's had enough of the Club."

I sit there secretly hoping to God that Tony buys this.

"Don't you dare fucking say that." Tony loves—absolutely loves—the Club.

"I just kinda wonder if things aren't getting a little predictable. You know, a little stale."

Chuck lights a Marlboro. "Must admit it's not as much fun as it used to be." He then whips off a one-liner, and I instantly crease up. "Mind you, they say the same about sex with dodo birds." I laugh at everything Chuck says; he just hits my funny bone every time. My laugh almost drowns out James Mason's nervy comment.

"I guess you've just got to look at the members who have left over the years." James dunks a chamomile teabag into a cup of hot water. There are already two other teabags sitting in there diffusing, and it's an accepted fact he likes a strong taste. "They must have had a good reason." James doesn't usually say much at the meetings, and if he's worried enough to bother talking to us rather than the voices he hears in his head, then it puts me on edge. I truly wish he'd go back to whispering to his dead mother, as for one horrible moment I think someone is about to question the real reason why eight—make that nine—of the original members don't attend anymore.

Tony looks a little sullen. "And this is my fault?"

"Who else we gonna blame?" Tallulah keeps on spoiling for a fight, and it's obvious to anyone that she's in a real grouchy mood. I'd put it down to her period if I didn't know she'd hurl an ashtray at me—like she did the last time I raised that particular line of thought.

"No one's blaming anyone, Tony," William whispers. "But I do think we need to maybe offer a little more than we do."

"Like what? Dancers? Maybe a raffle? Bring and buy—what?" Tony's face is turning red in his anger.

"Look, I only brought this up because Miss Lombard was pretty irritated at the way the Club was being run." Cher is keen to make her point.

"Are you questioning my chairmanship?"

"Of course not, Mr. Curtis."

"Sounds to me like you are. Sounds like you're blaming me for driving people away."

"Don't get so defensive."

"Hey, someone attacks, I defend—okay?"

"I just think we need an injection of something or other . . . a little light relief."

I notice Betty listening intently to the debate starting to rage around her. She looks ravishingly wholesome tonight, and after what Chuck said at the last meeting, I think I can see what he meant about her liking me. She keeps looking over at me—almost leering, in fact.

"I could always get up and tell a few jokes." Burt will jump at any and every opportunity to grandstand, and I for one am glad to see Tony ignore him completely as he casts his eyes over each one of us in turn.

"Anyone else ever hear Carole saying he was unhappy?" he asks.

"I could tell just from looking at him. The stink-breathed scum bucket." Tallulah lights a cigarette, licks her fingers, and douses the matchstick flame with them.

Tony is determined to get an answer to his question. "Did he or didn't he like the Club?"

I take a breath and slowly raise my hand. All eyes are suddenly upon me, and it makes me nervous. "Uh . . . I spoke to him, uh . . . at the last meeting, in fact. And I hate to say this, Tony, but he was pretty pissed at the way things were being handled."

"Oh, he was, was he? And just what was offal face sobbing about, Mr. Secretary?"

Tony looms over me, and I have to think fast. "He just said he was thinking about quitting and maybe moving on. Plus he hated his media name."

"I didn't pin the 'Brain Binger' on him."

"No, but I think it kinda added to his . . . well, his overall annoyance. I think he was hoping for something more upmarket." The atmosphere at the Club has turned pretty unsavory now.

"He knows the score. You want a good nickname, you sign it on the victim. Everyone knows that."

"I'm glad he's gone. His breath stank worse than a rotting polecat." Tallulah makes a screwed-up disgusted face. "And that's doing a big disservice to polecats."

Tony sits back and chews on someone's barbecue rib, sucking the sauce from the bone so loudly that a bunch of guys across the room look over. They look like a quiz team in hopeful search of a quiz—nerdish and toothy. I notice Betty looking over at one nerd in particular, and for a moment she looks like a lioness sizing up her prey.

"Okay, so Carole's taken a hike. Big deal. Personally I'm glad to see the back of him." Tony wipes his hands along his thighs. "We don't need trash like that."

My heart rate begins to slow, and I can look forward to relaxing and enjoying the meeting once more.

"What about the others, though?"

I immediately go cold inside, and my heartbeat hits two hundred.

You can always count on Richard Burton to put his big fat foot in it. Rich the Bitch, I call him secretly, on account of the fact that he possesses what look suspiciously like a pair of breasts, and this played on my mind so much that I just had to voice the very genuine concern that he is the world's first serial-killing hermaphrodite. Richard became very defensive about this—almost too defensive, in my opinion—but I'm afraid that no amount of bleating about gland trouble can make me believe otherwise.

"What about them?" I say this a little too abruptly and quickly cover myself. "Hey . . . like Tony says—who needs them?" I follow this with a little snigger. "Who needs trash?"

"Why don't they come no more?" Richard is a small-town hick from the sticks, slow talking, slow thinking, and totally irritating. "I was real fond of Errol Flynn. He had some good things to say."

Sure he did. Like how he butchered nine men on account of their likeness to a guy who once sold him bleached meat.

I lean forward. "I don't like to tell tales, but I once heard Errol complain about the membership fee." This is a blatant lie; it was actually me who spent a lot of time moaning about it to anyone who would listen—and to be perfectly honest, I had a good point.

"Jesus!" Tony breathes out a big breath, shakes his head. "Jesus fucking H!"

The quiz nerds look over at Tony's raised voice, and when I turn back again I see that both William Holden and Burt Lancaster are now eyeing them up as potential victims. I feel like I'm watching a nature program about big jungle cats.

Cher takes a moment, gets the words right in her head before speaking them. "Maybe we need to think bigger."

Tony instantly knows where this is heading. "We've said all we're gonna say on that subject."

"Just hear me out, Mr. Curtis."

Tony claps his hands over his ears and hums to himself so he doesn't have to listen. His fingers leave barbecue sauce prints all over the side of his head. Cher is determined to ride this one out and raises her voice.

"I vote we send a message to him."

The other members all look at Cher, and none of them like what she is saying. We have had this debate over and over, and it seems that Cher won't rest until she wins it.

"We've asked everyone else. It's only fair that we ask him. Come on, we've put this off for three years now."

"Who are you talking about?" Betty's soft voice breaks through, and I look at her as she scans the members hopefully for an answer. No one seems prepared to say anything.

Tony stops humming, takes his hands away from his ears, and scoops up a pile of peas from James's plate. He crams them into his mouth, spilling more than a few of them, and everyone waits for his next utterance. Finally he gives a great big reluctant sigh.

"Tell her, Burt."

This really bugs me. Can't Tony see he's just playing up to Burt's constant need to take center stage? I dive in before Burt can open his mouth. "We're talking about the Kentucky Killer, Betty."

"Oh my. . . ." Betty's hand goes instinctively to her mouth as her eyes bulge in their sockets.

I smile secretly at Burt's teacherly look of annoyance. That'll teach him.

Did I say teach him? The gags just keep on coming.

"The Kentucky Killer. Oh my. . . ." Betty breathes in deeply. And rightly so.

Because the Kentucky Killer is absolutely the number one skiller of all time. A living legend. The serial killer they all want to be. World-famous and with more kills than the entire Club combined. He is a total god when it comes to the slaughter of innocents, and his presence would really put the Club on the serial-killing map.

"Oh my," Betty repeats.

Later I feign an attack of food poisoning, which is easy for anyone to believe when they've had the dubious pleasure of dining here. That way, I leave the bar and grill before everyone else, and when no one is looking I climb into the trunk of William's car, finding, to my delight, that it isn't half as cramped as I thought it would be—but that it also smells like a cat's been living in there.

It is past midnight, and a full moon tries to break through the ominous-looking clouds overhead. The only sunrise William is going to see again is when I pour a gallon of gas down his throat and then set fire to it. William has done something similar to nine people and three guide dogs. The press have dubbed him the "Supernova Slayer," and the television psychiatrist became very animated about religious connections and the fire that purifies the soul. I just think William is a pyromaniac with a terrific tan. His two published reference books are really the same book written in different styles. The first is a thinly disguised denial of God posing as a study into the life-giving power of the sun. The second is also a disguised denial of God but contains cave drawings of big-chinned apemen bowing to the sun. According to William, the sun is God and God is the sun. His third factually based work was never published. Probably on grounds of self-plagiarism.

I peer out of the hole I secretly drilled a few days ago in his trunk and watch as William appears in the doorway to the bar and grill. He stands with Richard and Cher, and they are saying their good-byes.

My plan—which I didn't bother writing up—seemed to appease Agent Wade, and his whole demeanor brightened when I told him how brilliant and inspired it was. He wanted to know more, but I told him to wait and see; I could tell he was like a kid waiting for Christmas, but no amount of begging to know what the plan was made me tell him.

"Mr. Holden, Mr. Burton, I'll see you when I see you." I watch Cher give them both a Hollywood-style kiss on either cheek.

I note that she has never done this to me, but I for one really don't like that sort of empty affectation, and I think she knows this.

Cher walks off, high heels clicking on the damp sidewalk.

"Bye, Cher."

"Yeah, you be sure and drive careful, hon."

Will and Richard stop long enough to watch Cher get into and start up her sleek, low-slung sedan. They wave as Cher drives past, giving them a friendly beep. After that they start heading toward Will's car.

"I brought that video with me." Will pats his pockets, looking for his keys. "That *Sixty Minutes* show I taped a while back."

"Aw, gee, that's terrific of you, Will."

"I had to get it cleaned up after some punk jimmied the rear door of my car and pissed in it."

"They did? That's disgusting."

"I swear this world is going to the dogs."

Will still can't seem to find his keys as he checks through his pockets again. "You don't get a big mention in the video, but it's interesting what that TV psychiatrist guy has to say about you."

"Any photos of me, or closed-circuit footage?"

"None. You've been very careful."

"Still can't forgive myself for missing it. I had a blood

craze on that night. Always seems to come over me when there's something good on TV."

They stop right by the trunk, and I go very still. I wonder if they can see my eye staring out of the hole and hope that the moonlight doesn't catch my pupil and reflect off it.

"I popped it in the trunk in case the pissy punk came back for a crap."

I freeze instantly. I had been wondering what that sharp edge digging into my ankle was. I feel a swell of panic and can't seem to catch my breath.

William finds his keys. "Two weeks I've been trying to get rid of the stench."

The keys come out of Will's pocket, and I swear I now have rigor mortis because my whole body has clenched up so tight that my heart doesn't seem to be able to manage even a single beat.

Quarterback builder, quarterback builder . . .

How the hell am I going to explain this?

Quarterback builder, quarterback builder . . .

The key slides in.

Richard sniffs loudly, then recoils. "That sure is a putrid punk. . . ."

I rack my brains for a good reason to be in Will's trunk.

Quarterback builder, quarterback builder . . .

The clouds open and raindrops start pounding on the trunk. They're deafening me, and I clamp my hands over my ears. How am I meant to think with that racket going on?

Will sighs to himself. "Now the goddamn sky is pissing on us."

Quarterback builder, quarterback builder . . .

I've got it! I was locked in here by some putrid punks having a hoot. Yes! Four big and strong putrid punks dumped me in here, pissed on me, and . . .

. . . I'm a dead man.

Dead as dead gets.

And it's all down to that bastard Agent Wade hustling me into this.

Bastard!

The lock springs and the trunk is about to swing open when I suddenly hear someone joining Richard and William.

"Excuse me, gentlemen, but does one of you own that Ford over there?"

I know that voice—I'm certain of it.

"The midnight blue one."

It's Agent Wade.

"What's it to you?"

"It's just that it's on fire."

"What!? Jesus shit!"

Right now I think I love Agent Wade.

"Fuck!"

Richard lumbers off immediately, breasts no doubt slapping him in the face as he races over. I can't see what is going on, but I do hear the sound of Will retrieving a car fire extinguisher from under his driver's seat and then running over to Richard's Ford and spraying it.

"Stand back, Rich. You don't want any of this getting on your suit."

I decide to take my chance and start to climb quickly out of the trunk. I get about an inch when Agent Wade suddenly slams the trunk down on my head hard. My head spins as he speaks in a tight and unforgiving whisper.

"Next time, trunk boy, I make the plans."

William forgets all about the videotape and drives for three hours nonstop. He seems to make a point of running over every hole and rock in the road, and by the time he slows and pulls over, I feel like I've been shooting the longest rapids in history. I have now added a serious amount of puke to the overall putrid odor of Will's car.

William Holden blames the world for everything. He blames it for his lack of hair, his lack of voice, his absolute lack of personality, and he unequivocally blames it for turning him into a merciless killer. I've yet to hear any killer openly admit that they did the things they did purely because it cheered them up. Being a bald eight-year-old made William retreat into himself—not far enough, as far as I'm concerned—and he grew up a solitary figure. He initially tried to become a best-selling author—indeed, that is still his most fervent dream—but an alarming lack of talent persuaded him to go into research instead. During his investigations, he stumbled across some pretty weird stuff, and the murders he now commits are actually a homage to the great god Ra. He even has a little mantra he chants every now and then: "Ra-Ra Rarara." Just think cheerleader.

Will pulls over, and when I smell gasoline I realize he has stopped to refuel. I listen hard, trying to make out everything that is going on outside. Will dumps the fuel pump in the car, scratches himself, gives a few bars of his Ra-Ra mantra, and then, after jingling some loose change in his pocket, he walks off, probably to the men's room. He has left the gas pump sticking out of the petrol cap, and I want to tell him how dangerous that is.

I slip the catch of the trunk, and after checking out of the hole I made, I slowly open the trunk and look around. A four-wheel truck is pulling away and nearly crashes when the driver glances down and sees me emerging from the trunk. I quickly hide my face and wait for the four-wheel to skid back onto the highway and nearly cause a major pile-up—then jump out. I can barely bring myself to look at the mess I've made in the trunk, but Will's videocassette needs serious cleaning, that's for sure.

I gather myself, grab a few handfuls of the pale blue paper towels they considerately leave for drivers by the gas pumps, and wipe my clothes and face with them. As I do, I walk round to the front of Will's car and am leaning on his hood when he returns. He is naturally surprised to see me and is slightly put out by the amount of dry sick sticking to my clothes and hair.

"Hi, Will. . . ."

"Douglas!?"

"Excuse the vomit."

Will's eyes fall to my stained clothes. "You look terrible. What did you eat back there?"

Will knows I don't own a car and is probably trying to figure out how I managed to jog so far—and so fast.

I point to the sky. "Did you know it was a full moon tonight?"

"I, uh . . . I can't say I noticed." There is a querying look in William's eye.

"Look. Up there. See it?"

William is looking increasingly uncomfortable.

"A full moon." I look in supposed awe at the moon and find to my disappointment that it is completely obscured from view.

William doesn't bother looking. He is too busy staring at me—and wondering.

"Are you feeling okay, Douglas?"

I can see he is nervous. Not as nervous as some of his victims, but just a little on the edgy side. Will's kills—my phrase, not his; maybe I should take up writing novels—have all happened at night, and I have come to the conclusion that Will is trying to make it sunny by putting on his fireball act.

"I'm fine, Will. Absolutely triple A-OK."

"How did you get out here?"

"I was in the trunk of your car." There is no real point in lying to him. Besides, the look on his face, a real look of absolute and utter noncomprehension, is worth all the honesty in the world.

"Listen, if you'd wanted a lift, all you needed to do was say."

"That's very kind of you, Will."

He's making small talk to try to buy himself time. In his mind, there is a dim light going on. He searches for the meaning behind the light, and I realize he is trying that old favorite—putting two and two together. I can almost see the slow grinding of his calculations. First there were a lot of killers, now there aren't so many. He looks up, and I know he's made the connection. He's not a published author for nothing.

"You little punk!"

His hands are around my throat before I've got time to react. I realize the pummeling I have had in the trunk has slowed me down and I am not at my best. I gag as I feel the life being squeezed out of me.

"No-good little piece of shit!"

He is surprisingly strong for a hairless man, and as I find myself starting to black out, I do something I haven't done since I was a kid: I jab my thumbnails straight into Will's bulging eyeballs. He squeals, his grip eases, and I head-butt him as hard as I can across the bridge of his nose. As the stunned Will staggers back, I grab the gas pump and ram it into his mouth, clamping it there while I dump half a gallon of super-unleaded into him. His panicked eyes bulge when he sees my silver-plated cigarette lighter snap on.

"Ra-ra Rarara."

It is over in seconds, and I nearly get a tan from the sunburst. To be fair, there isn't a great deal of suffering, but I can always lie to Agent Wade about that.

I then turn and run. By my reckoning, I've got maybe eighty miles to cover. That's almost three marathons.

Behind me, the garage explodes with a deafening roar, and when I look back I see a garage attendant staggering around, engulfed in flames. I wince and call out, "Whoops. . . ." But he doesn't hear me as my voice is lost in another deafening explosion.

In my hand I clutch a memento—something I swiped from Will's glove compartment several days earlier. I don't really know what I'm going to do with a pair of false eyebrows, but I'm sort of hoping they'll come in useful around Halloween.

THE LIST

AGENT WADE pulls up beside a plastic Hannibal Hani-mal—a seven-foot-tall wolverine with a big canine-toothed smile. We're in a new drive-in burger joint, and the windshield wipers are on fast speed as the rain lashes down. Agent Wade risks being drowned as he leans out the window and talks into the intercom installed in the wolver-ine's chest.

"Gimme two specials . . . but make one a vegetarian."

"I'm not vegetarian."

Agent Wade regards me, frowns. "Yeah, you are. I saw the documentary on Grandson."

"I'm not Grandson, remember?"

Agent Wade considers this for a moment. "Right. . . ." Then he speaks into the intercom again. "Hold the vegetarian. Apparently I'm sitting with a doppelgänger." Agent Wade laughs to himself at this.

I turn away, watch the rain for a moment.

Agent Wade eventually leans back in the car and gives the plastic wolverine a thoughtful glance. "If that was real, I'd have to shoot it."

"Yeah?"

"Animals that big are a threat to national security."

I study him for a moment. "Listen, I never got the chance to say this, but thanks for the assist the other night."

Agent Wade gives me a dismissive look. "With a plan like that, you needed all the help you could get."

As we sit in the car eating our Hannibal Hanimal specials, which I paid for, Agent Wade gazes at the plastic Hanimals that litter the drive-in burger joint. Together with three more wolverines, there are four grizzlies, four leopards, three gorillas, five alligators, and what I think are a cluster of snapping turtles.

Agent Wade studies an angry grizzly rearing up in front of the car. "We should have gone to KFC. Portions are bigger."

Agent Wade then unfolds a typed page, and as I catch a glimpse of it, I realize it is a list of all the Club members. Agent Wade pulls out a pencil and flamboyantly puts a line through William Holden's name. Nothing is said, but there is a mutual feeling of accomplishment. I notice that Agent Wade has even put the list in alphabetical order, and I feel I have let him down badly by starting halfway down the page.

TALLULAH BANKHEAD
RICHARD BURTON
CHER
TONY CURTIS
DOUGLAS FAIRBANKS JR.
BETTY GRABLE
~~WILLIAM HOLDEN~~
BURT LANCASTER
JAMES MASON
CHUCK NORRIS

As I study the page, I become a little alarmed.

"Uh, I don't think I should be on the list. I'm not a serial killer."

Agent Wade looks at me. "You're not?"

"No."

"But I thought . . . ?"

"Of course I'm not." I give Agent Wade an indignant look.

He pauses before giving me a brief and uneasy smile. "Whatever you say, Doug." He puts a big thick line through my name. "My mistake."

TALLULAH BANKHEAD

RICHARD BURTON

CHER

TONY CURTIS

~~DOUGLAS FAIRBANKS Jr.~~

BETTY GRABLE

~~WILLIAM HOLDEN~~

BURT LANCASTER

JAMES MASON

CHUCK NORRIS

We eat the rest of the meal in silence, the rain refusing to let up even for an instant. The plastic Hanimals get soaked, and one of the leopards short-circuits, sparking and fizzing before smoke starts pouring out of its mouth. Agent Wade was right—we should have gone to KFC.

As he slurps his milk shake he looks at me, weighing me up in a slightly unnerving fashion. I'm glad when he finally speaks.

"So, how come you're still alive to tell the tale? I'd have thought the Club would've cottoned on to you by now."

"Oh . . . I'm a pretty clever guy."

"You are?"

"Like you need to ask. . . ." We share a knowing smile.

He holds my look. "Tell me all the same."

"The skillers come from all over, so no one knows their

real names, no one knows where they live, they know nothing about each other. Then when one 'leaves,' so to speak—the Club has no real way of contacting them to find out why. They try the small ads but soon give up when there's no sign of a reply. These ads cost money, and we don't like to waste Club funds."

Agent Wade glances back out the window, his ever-alert eye drawn to a waitress from the burger joint slicing through the downpour on Rollerblades to a waiting sedan and then slipping and falling hard—ending up lying sprawled across the hood.

"So if you're not a serial killer, Dougie, what exactly are you?"

I respond with a certain amount of pride. "I guess I'm the all-American hero. The answer to everyone's prayers. The Avenging Angel. That's me—Demon Dougie."

I watch the dark clouds scud across the depressingly gray sky, can see one that is shaped like a horse's head, a coal black stallion snorting its angry and willful rage over the earth.

Agent Wade has fallen silent, meditating, letting my words sink in. He blows out one last puff of smoke and then stubs out his cigarette in an ashtray. He runs his tongue around his teeth, then clears his throat. "I was going to be a dentist. That was my life plan."

"Really?" I take a moment to adjust from my newfound and glorious reverie, trying hard to focus on what Agent Wade is saying.

"I'm from a long line of dentists."

Despite this downswing in euphoria, I wonder if he could take a look at my upper-right molar, as it's been giving me a lot of pain recently.

"Thing is, I wanted to help people in another way, Dougie. Not just mend their teeth, but somehow mend their lives as well." This could easily sound crass, but somehow, coming from Agent Wade's mouth, it seems poignant. "Plus I was very keen on guns. A big fan. You know?"

I nod, take a big slurp of my milk shake, feel the ice cold liquid bring on that agonizing pain I get in my chest every time I drink this stuff.

"Some kids grow out of Cowboys and Indians. Not me."

I smile grimly as I remember my own childhood. "I was always the Indian. Being hunted down and 'scalped' by the other boys. I had to run pretty fast some days, I can tell you. It seemed everyone wanted a piece of Geronimo. That's what I used to call myself."

"Geronimo was FBI."

I stop, look at Agent Wade. He nods. Earnestly.

"Geronimo?"

"Not that it was called the FBI in those days."

"I never knew that. Geronimo, huh?"

"I forget what they used to call it, but I'm certain he was a member."

"Pinkerton . . . wasn't that what they were called?" I think I'm correct when I say this, but Agent Wade doesn't seem to acknowledge me. Instead he checks himself in the rearview, runs a hand through his hair, talking to me but staring at himself.

"So . . . who's next?"

TALLULAH
BANKHEAD

TETCHY TATTOOED TERROR

I DECIDE TO TRY to rectify my earlier mistake and start doing this alphabetically.

It hasn't rained for at least an hour, and when I get to the next Club meeting, I imagine everyone will be in good spirits. As I pass the nerdish quiz team, I notice they are now short one of their members and they appear a little on the solemn side. I don't get time to dwell on this because as soon as I get to the table, I know that something's wrong.

I feel myself turning pale when I glance up to the television that sits on high above our regular table and see a photo of William Holden glaring down at me. It is the one they used on the jacket of his first novel. His shiny face and head peer out smugly, and my stomach flips when they cut to the news-anchor, who looks up solemnly from behind his desk. "It took a high-class forensics team working round the clock, but the body has now been formally identified. More after these messages."

The Club members are all staring up at the screen. They are silent, and there is the unmistakable aura of concern and shock. I feel like turning on my heel and running for my life.

Tony is the first to catch my eye. He looks very somber. "You hear about this?"

To my horror, I find I can't speak. I look dumbly at Tony as my throat dries up. The other members are looking my way, awaiting a response, and Christ help me, I can't do anything but give them a low gurgle.

"I'll take that as a yes." Tony turns away and looks at the other members.

My heart is nearly in my mouth as I silently take my place, legs trembling so badly that I think my pants'll fall down from the vibration.

"Hoo boy . . ." Tony runs a large hand over his face. "Shit sure happens."

"Is, uh . . . is someone gonna say a few words?" James Mason sips from a very black-looking cup of tea.

Burt is in there like there's no tomorrow. No surprises there from the obnoxious limelight seeker. "I'd like to propose a toast." Members reach for their drinks and raise them in the air—I don't have one, so I just make a fist instead and raise it to the others. I note that my hand shakes violently.

Burt's words are tender and well-meaning. "To William Holden, a man first, a killer second—and a friend throughout."

Everyone murmurs, "William Holden," or "Friend," and I manage to mumble, "To Baldy," without anyone hearing. I then look around for the deaf waitress, wishing I knew the sign language for "Could you open a window?" The bar and grill seems very stuffy all of a sudden. I loosen my tie, unbutton my collar.

"I really liked that guy." Richard, the good ole southern boy, likes everyone he ever meets. God alone knows how he became a serial killer. "Even though he had no hair, he had some good things to say, him being an author an' all."

"What was that, Mother? What did you say?" James Mason looks all around him, and the rest of the members sigh or give tiresome snorts.

"Jimmy, get a life, will you? We're trying to talk here." Tony growls at James, who turns round and looks at the others, then shrugs in apology.

"Mother was just saying she wants the rice-and-bean soup."

"Jimmy, I'm warning you now. Cut it out, huh?"

"Tell the bitch to eat somewhere else." Tallulah gives a snide grin to James, who shies away and goes back to obsessively dunking a teabag into his cup of hot water.

"What I want to know is who killed Mr. Holden." Cher lights up, blows out her match, and does an actresslike shake of the head. It's like sitting in a movie theater being around her.

"There sure is some sick people out there, I can tell you." Chuck winks to make sure we know he is being ironic, and I have been so scared and so uptight that my laughter machine-guns out of me and causes everyone to turn and look my way. I immediately stop.

"Forgive me. I, uh . . . I think I'm in shock. . . ."

The faces turn away, and I am now desperate for a drink, but the deaf waitress seems to have disappeared.

"I guess I could try and look into it." Tony is a detective second grade. A pretty good cop by all accounts. Never takes a bribe, never plants evidence, never gets freebies from prostitutes. Which is all too rare these days and deserves special mention. "That's if anyone thinks it's worthwhile. Personally I'd like to just put it down to plain bad luck. Will was in the wrong place at the wrong time."

"But what about the way he was killed? That's some coincidence." Once Cher gets hold of an issue, she won't let it go.

"Will never blew up whole gas stations, Cher. He just blew up individuals he found hanging around dark alleys. It ain't his MO." Tallulah gives Cher a "boy, you're really dumb" look, and Cher glares back at her.

"Miss Bankhead, the mere fact that fire was involved and that Will was the one that got killed tells me things aren't sitting right here. Okay, honey? You got that into your tattooed skull now?"

"You always did think better pre–face lift."

Cher is out of her seat like a mongoose, ready to strike at Tallulah, when Tony manages to grab her arm and force her back down. "Ladies . . . this is not the way to honor Will."

Cher and Tallulah glare at each other, and I really don't like the bad air that is hanging around the Club.

The news program comes back after the ads, and sitting beside the anchorman is the television psychiatrist—they still trot this same guy out when something involving skillers turns up on the news. I haven't seen him in a while, and I note that he has had minor plastic surgery and all his teeth have been capped. He looks at least ten years younger. The Club is familiar with the psychiatrist, whom they find absolutely hilarious; his stupid theories and ridiculous profiles make for compulsive entertainment.

ANCHORMAN: I have here a copy of the book *Ra-Ra-Ra the Sun God,* written by the victim, and I believe you have something you'd like to say about it?

(The television psychiatrist takes the book from the anchorman and opens it to a premarked page.)

PSYCHIATRIST: Firstly I'd like to draw your attention to a particularly inflammatory—

ANCHORMAN: (laughs) Inflammatory. Very good.

PSYCHIATRIST: (serious) What?

(The anchorman realizes this is no time for jokes.)

ANCHORMAN: Sorry. Carry on.

(The psychiatrist gives the anchorman a stern look before turning back to the camera.)

PSYCHIATRIST: This passage in particular may well shed some light on why Turner Turner III was murdered.

I know everyone at the Club is just dying to phone in and tell the network that Turner Turner III wasn't William's real name, it was just an alias. Only Will could have made up a name that dumb. I finally get the waitress's attention and gesture that I would like a Bud.

PSYCHIATRIST: (reading) "It is my belief that the fear of eternal night drives mankind. The sun is our friend and our inspiration—our sanctuary from that round-the-clock terror. The perfect life would be chasing sunrises across the globe, never knowing night and thus never having to confront or dwell upon the consequences of death."

(The psychiatrist closes the book and looks up at the anchorman, who obviously hasn't understood a word of it.)

PSYCHIATRIST: I think someone read that and decided to kill him.

"If anyone killed him, it would have been his publisher."
I start laughing immediately, because Chuck Norris is speaking and I laugh instinctively at everything he says. I'm like a deranged hyena when Chuck starts up.
"Let's face it, his books were god-awful." The gag is obvious, and not everyone laughs. I get a cold look from Betty, and I am glad the deaf waitress's arm blocks her view as she sets down my Bud. Chuck flashes the waitress a warm little wink, which she enjoys.

"I figure his mother did it." James Mason is a quiet man who says little and isn't comfortable speaking in public. This surprises me, because James is a defense lawyer and I expected him to be much more aggressive and vocal. I often wonder just how many people this hopelessly timid man has defended successfully in a twenty-year career. I'm guessing about two. "Will told me he was going to write a book about her. Semiautobiographical or something. Maybe she read a rough copy of it and didn't like it."

"That's a good point, Mr. Mason."

James looks so amazed he's actually made sense, he nearly falls out of his chair. "It was more Mother's idea. . . ."

Cher continues, "We've got to remember that Mr. Holden was one of the few members we've had who hadn't killed their mother."

"Yet." Chuck is making up for his earlier weak gag, and again I find myself laughing.

"I'll go with Cher on that. Who's to say Mommy didn't turn the tables on him?" Betty is getting into the swing of things and becoming a lot more comfortable with the Club. She has combed a part into her hair and let it fall free tonight, and I like the way she keeps having to flick it out of her eyes.

Burt isn't convinced. "Let's think about this a moment. Would someone's mother really go out and kill their offspring like that? I mean, that's stretching things a little too far, don't you think?" I find I want Burt to die—right now.

"Actually, mine would have." I say this in a more petulant manner than I had planned.

"Like that's a surprise?" Chuck sniggers, as do a few others.

"Mine probably would have as well." Cher says this deadpan, cutting short the sniggering.

"Mine tried to." Practically her entire family has tried to kill Tallulah at one time or another.

Inside I smile.

Panic over. I take a big, satisfied swig of Bud.

"Thinking about it, maybe someone should call in and do his mother. Sort of in Will's honor." James, buoyed by the fact that he is being listened to for once, is now starting to call the shots.

Seven people around the table immediately respond with a very loud and very vociferous, "I'll do it!" I get mine in just a fraction after I realize this is what I should be yelling. Hands are raised in the air like schoolkids, and everyone looks so eager and willing that I can't see how Tony Curtis as resident chairman of the Club can possibly make a decision.

"Me. Pick me, Tony."

"No, me."

"Me, Tony, me."

"I'll do it." Tony says this in midbelch with cold eyes and an even colder delivery that ends any dispute before it can begin.

I take another huge and satisfying mouthful of Bud.

Two down, eight to go.

All through this meeting I have been sitting, on purpose, beside Tallulah. I study her for a moment and really can't think of anyone I've ever met who unsettles me as much as Tallulah does. Despite training at a top art school, she has ended up polishing the dance floor of a strip joint before and after performances. She wears charity shop clothes, lives in a dilapidated ghetto, and has no real ambition in life other than to kill as many people as she humanly can. She freely admits to hating all of humanity, and I happen to know that the feeling is mutual.

I study the tattoo on Tallulah's right forearm. It takes the form of a dagger, and at the dagger's tip, blood drips down, and the resultant pool of blood spells out "Art Is Dead." Knowing Tallulah, "Art" probably refers to some unfortunate guy she once knew.

"I've never had the nerve to say this before, but I'd really like to know where you had that done. I've got this friend who is looking for a good needle job." I talk as if I know the lingo of tattooists, and I think it sounds hip.

Tallulah looks up at me, eyes cold, gray, and hateful. "I did it myself."

"Wow. That's really, uh . . . really neat. So you're left-handed, then?"

"What do you think?" She has no need to sound sarcastic, but that's her way, I guess.

I give Tallulah a small, appealing smile. "I'm surprised you never entered the tattoo industry. Someone of your obvious quality."

Tallulah pulls a sarcastic face as she lights a cigarette.

"Wiping up after strippers—that must feel like a real comedown, especially when you have such a great talent." I have to needle her; I can't help it. Did I say needle her? "You know, your story really got me. . . ." I point to my heart. "Right here. I still can't believe you shared that with me."

"I told the whole group, not just you."

"I know that, but your story was so, uh, so . . . intimate . . . it felt like you were talking to me and me alone. I don't think I knew anyone else was in the room, your story was so compelling." I want to get under Tallulah's skin, making like the ink she uses to tattoo her victims.

In the background, James Mason opens up with the details on his latest kill.

"I had promised Mother that I would kill him. I saw it as a treat—for all the hard work we'd been putting in lately. He didn't quite fit the social group Mother and I have come to despise, those lowlife juror scum, it was more just a case of my saying to Mother, 'This judge would make a good kill.' Nothing more, nothing less. And I've got to tell you, I really enjoyed killing him. I can't defend myself here." As if he could anyway. "I hold up my hands and openly admit that he was a great kill. . . ."

Tallulah is only half listening to the story; she despises James like she despises all of us.

"That needle gun . . . what an implement. What a weapon. . . ." I shake my head and blow out a little air, as if Tallulah were the queen of killers. And even coldhearted and hateful, Tallulah can't help but warm to my indulgence in her.

"This friend of yours. Is it a big friendship?"

"Uh, no . . . uh . . . well, he's an acquaintance. Yeah, more of a work colleague."

"So he's male?"

"Yeah . . . at least he assures me he is." I snort out some laughter at this terrific gag. Tallulah doesn't even hear it as her eyes narrow.

"He ever tell you about seeing strippers? As in paying to see women demean themselves in front of a row of self-abusing losers?"

I pretend to think this over. "Actually, now you mention it . . . you know, I think he does go. Most nights he has free, in fact. He's a little bit like that. You know, a little bit depraved."

Tallulah's eyes widen, and I know I've got her.

"Set up a meet."

I had originally thought I was going to have to work hard on Tallulah. I hadn't counted on her killing agenda being so fervent.

"I'll tattoo him. From head to toe."

"I think he's only after a small butterfly design—"

"What *he's* after isn't my concern. When can I do this?"

"Soon as possible, I guess."

"Wednesdays are good for me."

Tallulah turns away. End of conversation. I study her lank, mousy blond hair. I imagine her on all fours wiping up peanuts and spilled beer, can visualize her growing hate as it courses through her, expanding in her chest until she's fit to burst. She probably gets yelled at by the perverts in the front row. I bet she yells back at them, and I know for certain they try to throw peanuts into her large, abusive mouth.

I smile to myself—not at the image, but because even though she'll never know it, Tallulah is planning to kill federal agent Kennet Wade.

And if I'm honest here, I wonder if I shouldn't let her do it.

There's a lot to think about, and later, after pretending to go to the men's room and sidestepping to the phone booth, I make a call to Agent Wade.

"Tallulah wants to meet you."

"Great. Hey, what a plan, huh? Worked first time."

"I had to tell her you like going to strip joints."

Agent Wade pauses. "How did you know that?"

I pause, a little surprised. "I, uh . . . I just, uh . . . I just thought you looked like the type of guy who likes a good time." I say this knowing it sounds weak.

"Yeah, well, there's nothing wrong with it."

"I didn't say there was."

"It's just hard establishing a solid relationship in my line of work."

"Absolutely."

"A lot of the guys go. . . ."

I'm not really listening to Agent Wade because I'm more engaged with the thought that Tallulah might just take it upon herself to tattoo him to death. I can even picture the slogan she'll jab across his tanned and healthy-looking skin.

"Agent Wade Is Dead."

And maybe I could add something to that.

Like "Long Live the Club," for instance.

It is sorely tempting.

NEEDLE GUN

I SWEAR ON WEDNESDAY nights it rains harder than ever. One thing you don't do in Chicago is walk your dog on a Wednesday evening. You just sit in and let the dog whine itself into a frenzy rather than see little Rover get washed away by a flash flood.

Agent Wade is standing on the corner of a deserted street, the rain is coming down in sheets, and I'm sitting beside Tallulah as she drives her vile and tacky car through the flood. Agent Wade suddenly flashes a bright grin through the rain and starts waving us down. He looks excited, and I'm a little disturbed by his apparent lack of cool. He wears a baseball cap and is dressed just like any guy you'd see in a strip joint—lumberjack shirt and sawdust-stained jeans. Tallulah glances across at me as she slows.

"That the jerk?"

I don't answer as I open the door to her car, and as Agent Wade scurries toward us I note that this is about the ninetieth day running that I haven't felt so much as a breeze. Nothing is ever going to blow these rainclouds away.

Agent Wade climbs in beside me, gives me a big friendly nod. "Hell of an evening."

"Yeah. Sure is."

I turn to Tallulah. "This is my friend, uh . . ."

"Barclay. Barclay Moone. You can call me Bark." I'm impressed—an alias. This guy's good. The name is so much better than anything William Holden could've dreamed up.

I spend the rest of the journey listening to Agent Wade combating Tallulah's dry, hateful tones as they spear across me. It's almost like I'm not even there.

"I've wanted a tattoo since I was so high." Agent Wade—or Bark to his new friend—grins across me, staring bug-eyed at Tallulah while she drives. He is really on a high, and I can only presume it's because he's never met a skiller before. Not a live one, anyway. "Mom wouldn't let me have one. Refused point-blank. I must've asked her a hundred times."

"She still alive?" Tallulah is like her needle gun—straight to the point.

Agent Wade pauses. A lump swells in his throat. His voice seems less solid. "Domestic accident."

These two anguished words are enough to convey everything that Tallulah need know. The matter should be closed.

"You see it happen?" Tallulah and tact have never met.

It takes a while, but Agent Wade gives a small but positive nod. He's playing his part well. The FBI have obviously given him the best training possible.

"Gunshot?" Tallulah doesn't take her eyes off the road as she jabs out her words.

"Arrows."

"How'd it happen?"

"Me and a few pals, we were playing in the yard. Could only have been eight or so. I was always real keen on taking the suckers off my arrows, you know, and then, uh . . . sharpening them. We couldn't get real bullets, but we could get close to a real arrow." Agent Wade sucks in his bottom lip, his chin quivers, and I can't help but think this is a really terrific act he is putting on here. "Mom took three arrows in the chest. Full on."

"My mother was murdered."

Agent Wade looks up, takes time, as if to let this awful, hideous truth sink in. "That must have been terrible for you."

"Trussed up like a chicken and pretty near plucked like one, too. If you can pluck skin, that is."

"Truly awful."

"I kept telling her to use moisturizer."

I listen to this, and although I've heard Tallulah mention this before, I still don't get it. Moisturizer?

Agent Wade nods as if he understands implicitly what Tallulah means. "I hate wrinkles."

I make a mental note to ask Bark to explain this to me.

We near our destination, a small motel on the edge of town, where Agent Wade, no doubt using his false name, has rented a room. He already has the keys, and we hurry from Tallulah's vehicle through the heavy rain and over to the run-down motel room. Agent Wade opens the door, and we all step inside. I'm last in, and as I step forward I suddenly feel Tallulah's tattooed arm block any further progress into the room. Agent Wade has walked over to the bed and is trying to switch on the lamp.

"Bark's mine," she growls.

I'm immediately plunged back into that deep and cavernous quandary. I would love to be famous and adored—who wouldn't?—but equally I can't deny there's something scratching deep within me that says I should put an end to Agent Wade.

I study Tallulah, wishing she weren't so full of hate and had a soft spot somewhere. Something I could make contact with. Agent Wade finally gets the lamp on, and he is a little surprised to find that there is a red bulb in the lamp. The room is suddenly glowing in this scarlet hue, and I can make a good guess that a prostitute or her client will be the first to find the murdered body.

But whose body?

Maybe it's knowing that Tallulah tattoos her victims, then strips off the newly patterned skin and mails framed examples of her work to art galleries, but I come down on Agent Wade's side.

If I think hard enough, I know it gets down to the fact that he said "please" when we first met. There was a certain humanity in that. Agent Wade didn't have to be polite, but as Tony Curtis is fond of saying as he belches, "Good manners is everything."

I close the door behind me and pull on a pair of calfskin driving gloves, and as I feel that familiar surge of adrenaline mixed with fear, I leap on Tallulah from behind.

"Die!" I think it has something to do with having an audience, but for some reason I feel the pressing need to make this as dramatic and compelling as I can. "Die, die, die!!"

Tallulah is fast, though—much stronger than I realized—and she easily tosses me off her before I can get my fingers clamped around her throat. I am aware of Agent Wade standing back and watching things unfold, and I half feel like yelling to him for some help when Tallulah whips out her needle gun and comes at me with it.

"Little fucking freak!" I get ink dots embedded, probably forever, in my wrists and forearms as she drives me back, stabbing and slicing relentlessly, until I find myself in a corner watching as thick white saliva builds around the corners of Tallulah's mouth. "Little fucking scum bucket you turned out to be."

As she goes for me, I grab up the lamp, and with my eyes

closed in sheer terror, I swing the lamp back and forth wildly, lashing out at Tallulah, not connecting with anything, just flailing desperately at her. I swipe at her like I'm trying to hit a fast-moving wasp and manage to get out of the corner she had me trapped in. I look around, and Agent Wade is there one moment and then gone the next as the red bulb explodes and plunges the room into darkness. For a moment I can't see a thing; my eyes can't adjust to the sudden light loss, and I peer out, not knowing where Tallulah has gone. I can see a shape move first one way, then it seems to be moving in the other direction.

"Bark? Is that you? . . . Bark!"

I look around, knowing an attack is going to come but not knowing from where—Tallulah could be anywhere.

"Time to get inky!"

Tallulah suddenly comes at me again, like a giant savage rat, and I feel myself crumple under the weight of her attack. I take her down with me and get the wind knocked from me as her knee lands hard in my gut.

"Jesus! Help me, can't you?!" I gasp as I feel Tallulah's fetid breath burning my face.

"Inkier and inkier!" Tallulah's eyeballs catch the moonlight streaming in through the window, and for a moment they look like they belong to a cat. Her arm arcs up, and I know she's going to drive her tattoo needle straight into my brain. A light suddenly comes on—a searing, blinding flashlight—catching Tallulah momentarily off guard. A dark shape looms up behind the light, and although I can't make out the cause of it, a sickening thud rings out—something heavy hitting something soft. And the next thing I know, Tallulah's rank spittle sprays all over my face. Only when it trickles into my mouth do I realize it is her blood.

Tallulah pitches forward and lands heavily across me, and

as the searing flashlight finds my eyes, Agent Wade squats beside me and gives an almighty and sardonic sigh.

"Ready when you are, Dougie. . . ."

Tallulah's blood keeps running into my mouth, and my only response to Agent Wade is to gag on it.

Later, it comes as a shock to find Agent Wade snatching the needle gun from me, plunging it into a bottle of ink, and then tattooing Tallulah's lifeless arm. I have just finished what I consider to be a rather neat version of a black cat, but for some reason he is mortified, telling me in no uncertain terms, "We have to get this right, Dougie, we have to make it look like the work of the Tattoo Terror. . . ." Agent Wade gives Tallulah eight tattoos that night, all of them bearing the inscription "Mom."

I grab up a bottle of ink as a memento, and after Agent Wade wipes everything down, removing our fingerprints, we sneak out into the rain and walk briskly uptown.

"You learn tattooing at the academy?"

"You learn everything at the academy, Doug. Everything."

I glance up at Agent Wade's fine movie-star profile and know for certain that he must be a real asset to the Bureau.

MURDER RAP

~~TALLULAH BANKHEAD~~

RICHARD BURTON

CHER

TONY CURTIS

DOUGLAS FAIRBANKS Jr.

BETTY GRABLE

~~WILLIAM HOLDEN~~

BURT LANCASTER

JAMES MASON

CHUCK NORRIS

I STUDY THE LIST and wonder why the line going through my name has been erased. Agent Wade and I are standing outside the monkey pen at the zoo where I work; a few visitors are laughing and throwing peanuts to the apes, who I note are getting lazy and fat thanks to their high-sodium diet. A sign says DO NOT FEED, and I hear Agent Wade whisper, "I could get all of these perps on a federal rap."

"I, uh . . . I see I'm back on the list."

"What?" Agent Wade looks genuinely alarmed. He snatches

the list from me. "What was I thinking? Sorry about that, Doug . . . really."

Agent Wade then picks up some spilled peanuts and hurls them at, rather than for, the monkeys. Under his breath I swear I hear him mutter, "Choke on this. . . ."

Later I take Agent Wade for lunch in the zoo workers' canteen. I order a giraffe-shaped burger, and he has an elephant pizza, so-called because it comes in the shape of an elephant's ear. Agent Wade claims he has left his wallet behind, and I am forced to pay for the meal. We share a can of Dr Pepper.

"Tallulah sure put up a hell of a fight." I pour my half of the Dr Pepper, then hand the can to Agent Wade.

"Some women are like that. They're wildcats."

"She gave me the most trouble I've ever had. Was lucky you stepped in like you did."

Agent Wade takes a sip of Dr Pepper. "My guess is she was on steroids. Probably taking enough to beef up an entire Olympic squad."

"You think so?"

Agent Wade nods with complete conviction. "FBI Directive Eighteen. Chapter twelve, verse four."

"Verse four?"

"Did I say verse? I meant paragraph four, subsection thirty-four. 'Steroids induce anger, unreasonable belligerence, and instability. When investigating a case with steroidal intimations, use maximum force.'"

I let out a low, complimentary whistle. "You sure know your stuff."

My giraffe burger arrives with Agent Wade's elephant pizza. I smile at the waitress, who I note is new here. She is also devastatingly pretty.

"Just started?" I give her a pleasant grin.

"Actually I've been here four months." She yawns, and I can tell she's coming to the end of a long shift.

"Really? Four months? So where have you been hiding that I haven't seen you around before?"

"Oh, I've seen you around before." The waitress walks off, and I admit I don't quite get the gist of this. She may be pretty, but her conversation is badly lacking.

Agent Wade watches the waitress for a moment, cutting into his pizza as he does. "Cute."

"Hands off. I saw her first." I say this with a gentle laugh but find that in truth I really mean it. It may have taken four months, but I did see her first.

Agent Wade shrugs. "She's not my type, anyway."

I can only presume this is because she doesn't work in a strip joint.

Agent Wade finishes off his half of the Dr Pepper, then gives me a thoughtful look. "I guess you want to know what's gonna happen at the end of the two months?"

"I'll admit it had crossed my mind."

Agent Wade smiles, takes his time as he lights a cigarette. "If you finish the job, then I'm gonna let you go."

I sit very still, knowing I should be thrilled by this, but there's something in the way he says it that tells me he's lying.

He blows smoke toward the ceiling. "Bet you never figured that would happen."

"No, I sure didn't."

"You're gonna be a free man, Doug. After you're done, I'm outta here. Sayonara, au revoir, vamoose, all those things."

I hold Agent Wade's unwavering look, offering him a thin smile, hoping to convey some sense of joy at this news. But inside I don't believe him.

Not for one second.

Agent Wade keeps smiling at me. "Listen, there's something else I need you to do for me, Doug."

Agent Wade takes a moment and then leans forward across the table. I feel compelled to lean toward him, and we talk conspiratorially.

He takes his time. "I want you to get the Club to offer the Kentucky Killer a membership."

I immediately shake my head. "They won't do that. We've discussed it a hundred times over."

"Dougie . . ."

"It's impossible."

"Dougie, just hear me out."

"You don't know what you're asking."

"He's just another killer, Doug."

I shake my head firmly. "No. No way. He's the king of killers. What's he up to now? Two hundred and ninety victims."

"Two nine eight."

"The Club can't compete with that—their combined total isn't even half that. If he started telling stories, we'd still be listening six months later. You're talking about a lot of egos getting crushed beyond recognition. KK's had masses of stuff written about him, MTV specials have been broadcast, he's had TV movies made about him, there's even talk of a serial killer soap opera. We're dealing with the equivalent of Elvis here, the members are cruise ship crooners in comparison."

"Which is why you've got to get him to join. You have to take out the top guy. He probably inspires as many people as he kills. It's not a good thing him being out there. Besides, I want every last serial killer, Dougie."

"How, though? The cops, the CIA, even your FBI people can't catch him. How d'you think we're gonna do it?"

"You know how to communicate with him, to draw him out. Sure, he might be more famous than an astronaut, but no one has any idea who he is. Those movies they made of him, in one he was Caucasian, another Hispanic, another he was African, another he was in a wheelchair. He could be anyone. You. Me. Anyone."

I shake my head again, knowing this is crazy. "If Tony says no, then Tony means no."

"Think about the victims a minute, Dougie. You want to be a hero, right? Then save all those people who are going to buy some fast food, walk out into the midday sun, and then be found half an hour later with a KFC family meal carton dumped over their heads. Abject souls with lemon-scented hand wipes stuffed down their throats and the menu for a new secret recipe stapled to their foreheads. What about them, Dougie? Huh? Come on, hero—what about them?"

I look away, don't know how to answer that.

"Imagine your last moment on earth being an argument with a KFC employee as you try desperately to make them understand your order. Life can get cheap, Dougie, but that's no way to use up your last few minutes before KK strikes."

"Tony won't allow it. . . ." I know this sounds weak, and Agent Wade comes in for the kill.

"Five years he's been out there killing roughly one a week. And you're right, we can't find him because we can't man every single KFC outlet, it's impossible. You're the last chance we have, Dougie."

"I wish I could help . . . I honestly do. But—"

"Get them to invite him, Douglas." Agent Wade gives me a no-nonsense look, spelling his words out, making sure I understand fully what I've got to do. "He has to join."

"No."

"Do it for me, then. For your old pal Agent Wade."

"The Club'll get suspicious—they're already asking a lot of questions."

Agent Wade is not going to take no for an answer. "Who saved your life, Dougie? Who did that, huh? Not once, though, but twice. Who was there for you?"

I hate to admit it, but I think he's got me there.

"Agent Wade came good for you, Dougie, so it's time you came good for Agent Wade, don't you think?"

I give him a reluctant shrug, know he's got me backed into a corner. "I guess I could try. But I can't promise anything."

Agent Wade suddenly switches tack and gives me that handsome grin of his again. "Dougie . . . you're Club secretary, you've got sway. And I've seen the way you talk to girls, I know you can charm anyone into doing anything. Trust me. You're a natural. . . ."

I can't help the sudden and glowing sensation spreading through me.

Agent Wade finishes the can of Dr Pepper in three big, greedy gulps and then gives me a proud wink. "You're the man, Dougie!"

TENSE WITHOUT TALLULAH

AGENT WADE has made me take the rather clever precaution of hiding the ink dots I received from Tallulah's needle attack under two sporty-looking wristbands. We went shopping together, and he helped me choose several pairs in different colors, and the red ones currently match the jersey I have tied around my shoulders. I turned up at the Club carrying a sports bag with a tennis racket inside it to help the overall image—I took this as a memento from Stan Laurel, who toured as a pro for some years.

"Hey, everyone, look at the athlete." Chuck points to me and grins as the others turn. I nod back to them, feeling good that they've bought the image.

"They lower the net specially for you?" I pretend to enjoy this joke from Burt, laughing along with Betty and the others, though secretly I want to bury my tennis racket in Burt's face.

"Tallulah's late." Tony licks Cher's soup spoon before plunging it into what's left of her chicken broth. How polite of them to start without me.

Tony's voice seems heavy and weary, and he isn't interested in any of the gags flying around.

"She's never late." Richard shifts in his seat.

There's an undeniable tension in the air that is mush-rooming over the table. "I really like Tallulah."

The contempt I feel for Richard is slowly eating away at my insides. So far, he's told everybody but me that he likes them.

"Mother says she may have just got held up." James Mason offers this, even though he knows it sounds weak.

"Maybe her needle jammed." I can't help myself. I have to laugh along with Chuck.

Cher isn't amused. "What's happening, Mr. Curtis? What the hell is going on?"

"Jesus . . . cool it, will ya? Like Jimmy says, maybe she's stuck in traffic."

"Mother said it, not me," James corrects Tony.

"Crawl off and die, Jimmy." James is making himself a strong candidate for Tony's next kill.

I lean forward, putting on my best helpful look. "I heard flash flood warnings over the radio." I don't even have a radio. Not one that works, anyway.

"There you go, then. Little Dougie there's just given us the answer."

I bathe in Tony's gratitude, but Cher isn't convinced.

"Miss Bankhead would get here whatever. I know that for sure."

"And how'd you know that, exactly?" Tony is quick to jump on this. I find that I'm enjoying their sparring session.

"I know how much the Club means to her."

"Sounds like you and her are pretty tight. Anything else you want to tell us?"

"Like what?"

"I'm waitin' to hear."

Cher glares at Tony, who glowers back. I catch sight of Betty, and she looks very nervous. She obviously isn't a big fan of confrontation. I then see Burt sneak her a furtive smile of assurance. I don't like that—I wanted to do that.

Tony and Cher are still eyeballing each other.

"Why's she not here, Cher?"

"You tell me."

"Hey . . . I asked first."

"Come on, guys, huh? This is crazy." Chuck stabs out his Marlboro. "Lighten up. The Club's meant to be a fun night."

"It will be without Tallulah around." I throw in this great joke and laugh heartily. It takes me ten seconds to realize that everyone is scowling at me. Even Betty. "Drink, anyone?"

"Fuck Tallulah, I don't give a pig's nipple about her." Tony is sure in a foul mood tonight. "What I wanna know is, which one of you chooks did this?"

Tony yanks a crumpled copy of the evening edition out of his jacket pocket and hurls it onto the table in front of everyone. It is open at the personals column, and I go weak at the knees when I see it.

King of Kentucky,
It's time to chow down with your brethren. Looking forward to some fast food and fast times.

Yours,
Chairman Tony

Tony glares darkly at all of us in turn. "I'm waitin'."

There is complete silence. I look at Betty. She in turn looks at Burt. Cher glances at Chuck, and I turn away when he looks at me, only to find James staring my way. Richard reaches over and turns the newspaper around so he can read it. Or, in his case, try to read it.

"What am I meant to be looking at?"

Tony shakes his great head. "Fuckin' half-wit."

The silence stretches and expands until it seems the very air around us is going to burst.

"Who ran the ad? Come on . . . spill."

"It sure wasn't me—or Mother."

I realize that we are spaced farther apart around the table, and this lends a sense of isolation to each of us. I feel like I could swing a cat round my head and not hit anyone. I don't like being so prominent, because the one thing I can't do now is draw any attention to myself.

Tony is still waiting for an answer.

"I'm gonna find out one way or another." He says this directly to Cher, and I guess with the way she is so keen to get KK to join, it's only natural that he suspects her.

She knows this and looks edgy. She scans the faces of the others and realizes they are thinking the same thing. "Why's everyone looking at me?"

"Why do you think?" I see no harm in really pointing the finger at her.

Cher's face reddens with anger. "You're Club secretary, you're the one who runs the ads."

"Which would be pretty stupid of him to do this, don't you think?" Chuck squeezes out an ironic laugh, and I hold out my arms and shrug like an Italian toward Cher.

"Totally dumb."

"Maybe it was Mr. Fairbanks, then. Cuz it's obviously the work of an asshole."

For some reason, the longer I know Cher, the more I find myself hating her.

"You're the only one who wants him to join, though." Betty's lilting voice soothes my inner panic, and I look up at her, giving her the broadest smile I can muster. I stay that way long enough for her to get the message that I'm very grateful to her.

"Could someone read it to me?" Richard's illiteracy is irritating the hell out of everyone, and they are glad to have a target to aim their pent-up tensions at.

"Mr. Burton, don't you think it's about time you learned to read and write? I mean, how old are you, for chrissakes?"

"Yeah, I'm sick of reading the menu to you every time we meet here." Chuck eyeballs Richard. "A fetus is brighter than you are." God, I enjoy that.

Tony snatches up the evening edition and starts tearing it angrily into strips. "One thing I won't tolerate is disobedience in the Club."

Cher doesn't like the way Tony is still staring at her and bows her head and tries to force down a mouthful of raw-looking venison that has just arrived in front of her.

"Let's just hope ole KK doesn't see this."

"But what if he does?" Burt considers Tony for a moment. "What if he responds?"

"We are getting kinda short on members." Richard sticks out a flabby finger and starts counting out loudly. "One, two, three, four . . ."

Tony bats the finger down hard, and Richard recoils. "I think I've noticed."

"Sorry, Tony."

There is no sign of any lightening up for the rest of the evening. It is a bleak and tense meeting, and as if to reflect this, the darkest clouds I have ever seen gather in the hundreds outside. Not even the television psychiatrist revealing a new and quite hilarious method for catching skillers can break the bleak mood. From what I could make out, it has something to do with urine samples and a test scientists can then carry out. So far, the idea is only in its infancy, as it would entail the whole of America sending their labeled piss to a small three-man lab in southern Alaska.

Later Chuck decides he needs to help lift the mood and rises to tell the story of his latest kill. If anyone is going to get the night back on track, it's going to be the great Chuck Norris. Cher calls him our movie star killer and she would know, considering she's our rock star killer.

"So I'm in this girl's closet. One of those walk-in closets that you always see in horror movies, you know, with the thin white slats in the door, all the clothes hanging up behind you, and the killer's in the bedroom, thinking, Duh, I wonder where she's hiding? And it never occurs to him that she's in the closet even though it's about the only place she can be hiding, and he's not only walked slowly past it five or six times, but he's just got to have seen at least one horror movie in his life. So you think he'd figure it out, right? Anyway, things are different on this particular night, cuz the killer is in the closet this time, and the girl, who is running late by the way, should in fact be in the bedroom."

I immediately laugh. "That's hysterical."

No one else seems to get the joke and I feel I have to point it up. "It's usually the killer who's outside the closet. But Chuck's inside it."

I get a few blank looks but most people are waiting for Chuck to continue. I shake my head, turn to Chuck. "Don't worry, I get where you're coming from."

"Would you shut the fuck up?" Tony glares at me, and all I can do is shrug at him.

"I'm just—"

"I mean it, Junior. Another word and you can go sit in the kitchen."

I shake my head, making a point of sighing loudly. Sometimes I think I'm too good for them.

Chuck replays a little of what he's already said, trying to find where he left off. Then he clears his throat and continues.

"Anyway, I'm in the closet. And after an hour of sitting with her lingerie draping itself around my ears, I'm wondering where the hell my victim has got to. I've stalked her for a month and I pretty much know her routine by heart. Tonight, Thursday, is the night she comes home from work, runs a bath, then watches her favorite TV program, taking advantage of the commercial breaks to go check on the water or add some bath salts."

"She only bathes once a week?" I am stunned by this.

I ignore the scowls that shoot my way from the members.

"She showers the other days," Chuck explains, and for a moment he looks tired. I'm starting to wonder at just how long he was in that closet. It seems to have drained him of his usual sparkle.

"But she doesn't show. I'm waiting to hear the key in the front door any moment, but there's nothing. Another hour goes by, and by this time, I've counted all the slats in her closet door."

"How many were there?" I think that's a fair question.

"Eighteen million," Chuck responds rather dryly.

I definitely think he's got a case of closet fever. God help him if the police ever catch him and toss him in a cell. He'll go nuts within seconds.

"So where was she?" Betty's timid voice is barely heard.

"Exactly what I was asking myself," Chuck responds. "So after what must be three hours, I finally come out of the closet."

"Hey everyone, Chuck's gay." I'm always reading how women find men who make them laugh hugely attractive and I can clearly see that Betty is trying her damnedest to control her laughter. She's good though, barely a smile creases her lips and I admire that amount of self-control.

"One more interruption and you're going in the fucking kitchen. To be cooked." Tony leans toward me, his eyes blazing. I immediately sit back in my chair, hunkering a little lower, annoyed that so few people have a sense of humor these days.

Chuck starts again, looking more world-weary by the second. He seems to have lost his enthusiasm and this story is taking its toll on him. His delivery is routine and that wonderful stage presence of his has all but evaporated. Poor guy must be sickening for something.

"Anyway, I'm in her bedroom, I'm looking through her Rolodex, cuz I want to find out where she is. I call her friends, her family. 'Hey there, have you seen Penny tonight?' 'Hi, I'm looking for Penny.' I make about a dozen calls but no one's seen her. Some of her friends sound real nice, and her father is just the greatest guy alive. I talk to him for maybe half an hour, then her mother comes on the line, then her sister, and I gotta tell you, they are some family. When I hang up I feel like I've known them for years. I even got invited to dinner."

No one laughs at this; Chuck has lost his audience and he knows it.

"So did this Penny ever show?" Cher is probably the only one still listening.

"Well, that's the weird thing. She got knocked down by a car. Stepped out into the road without looking. How careless is that? So I guess if your number's up, well, your number's up. Car, serial killer, it doesn't matter which. Least I got a free dinner out of it."

Again no one laughs, despite Chuck's hopeful smile. This is probably the worst story Chuck has told, and when I think about it, what he needed were more jokes and better timing. I tried to help lift the story, but in truth, it was beyond saving.

When I get home I find Agent Wade sitting with his feet up on my bolted-down sofa. He has had house keys cut, and I can smell eggs boiling in the kitchen. He is watching a late night movie and seems to have made himself at home. There is a battered typewriter sitting in his lap, and several typed pages lie on the immovable coffee table. Agent Wade flicks the remote, killing the sound on the television.

"Like the ad?"

"It was you?"

"Who else?"

"Everyone thought it was Cher."

"That should flush KK out."

I try to stifle a yawn; it's been a long day. "It might take some time for him to bite. Could be that we run over the two-month cutoff point."

"He'll come. I know he will. Can almost smell the lemon hand wipe."

Agent Wade takes off his shoes and then brings his feet up on my sofa, stretching out as he does. "I've been doing some thinking, Dougie. . . ."

Agent Wade studies me, and I don't like the way he does this.

"I think I'm gonna stick pretty close to you from now on. You know, move in with you."

He takes off a sock, sniffs it, then tosses it toward his shoes. "My stuff's in the car, if you want to bring it in for me."

I stop. Who does he think he is?

Agent Wade sniffs his other sock and then tosses it toward me. "I've got a ton of laundry in one of the suitcases." He turns the sound back on and concentrates on the television again. "The keys are on the side there."

I don't believe this.

"Lying on the list."

I say nothing as I trudge slowly over to the side and reach for the keys to his sedan. As I take them off the list, I can't help but glance at it again.

It doesn't surprise me to find that he hasn't scored my

name off yet, so I reach for a pencil lying in a fruit bowl and quickly draw a line through it.

"What are you doing, Dougie?"

I pause, not believing that Agent Wade could have heard me. I turn to him and see him giving me an unrelenting stare.

"Nothing . . . nothing at all."

"Good, 'cause when you're done with my stuff we can start making another plan."

"Already? But . . ."

"But what?"

"Aren't we going a bit fast? Barely had time to catch my breath."

"Which is exactly what I want, Dougie. If I let up the pressure on you, even for a second, then you're going to blow it—I know it."

I'm outraged. "Hey, I survived this long. That takes great skill and determination."

Agent Wade puts a hand to his mouth and feigns a big yawn. "No need to get so bigheaded."

That remark hurts, and I turn away, not wanting to look at him anymore. He can obviously see that he has upset me and tries to get back in my good books.

"Okay, you were skilled and determined. But we really don't have the time. I want them wiped out ASAP. Who's next on the list?"

"Richard Burton."

"Then Richard Burton it is."

"The Club is going to go crazy when he doesn't show."

"The Club is crazy anyway."

Agent Wade eases back into my sofa, stretches, picks up the remote, and starts watching television.

"By the way, I like my pants pressed with a crease you could cut your wrists on."

RICHARD
BURTON

LIBRARY OF LOVE

AGENT WADE spent most of last night typing, and the sound of *clack-clack*ing until four in the morning nearly drove me insane. I tried to ask him to stop, but he claimed the FBI like their reports in triplicate and just kept banging away at the keys. As I lay awake listening to the equivalent of a marching band tramping through my living room, it dawned on me that I needed to talk to someone. And more important, I need a way out.

Betty Grable stamps the book of a nerdy-looking fifteen-year-old, watches him blush as their eyes meet for a moment, and then almost collapses in a heap when I walk up to her with a copy of a book entitled *Paddle Steamers—The Proud Years*. Betty's jaw drops, and she takes an involuntary and nervous step backward. I say nothing, just offer a smile, present my book, and watch as she swipes my library card through her machine. I then walk off to wait for closing time.

I catch up with Betty as she crosses the street to board a bus and jump on in near perfect synchronization with her. Although she is flustered at the sight of me, I have the feeling she knew I'd be waiting for her.

Her eyes blink up at me from behind her large pink glasses. For a second, I remember her wiping away tears of laughter with part of a tablecloth, and I know I have chosen to speak to her purely on account of that. I am also experiencing an undeniable feeling of excitement whenever I see her, and this is the first time I have felt this way about anyone in years.

Betty speaks first, looking at me shyly from beneath hooded eyes.

"Douglas."

I smile, trying my best to look warm and approachable.

"Betty."

"Did you, uh . . . Did you come in the library by accident?"

Betty is wary but also reveals an alertness that I didn't know she possessed. She's just been too shy to make much of an impact at the Club.

"Yeah. An accident. Pure and simple." I have to lie because I don't want her panicking. If she does, then I'm not going to get through to her.

"Knew it must've been that. You live round here, then?"

"Pretty close."

We fall silent for a moment, and I want Betty to think that this meeting is definitely an accident by stretching it out to an embarrassed and altogether stupefying silence. Like I haven't got a thought in my head or any talent for conversation. Just a stupid weak grin.

I smile stupidly at her for what seems like hours, and I can see she is uncomfortable with this. It forces her to break the cloying muteness.

"I had to ask . . . just to make sure."

I nod but keep on grinning—playing the "stupid grin ruse" to perfection.

"I'm just a little jumpy right now. Especially since William

Holden died. Plus there's still no word on Tallulah." Betty keeps talking, through sheer nerves more than anything else. "I know I'm still new to the Club, but it's kinda scary."

"It's a scary world." I remember the television psychiatrist saying this once, and uttering it works like a magic spell; suddenly I am back in the land of the supreme conversationalist. "Though I'll be the first to admit I never liked her. Do you know, she never paid her full share of the check at the end of the night?" By my calculations, Tallulah owes the Club nearly $90 all told.

Betty seems a little stunned by this, and I quickly try to make up for it by pretending it was a joke and breaking into the sort of laughter you hear in operas. Loud, deep, and tuneful. Ho-ho-ho.

"Joke!"

Though I have to admit, if there's one thing I don't like, it's a tightwad.

I watch Betty smile weakly, and I notice her dimples, big gouges running through what would be a perfect complexion if she bothered to sign up for an intensive facial every second month or so. She looks up at me with timid eyes.

"Tell me if you think I'm crazy, but do you think we're in danger, Douglas?"

I try to look confused, as if I don't follow her. "Danger?"

"Well, it's just that I know a few things. . . ." Betty gets a slight blush in her cheeks.

My veins freeze inside me.

Betty starts to say more but loses her nerve and turns away with a small tut. "Forget it. I'm just being paranoid."

I have to keep her on track.

I play it casual, cool. "Know what things?" My predicament with Agent Wade is suddenly becoming a thing of the past. It's looking as though I might have to kill Betty before I can kill Richard.

She shrugs, thinks things over, then lowers her eyes as she speaks. "It's actually Tony's theory. He said not to tell anyone . . . but God, Douglas, I am so spooked."

I stop.

Tony?

Did she just say Tony?

I don't want to ask, but I have to.

"Tony as in . . . ?"

"Yeah. Tony Curtis. The Club chairman. My brother."

I could easily fall out of my seat at this point and can't hide my stunned look. Betty offers another nervy little shrug. "We both had the same mother." And I guess that explains what needs to be explained. "You won't tell anyone, will you?"

"Of course not." I know what Tony does, and I am not going to tell anyone a single thing. "What, uh . . . what's his theory?"

"There's a rat in the Club." The phrase doesn't belong to Betty, but I can see it erupting from belching Tony Curtis's big fat mouth.

"A rat?" If Betty can't hear my now thudding heart, or see my stomach flipping over, then she must be both deaf and blind.

"He thinks someone at the Club is out to get us." The words smash against my temples, fall back, then crash again at my now throbbing head. "He's been investigating, and uh . . . well. He told me not to tell a soul, but he's been doing a lot of backtracking and managed to get hold of some details."

I'm being attacked by wave upon wave of nausea. I grip the handrail as tight as I can, hanging on for sweet dear life as the world does backflips in front of me. My voice has become a miserable little William Holden whisper.

"Details? What details?"

"I can't say. Really I can't. Tony was very adamant about keeping it a secret for now."

I'm pretty positive I haven't lost my voice altogether, but the sudden pressure on my larynx is making it a real struggle to get my words out. "Please. I'd like to hear it." I clear my throat, cough up phlegm, and spit it quickly out of the window. I hit a workman. "After all, I am Club secretary . . . and hell, Tony does think an awful lot of me."

Betty gives me a big frown. "Really?"

I decide to let it go; there are more important things to deal with here. "These, uh, details . . . ?"

Betty thinks it over for a long moment, and if she doesn't start talking soon, I'm going to have to take her somewhere quiet and beat the truth out of her. Finally she gives a vague shrug. "I guess it should be okay to tell you. Tony said the killer had to be someone really very clever, so . . ."

Betty smiles awkwardly rather than finish her sentence, and I have this sudden and overwhelming desire to smear her grin all over the sidewalk.

"He contacted a lot of police departments across the country, managed to get a few photos faxed over from morgues, and, uh . . . well. It seems like a lot of the members who supposedly quit the Club, uh . . ." My heart is now going like a jackhammer. "Well . . . they were murdered."

There is a huge pause, and then for some reason my machine-gun laugh fires out and I only just refrain from slapping my thigh like an old-time vaudevillian.

"Is this some kind of sick joke?" I say this sarcastically and without a hint of integrity. "Jesus, what's your brother on? Jeez . . . that's funny. Sick but funny."

I know I am overdoing this, and I truly hope to God Betty

doesn't tell Tony about this conversation. But I can't seem to help myself.

Now I do slap my thigh like an old-time vaudevillian. "That's the funniest thing I've ever heard . . . the absolute funniest thing." Another slap. Another big opera ho-ho-ho.

"I think he's on to something." She says this calmly, as if my laughing and thigh slapping hadn't happened. She cuts right through me with her simplicity. I look at her, swallow, straighten up, assume a more serious tone.

"You do?"

Betty looks at me with pale and ominous features. "Someone's out to kill us, Douglas. All of us."

I fall silent, try to gather my thoughts, but Betty's simple argument is grabbing and twisting at my insides. Reaching in and yanking handfuls of intestines this way and that.

I have to force my words past the rising bile smothering the back of my throat. "Does he . . . uh, have anyone particular in mind?"

Betty and I are seated in a little cafeteria; it's quiet and we are over by the window, life dragging its weary, rain-sodden self past us outside. I am feeling only slightly less anxious, but as the moments tick by I realize that I'm going to need to find a really clever way out of this. What I have to do for now is just bide my time and go with the flow. I get a little distracted by the smell of a dog and wonder if the cafeteria serves animals as well. I look around for a sign of one but don't see any dog bowls or poop-a-scoops.

I look back at Betty, try to collect my thoughts, and give her the most earnest look I can muster. "I love Tony."

Betty looks up, surprised.

I try to beat her to her next obvious conclusion. "Well, not love in the strict valentine sense, but he really is a helluva guy."

Betty doesn't bother replying, and I feel I have to fill the gaping silence that is stretching out between us. "I think he is the best chairman we have ever had. The absolute best. And you can tell him that from me."

Betty watches the raindrops snaking down the window for a long moment, lost in thought, and then finally looks round at me.

"Is it a medical thing? Your height?"

I am not sure how to respond to this. Betty must see that I look a little on the crestfallen side, and she offers what she thinks is a warm look. "Working in a library means you get to read about these things."

I nod slowly and find that my lips feel tight and bloodless for some reason.

"There was a fourteen-year-old at the Club. Shirley Temple. And she was real small. Tiny compared to me. That was definitely a medical thing."

"Fourteen? Really? How frightening."

"It was. She couldn't get served."

"What happened to her?" Betty gives me a fearful look. "You don't think she got killed, do you?"

"She got herself arrested." The spoiled little brat used to irritate the hell out of me until she stupidly went and got caught. "She's incarcerated and kept sedated somewhere. Won't be seen again till she's like eighty years old. Sure like to see her try and kill someone then."

A pretty waitress who isn't deaf brings over a large cappuccino for Betty and a double espresso for me. Earlier, I had jokingly asked for a quadruple espresso, and the waitress thought about it for a second before telling me they didn't stock cups that big. I know it was a silly joke, and probably one she hears every day of her life, but she could have at least smiled. After all, I was trying hard to put Betty at ease.

Betty sips at her cappuccino and gets a small, browny white foam mustache for her trouble. I want to reach over and wipe it off but instead spend the next minute trying not to look at it.

"So Tony Curtis is your brother. I can't see much of a resemblance."

"He's a half-brother."

"And half-bastard." I leap in like there's no tomorrow with this one. I find it hysterically funny but swallow my laughter when I see Betty frowning at me. "Sorry. It's an old joke. I didn't make it up, I was just repeating it." I am now hoping that Betty likes nervous, edgy men because this is definitely what I have turned into. I grab a napkin and dab her top lip with it before either of us knows where we are. She arches her neck and head back, trying to escape the napkin, but I am determined to wipe her mouth clean and clamp the back of her neck tightly with one hand while I rub her top lip.

"You've got foam . . . cappuccino foam . . . Look. See it? There. Look." I thrust the napkin under her nose, and she peers down at the napkin, starts nodding, offering a weak smile.

"Uh, yeah . . . I see it. Thanks. Thank you."

I'm hyped up, and the espresso isn't helping. I pop a raw cane sugar cube into my mouth, start crunching it loudly.

"You know, I never said this earlier, and maybe I should have, and then again maybe I was right to hold back—but can I trust you, Betty?"

"Trust me?" I'm now trying to look at Betty with big dog-like eyes, as I think this might be the thing that she likes in a man. She likes him to look at her like a dog. This is just a wild guess on my part, but I am sure I can smell dog on her.

"You told me all that stuff about Tony, so I guess I can."

Betty starts to look alarmed. "What is it, Douglas?"

"I'm in real big trouble. Really big stuff. You know it's, uh . . . it's total shit that I'm in. Total and utter shit." I reach for another sugar cube, crunch hard on it.

"What sort of trouble?"

I continue crunching loudly. "There's this guy. He's making my life hell."

"What guy's this?" Betty's voice is soft, warm.

"He's just this . . . this guy. He won't leave me alone."

"Why not?"

"He just won't."

Some people crumble under pressure; me, I guess I just rise to the occasion. All of my previous anxiety is dropping off me like leaves from a dying tree. I've got the plan to end all plans.

I am a genius.

"Douglas . . ." I find that I am looking straight into Betty's warm, sparkling eyes and figure I could sit here forever if she asked me to. "Tell me why he won't leave you alone."

"Uh . . . I can't."

"Douglas, please. Just tell me."

I pause, feel the sweet residue of the sugar lumps eating into my teeth. Maybe I will need dentures one day—and I know that when I do, I won't be fooled into buying that obnoxious brand of denture paste that Carole Lombard used.

"This, uh, guy—he knows."

"Knows what?"

"He knows what I do."

Betty knows what I do, or at least what I lie to the Club about doing.

"Can't you just, uh . . . You know . . ."

I shake my head, slowly, painfully. A heavy head on a weak neck.

"Why not?"

"He's got pictures."

"Of you?" I nod. "Doing . . . ?" I nod again. Then she nods. Slowly. My big dog eyes peer out at her from under heavy dog eyelids. "This, uh . . . this explains a lot. About your, uh, odd behavior. . . ." I nod again, secretly pleased that my "act" is working so well.

"Have you told anyone else about this?"

"Only you. And I don't even know why, to tell the truth."

"This is awful, Douglas. As if we haven't got enough problems. Is there anything I can do to help?"

Yeah, you can kill Agent Wade for me.

"This is my problem. I should sort it out."

"I take it he's after money?"

"Yeah. Money. That's it. Money that I don't have."

"Let me think about this. . . ."

"Please. I don't want to involve anyone else."

"Look, Douglas, there's a way around this, there always is. Right now you're too worked up, too emotional. Me? I've got a clear run on it. I could help you."

"But why would you want to?"

"Because . . . because I just do. I don't know why, but I happen to find this sort of thing to be totally unfair. You shouldn't be subjected to this. Not someone in your state." What state? What's she saying here? "You're probably a very nice guy underneath it all."

I look at Betty and can't believe I'm talking to a serial killer. All I can see sitting before me is a good woman with soft white skin and big glasses. The sort of girl I would be proud to take as my wife.

"You're a very kind woman, Betty. An angel."

"I don't know about that, Douglas. . . ."

"You are, though, Betty. The kindest woman I've ever met."

Betty blushes, shifts in her seat, looks away for a moment. I take this opportunity to lean forward and give Betty a surreptitious sniff, which I don't think she spots.

"Labrador, am I right?"

"Sorry?"

"You own a dog. I'm guessing Labrador." I breathe in as if I'm inhaling the very best scent money can buy.

Betty looks uncomfortable. "I don't own a dog."

"You don't?"

"Are you saying I smell of dog?"

I hesitate a moment, then quickly turn to a pretty but very thin woman drinking an espresso behind me. "Labrador, right?"

I turn back to Betty before the thin woman can respond.

"Let's get out of here. It's like being in a kennel."

WADING IN

AGENT WADE flicks cigarette ash onto my living room carpet and doesn't seem to care. He's watching an afternoon matinee with John Wayne heroically killing men in wide-brimmed hats. He is only half concentrating on the movie because every now and then he hits a typewriter key hard with his right index finger, as if punctuating his anger.

"Why did you go and see Betsy Grable?"

"Betty."

"Whatever. Why did you go and see her, Douglas?" He bangs a couple of keys. I hadn't for a moment thought that Agent Wade would be following my every move. The revelation has made me feel very vulnerable—and horribly invaded.

It reminds me of when he first squeezed my shoulder at the urinal, and a shiver runs through me.

"I didn't go and see her. It was just a coincidence. I wanted a book."

Agent Wade doesn't believe a word of it. "You wanted a book?" He mockingly repeats the words in a slow, southern-style drawl. I don't know why because I don't speak like that. "I thought I told you Richard was next?"

"You did?"

"Look at the list. He's next."

"Yeah . . . I know that."

I can't shake Agent Wade's unblinking eyes as he stares straight into me. "So what were you and Betsy talking about? You looked pretty cozy in that little café."

I sit down and wish he'd lower the sound on the television. All I can hear is John Wayne shooting at anything non-American.

"This and that. You know."

He bangs some more keys, and I swear he'll puncture the paper. "Listen, Dougie. I know you. Remember, I profiled you. I know what you were doing."

I start to panic, thinking that maybe Agent Wade has planted a bug on me, a listening device of some sort. "You, uh . . . you do?"

Agent Wade gives the typewriter one last hard bang, but he misses and gets his finger caught between the keys. He grimaces, yanks out the finger, and blows on the broken skin.

"Can't leave the ladies alone, can you?"

The prickling sensation I have been feeling all over my body starts to die away. Agent Wade sucks his finger and then wipes the small show of blood into the arm of my sofa.

"Forget your pressing need to mate, Dougie. Just for now, huh?"

"It's hard for a guy like me. She's attractive, she's available, and she's exactly my type."

"I want you to kill them, Dougie, not date them."

"But I like her."

Agent Wade gives me a pitying look. "You like her? Have you any idea what that woman does to men?"

"Of course I do. But just because she kills people doesn't necessarily mean she's all bad."

"She's sure cast a spell over you, hasn't she, Dougie. Huh?"

I feel myself blushing. I hadn't realized that I liked her this much. "I think it's pretty mutual, to be honest."

Agent Wade gives a huge and raucous snort of derision, then wipes his finger along the arm of my sofa again. He starts shaking his head—firing out this tut-tutting sound. The kangaroos at the zoo make the same noise, but it more often than not means they are ready to mate.

"Dougie, come and sit here a minute. . . ."

Agent Wade pats the sofa, and I feel utterly reluctant to join him on it. He winks at me. "Come on. . . ." He pats the sofa again, and I walk leaden footed over to him and sit down. He looks round at me, grins hugely.

"There's a time for romance, and there's a time for ridding the world of serial killers. Now guess which administration we're currently operating under?"

I look at Agent Wade, knowing he doesn't want an answer, that he's telling me how things are and that's it.

"Betsy is—"

"Betty—"

"Dangerous. Worse than any animal you clean up after. She's a killer, Dougie, and she has to be stopped."

"But I like her." It's a weak response, I know, but the more he tells me to forget Betty, the more I seem to want her.

Agent Wade puts an arm around my shoulders, pats me on the back like I'm his son in need of a man-to-man talk.

"Just because she makes your pants stick out doesn't mean you've got to go gooey on her."

BITCHFORK

O
N THE PLANE TO L.A., I keep thinking about Betty. I
can't get her out of my mind. The thought of having to
kill her makes me sick to the pit of my stomach, and a
depression hits me—sapping me of any real spark of life. Even
when I'm sitting in the back of a cab, looking out at the dazzling world that is Los Angeles, I fail to see anything about
human existence that makes it worth living. Not even the taxi
driver nearly running down a minor television celebrity can
bring anything more than a muted response from me. When I
finally arrive at my intended destination, I feel so down that I
tip the driver only a quarter, because depression like this
should be shared.

Richard lives in a condemned loft near some major porn film
studio that everyone pretends isn't really there. I had hoped to
get away from the incessant downpour of Chicago, but the thun-
derstorm raging all over town puts paid to that idea.

As a child Richard was an orphan, a fat boy, and intellec-
tually subnormal. Upon reaching adulthood, Richard found
himself to be illiterate and carrying a rare strain of herpes.
Despite these setbacks, he managed to trace his original par-
ents to Hollywood and was horrified to find he was the prod-
uct of two 1970s porn stars' overindulgence in front of the

camera. Pitchforking sixteen porn stars to death was perhaps a little uncalled for, but "Farmer Fear"—you can tell Richard made that one up—claims he doesn't want any more people coming into the world the way he did.

The only thing that can lift my mood tonight is killing Richard.

I press the buzzer for his loft. I want to make him nervous, and if someone presses your buzzer at two in the morning, it's bound to put you on edge. Agent Wade told me that this was one of the first things he learned at the academy, and I admit to being impressed.

Even though Richard's voice is scratchy because of the intercom, I swear I can hear fear caught in the back of his throat. "Who's there?"

"FedEx delivery."

"Huh?"

"Special package. I'll need your autograph."

"Huh?"

Get with the program, you dumb-ass, it's freezing out here! I sigh heavily. "It's an overnight, has to be signed for."

"This a joke?"

"You want this package or not?"

Richard debates for a moment, and then I hear the automatic door lock click and I push into the abandoned building. The place is functioning only on an emergency power supply, one that Rich, amazingly enough, got up and running all by himself. I walk to the elevator, only to find that it is out of order. All there is is a long, deep shaft going all the way up to the top floor, and there isn't actually an elevator inside it. I turn, look at the stairs, and wish Richard had opted to slum it in a ground-floor apartment.

I climb what feels like a thousand steps until I finally reach Richard's landing. It is pitch black, and I can hear rats scurrying behind me. The howling gale outside and the stagnant darkness inside would make me nervous without having to do what I have to do, so I take some deep breaths, sucking in air and exhaling slowly, until I think I am ready.

"Ra-rarara. Ra-rarara." I hum this lightly under my breath and find that it does allow a certain calmness to creep back into me. William Holden may have hit upon something there.

Richard's place is the only one with a door, and I go over and knock on it. I am surprised when the door swings open to reveal an empty, silent loft. I hear the rats scurry again. They seem to be getting closer.

I peer into Richard's dark and barely furnished room. I don't know how he has managed to live like this for so long, but as I look into the room I can see that he has tried to make it homely by putting plastic flowers in the window.

Outside, thunder suddenly booms across the belligerent sky, and the rats go silent—freezing in their tracks.

I peer into the loft. "FedEx man. Anyone home?"

"I don't remember ordering nuthin'."

The voice comes from behind me.

I swivel, and as I do lightning skewers the night and illuminates Richard, freezing him in a brief ultraviolet tableau. He is wearing pajamas with *Star Trek* characters printed on them; they are unbuttoned at the neck, and I can see his bulging cleavage. It's a disgusting sight, absolutely disgusting.

He then raises his pitchfork.

"Fuckin' no-good dwarf!"

How no one saw Rich carrying a pitchfork from murder scene to murder scene is one of the great mysteries of the modern age, but one I don't get the time to dwell on because the pitchfork is now slicing angrily through the air toward my throat.

"I sure know what you've come to deliver!"

I dive to one side, and sparks fly from the tips of the pitch-fork as Richard strikes the metal jamb of his loft door.

I grab for the knife I have in the waistband of my jeans and whip it out, only to feel instant dismay. It's at least twenty-four inches shorter than Richard's pitchfork. I could kick myself. I thought this was going to be so easy, that the thick slob would be too stupid to do anything but roll over and die for me. Lightning flashes again, and the sharpened tips of the pitchfork come straight for me and this time catch my sleeve, searing along my arm as they do. I drop my knife as the agony makes me unclench my fingers.

"Little pissy punk . . ."

I feel myself lifted off my feet as Richard heaves the trapped pitchfork into the air. Jesus, he's strong! I can't get free as he then starts half shoving, half carrying me toward the elevator shaft.

"Fuckin' never liked you."

I feel myself about to be hurled into the abyss of the eleva-tor shaft but manage to grab hold of either side of it, and we come to a momentary standoff as he shoves hard on the pitch-fork handle and I resist as best I can. My feet scramble for and then find the landing. Richard looms up, a dark monolithic shadow; his teeth are clamped tight, and his great breasts heave and glisten with sweat. He pushes harder and harder on the pitchfork, and it is all I can do to stop him from shoving me over the edge.

"Soon as I set eyes on you, I wanted to do this."

Richard shoves even harder, and I can feel my fingers starting to slip from the sides of the elevator walls—I'm going over, and there is nothing I can do about it.

"Fuckin' putrid pissy pisser . . ."

With one last heave, Richard shoves with all his might. His great chest rises up and flops back down, such is the effort, and as I realize it is all over for me, I hear my sleeve finally tear free from the prongs of the pitchfork. I immediately drop low, leaving Richard to suddenly discover that there is nothing resisting him, and he stumbles helplessly, relentlessly forward. He can't stop himself as he careers headlong into the elevator shaft, my last sight of him being his great fleshy backside mooning over the top of his loose pajama bottoms as his ass goes past my nose.

I sink to the floor, feeling exhausted and numb. I was an inch away from certain death. I came that close, and as the aftershock hits me, I notice that I can't stop my hands from trembling.

I take a badly constructed matchstick model of the starship *Enterprise* for a memento—it could also make a thoughtful birthday present for someone—and as I step out of Richard's loft, I go over and peer gingerly down into the elevator shaft. Somehow I have to make it look like Farmer Fear killed Richard. I grab his fallen pitchfork, and taking as good an aim as I can, I hurl the pitchfork down at his lifeless body. The next lightning flash sends me—more from the sheer relief of it all than anything else—into a fit of giggling as I catch a glimpse at where the pitchfork hit. It wavers back and forth in Richard's upturned butt and looks so hysterical that I double over, weeping openly.

On the flight home, I stop laughing and the shock of how close I came to getting killed kicks in hard. My grazed arm is stiffening and giving me immense pain into the bargain, and I'm starting to think that maybe it's time to make a run for it. I'd really miss Betty, but it seems that if Agent Wade gets his way, I'll be missing her regardless.

I come home to a pigsty. The house is a mess of abandoned and unpacked clothes and empty KFC bargain buckets. Agent

Wade is pressing his powder blue pants when I walk in, trying to get the crease razor sharp. I find that my arm is now completely stiff, and I have to hold it close to my chest in an attempt to relieve the throbbing pain. Agent Wade glances over at me.

"How was L.A.?"

"Overcast."

"You do Richard?"

I nod silently and walk to the list and score out Richard Burton's name. Just for good measure, I put a line through my name again, the previous line having disappeared again, surprise, surprise.

I then notice that some of Agent Wade's report lies out in a chair nearby, and I take a step closer and try to read the top page.

"Nosy."

I turn suddenly, and Agent Wade is standing right behind me. I hadn't even heard him, and I catch my breath. He reaches past me and grabs the thick volume of pages.

"You've got your own book to read. Remember? The one from Betsy's library?" He holds the pages rather guardedly to his chest.

"Betty. Her name's Betty."

He pats his precious sheaf of pages. "This is mine." Agent Wade hands me his blue pants. "Hang them up when you get a moment."

He returns to my—or should I say his—sofa and slumps down in it. He's getting to be like a dog who has taken up residence there. I study him for a good long while and realize that I'm exhausted. That I think I've had enough.

"Listen, I had a few thoughts on the plane."

"Yeah?"

"The Club's getting to be a dangerous place, and seeing as

I know where all of the skillers live, there isn't really any need for me to go there anymore."

Agent Wade sits up sharply.

"They'd just look on me as any other skiller who's suddenly disappeared."

"Not turning yellow on me, are you, Dougie?"

"No."

"Sure sounds like it."

"I don't need to go there, that's all I'm saying."

"Thought you liked the Club?"

"I do, but . . . well . . . there isn't going to be one for much longer, is there?"

"You disappoint me, Dougie."

I try to reach a middle ground. "We can still kill them."

"We? I'm no killer."

"Well . . . I can."

"Maybe I want you at the Club. Ever thought about that? Maybe it's all part of the strategy."

"It's getting tense there. I don't want to blurt out something I shouldn't."

"I need you in the field, Dougie."

"Why?"

"Because I like to make things interesting."

I pause, see a glint in Agent Wade's eye.

"Discussion over."

I sit in numb silence, watching the television for a couple of hours until I look over and see that Agent Wade has fallen asleep, using his thick report as a pillow. It occurs to me that if I'm to make good my escape, I should try to find the photo he has of me. But despite searching all over, I can't locate it anywhere.

Even a search of Agent Wade's car brings nothing. Apart from a strong lemon odor that not even a full blast of air-conditioning can get rid of.

BURT
LANCASTER

RECAP ON DECAP

I ARGUED LONG AND HARD with Agent Wade about the fact that I thought we were doing this alphabetically, but he eventually confided in me that that was just a big ruse of his. Someone might figure out what was happening, and then realize it was alphabetical as well, so now was the time to toss in a wild card and not go for the obvious.

Despite my growing reservations, I continue to have nothing but admiration for the first-class training the FBI has given Agent Wade. I was then only too eager to listen to what he called "the alphabet ploy," which he said would hopefully keep me alive and active at least a little while longer. That's so reassuring.

At the next hastily arranged Club meeting, Betty and I pretend not to know each other and nod very formally and correctly in each other's direction. As I glance around the bar and grill, I note that the quiz team is now down to two members. They look forlorn and sad, and I think about sending them a secret message telling the surviving two to go and eat somewhere else. I have my arm in a sling and have been told by my doctor not to do anything energetic for a while, which pretty much rules out murder, I guess.

Earlier on in the evening, it almost came to blows when the management tried to get the Club to move to a smaller corner of the bar and grill. That would have meant we wouldn't have been able to watch the television, and the psychiatrist was scheduled to speak on *60 Minutes* later. As I watched the manager and his headwaiter arguing with Tony and Cher, I could feel the bloodlust in the others boiling nicely into a murderous rage. Vultures one and all. Apart from Betty, of course, who happened to be in the ladies' room when the worst of the argument took place.

Burt takes a look at his watch, then states the obvious. "Richard's not coming, is he."

"Sure don't look that way," Tony grumbles as he and Betty share a furtive look.

"Where the hell is he?" Chuck tenders this in a slightly nervous manner, and I am surprised because Chuck is usually the epitome of cool.

"Good question, Mr. Norris. Any ideas?" Cher gives up on her lamb cutlet, which I note is bleeding all over her mashed potatoes.

"Why would I have ideas? What's that supposed to mean?" Chuck lights a cigarette, takes a huge drag on it, and it is many seconds before he eventually exhales a huge plume of smoke. He then looks at me, and for a moment his eyes rest on my sling. He studies it and then raises his eyes to meet mine. "What's with the arm?"

Agent Wade has already briefed me on how I should respond. How he knew the question was coming, I don't know, but he sure is a terrific federal agent. They should be proud to have a man like that wearing their shield.

"One of the animals in the zoo bit me."

"The zoo?"

"I work there. Senior cage cleaner." I'm pretty proud of myself for staying so calm. None of the Club members are meant to know too much about one another's private lives, but Agent Wade figured it would help show them how deeply honest I was.

"What a shit job." Tony belches.

"It's not so bad," I offer calmly. "Lots of perks."

"What? Like getting bitten by a lion? Or having a snake slither up your ass?" Everyone laughs at Chuck's joke, but I ride it out. I am very proud of what I do, and I can tell that the animals truly appreciate my sterling efforts.

Burt's eyes narrow as he squints over at me. "Anyway, lion bite notwithstanding, you any idea why Richard's not here?"

"Me? Why would I have any ideas?" I offer a wide-eyed, innocent look, knowing for sure that they will buy it.

"Yeah, what's your reason this time, Mr. Fairbanks?" Cher eyeballs me.

"You've always got a theory." Tony looms over, and as I realize that they are all studying me intently now, I can't get this image of hungry animals out of my head.

"C'mon, Dougie, spill." Chuck's earlier nerves have been replaced by a more determined, almost accusative look.

I don't like the way they are all homing in on me.

"We'd sure like to hear it, Gob. . . ." As James adds his unnerving presence to the proceedings, I realize I have just bitten my tongue.

I can't speak. Agent Wade never gave me any more than the animal bite theory. I'm floundering.

"Uh . . ."

"Uh? What's 'uh'?" Tony's face seems to be pressing closer to mine, his eyes bulging, and I can see his cheeks are flushed with the beginnings of rage.

"Um . . ."

"He's umming now." Chuck also leans forward.

I swallow, heartbeat quickening. "Well, uh, um, uh . . ."

"Maybe Richard was the one who ran that ad asking the Kentucky Killer to join and felt too guilty to come in." I look over at Betty.

My savior!

She gives me a half-smile, and I feel like kissing her full on her thin-lipped mouth.

The others immediately look her way. She gives them her beautiful shrug. "It kinda makes sense, doesn't it?"

"Richard couldn't spell VD, let alone write an ad." Burt is quickly in with this, and I look back to Betty. She stalls, loses her way, falls silent.

"You don't need to be able to spell to dictate something over the phone." Nice going, Chuck. Nice going.

"So that's how you run these ads, is it?" Cher leaps in.

Chuck faces her off. "What are you trying to say here?"

"You seem to be a bit of an authority on ads, Chuck."

This comes from me and is out before I even know I'm ganging up on my all-time favorite member.

"An authority? What are you talking about, you runt?" Chuck looks questioningly at the rest of the group. I can't help but shake my head somberly. I then give a big and unqualified shrug of the shoulders.

"Just seems like you're the expert on posting ads."

"You little shit." Chuck gives me a seriously unsavory look.

Tony belches as he speaks. "Look, forget the fucking ad."

"What about Richard, though?" Burt pushes his plate of fried fish away from him and instead reaches for a strong-looking cup of coffee. "Are we just going to write him off? Like the others?"

Tony takes a long moment, rubs his face with his hands,

and then yawns, revealing some fairly gruesome-looking teeth. "I'm looking into it, okay?"

"'Fraid that's not good enough, Mr. Curtis. We have a right to know what's going on here."

"And when I know, I will freakin' tell you. Okay?"

Tony absentmindedly blows his nose in part of the table-cloth. He finishes, lets the tablecloth drop, and then looks at the anxious faces of the Club members. He plays it calm, keeping whatever clever scheme he has devised under wraps. "Let's just ease off the throttle. Everyone's getting a little jumpy."

"What'd you expect?" Again Chuck reveals more of this previously unknown jittery side of his. "Where have they gone? I mean, someone must know something. We know William was killed, maybe the others were, too."

I'm starting to wonder if maybe Chuck isn't a bit of a coward underneath it all.

Tony gives him a dark look. "Listen, worrywarts, I said I'm lookin' into it."

Chuck gives a sour look in return and then takes a monumental toke on his cigarette. "Who else knows about this Club? I figure someone musta said something to someone, maybe a friend in passing. That's what I figure. That someone got wind of these meetings and decided they don't like it. Not one bit. Someone's blabbed. Who was it?"

"I'm gonna slap you across the lips if you don't shut up." Tony belches this out, then yawns again, and before he closes his mouth he crams half a lettuce from Betty's plate into it.

Chuck turns away, looks entirely pissed off. "Something ain't right. Truth is, everything's starting to stink."

Chuck's somber dark words hang in the air for the rest of the evening, and not even Burt Lancaster telling a funny story makes anyone feel any better. The Club is dying, and inside I feel like crying.

Sure, I want to be a hero, but there's still a big part of me that will forever be the Club.

I catch sight of Betty's profile. She must be aware of my looking at her because she turns and our eyes meet. We stay that way—looking at each other silently—for what seems like eternity. I am drowning in her gray blue eyes and want never to come up for air.

Later, in the men's room, I am relieved to relieve myself. The awkward darkening atmosphere of the Club is weighing down on me and giving me a migraine. Tony Curtis walks in, mid-belch, and stands right next to me. He is surly, and I know his blood pressure is rocketing.

"Burt's about as funny as a pulled sphincter muscle."

I stick to my gambit of immediately agreeing with any viewpoint Tony has.

"Absolutely. He peaked the other night, you ask me."

Tony lets rip with a hot and hard torrent of urine.

"Of course, you know why he's not so funny tonight."

Tony looks across at me, raises a querying eyebrow. I have said this on purpose, because I intend to stay alive despite everything.

"Whyssat?"

"Well, I don't want to say anything . . ."

"Yeah, you do." Tony crashes through life in a spectacularly blunt and tactless way. I really admire that about him.

"Well . . . and this is between me and you, okay? But I think we've got a rat in the Club."

The washroom goes deadly quiet. Tony pauses an awful long while before he shakes himself, then zips up. He wipes his hands on the front of his shirt. He looks at me, runs a hand over his mouth and chin as he contemplates words that he himself originated. "A rat, huh?"

"Yeah. A rat."

Tony looks around suspiciously. He is weighing me up, and I know he is connecting with me.

"You finished?" He motions to the urinal.

"Uh, yeah . . . yeah. . . ." I zip up. I turn and walk past Tony to the sinks. I start washing my hands, all the time feeling his eyes boring into the back of my head.

"And you think this rat is affecting Burt's performance tonight?"

I look up, and in the washroom mirror I can see Tony looming over me, staring straight into my eyes. I blink, feel the beginnings of an anxiety attack. But I hold it all in as I nod, slowly and quite purposefully. "It has to be."

"How come?"

I pause, blink again. "Burt is the rat."

As soon as I've said it, I feel a slow release of tension. Five seconds after that, I want to hang myself. The repercussions of what I have just said may well signal the end of me. I have no proof, no FBI pictures, nothing. It's my word against Burt's.

Tony remains calm. He then takes two steps over to the cubicles, pushes open one of the doors. He looks at me, starts to belch.

"Step into my office a moment."

I truly don't believe I can move a muscle. The cubicle door seems to open into complete darkness, a never-ending night. Tony steps aside to make way for me.

I wish this were on tape and I could press rewind.

Somehow or other, I manage to get my legs to move. I am very stiff, though, labored, and the floor seems to be made of molasses. The cubicle door awaits me, the darkness calls to me, and I know there is no way back.

"Take a seat." Tony bolts the cubicle door behind us and

then turns to face me. The cubicle is half the size I remember it, and his huge, gassy body looms over me, his giant thick head bending forward, his dark, soulless eyes staring deeply into me.

"Go on. Siddown." Tony lifts a giant foot and knocks the lid down. It bangs hard behind me, and I realize he wants me to sit on it. I do so and find that even though I'm probably a dead man, I feel just a tad silly.

"You a faggot, Junior?" I don't know why he asks this; surely it's obvious to anyone that I'm not. "Coming into the john with a stranger. . . ." He makes a big fist, raises it, and then laughs and knocks my shoulder playfully with his fist. "Joke."

I laugh my hyena laugh. And this is a star turn. This laugh is so big and enthusiastic and false, even I recoil at the horrendous depths of fawning I am plumbing. But Tony laughs heartily as well, enjoying his joke so much that he farts. I pretend not to hear it but do close my laughing mouth in case I end up eating the fart.

Tony leans back against the bolted cubicle door. "So . . ." He lets the laughter settle.

"So . . . ," I echo, but not with half as much resonance.

"Burt's a rat."

"Total vermin."

Tony starts to nod, musing to himself. He isn't smiling now, and all joviality is at an end. "How'd you figure this?"

How indeed? I brace myself, trying hard to think of something. "I uh . . . well . . . it's kind of a long story." Or it would be if only I could remember what I'd planned to say.

"I'm not going anywhere."

Come on, Dougie, think.

"It's like this, Tony. . . . Burt, uh . . . Burt tried to behead me."

Tony's eyes widen in surprise; he is momentarily taken

aback by this. This wasn't quite how I'd rehearsed it, but it'll have to do.

"What?!"

"He tried to cut off my head."

To my surprise, Tony laughs. "He did? Fuck. This a personal thing?"

I frown. "I don't follow."

Tony is as blunt as ever. "It's just I know how irritatin' the members find you." Those bastards. He laughs quite blatantly. "I never knew one guy could fit so many different killers' victim categories."

I can feel a red mist descending slowly over me, and all I can think is, I'm going to kill those—

"I don't think it was personal. He looked to be in a real bloodletting mood. I mean, for chrissakes, I woke up to find him kneeling on my chest with a big ax in his hand."

Tony studies me. He is curious, suspicious. But I think that if I can just remain calm and levelheaded, I can get through this.

Maybe.

"He was foaming at the mouth . . . saying things, really evil things. I'd never seen so much hatred. I kept asking him, 'Why? Why are you trying to behead me?'"

"And this is why you think Burt's a rat?"

"It is kind of a strong indication, isn't it?"

Tony gives a rippling shrug of his big, flabby shoulders. "How'd he even know where you lived?"

"He obviously followed me. Like he . . . like he followed the, uh . . . the others. . . ." I lick the sweat from my top lip. I lay the palms of my hands firmly on my thighs, pressing them in hard, to try to stop my legs from shaking.

"And what others are these?"

"The, uh . . . the others. You know. The dozen or so Club members that, uh . . . well, that don't attend anymore."

Tony studies me, purses his lips. I feel I have to continue, to get the point across.

"You know . . . that, uh . . . that Burt has . . . you know . . . has killed." I manage to stammer all of this out, but it's hard to talk when my tongue keeps darting out to lick my top lip.

Tony has a hugely imperious look on his face. "Lemme get this clear. You say Burt's been killing members of the Club? My Club?"

Tony's eyes bulge as his anger starts to boil. He lets this question hang in the air. And it hangs around long enough for me to realize that I couldn't plan a walk in the park.

"Why, June? Why d'ya think Burt's doing that?"

Did Tony just call me June? As in June for Junior?

"Huh, June?"

Oh Christ.

I really believed Tony'd buy the story straight off. I can't think. I can't breathe. I can't do anything but stare dumbly back at Tony.

Quarterback builder, quarterback builder . . .

"C'mon, June. You know something I don't?"

A tiny little voice somehow scratches its way from between my lips. "He told me . . . he said it outright. 'I killed the others, Dougie, me, little ole wiry-haired Burt, I did them all.' It was like a boast. You know how bigheaded Burt can be."

"He came straight out with it, just like that?"

"Yessir. That's what the rat said. . . ." I nod, possibly too hard and for too long, but Tony doesn't seem to notice this.

"So you're saying Burt Lancaster sat on your chest braggin' about murderin' everyone and then damn near gave you a southern haircut?" I nod feverishly. "That doesn't really fit the killer's MO, does it?"

I immediately shake my head as hard and as fast as I was previously nodding it. If I'm not careful, my head will fall off.

Then I stop. "It doesn't?"

"You see, June, I've been doin' some investigatin' of my own, and it just don't tie in."

Where's Agent Wade when you need him? Why's he stretched out on my sofa when he could be here arresting Tony?

"Uh . . . tie in to what, exactly?"

Tony doesn't bother answering, preferring to reenact an interrogation scene instead. "How come he didn't manage to kill you?"

"I, uh, I fought him off."

"But he's here tonight? And so are you. And nothing's been said. Not even a murmur between you. Whyssat?" Tony is getting real aggressive, playing good cop/bad cop with me. Keeping me on my toes, not allowing for a single moment's relaxation.

I'm going to blow this, I know it. The quarterback's just been crushed to death, and the builder is hurtling toward the sidewalk.

"He threatened me. Threatened to cut out my heart if I told anyone," I say nervously.

Tony isn't buying this. He frowns at me. "So he's changed to hearts now?"

"Yeah . . . I guess he has."

Tony stares into me, straight into me, and I keep getting this stupid rhyme in my head, "Demon Dougie, eyes are buggy."

"At last . . . now we're getting somewhere."

The rhyme starts to fade.

"It's obvious. . . ."

It is?

"Burt's gettin' confused." Join the club, Burt. "Between his usual MO and his copycat MO. He's losing it big-time."

I sit there, dry mouthed, but with at least some color returning. I want to nod, but my neck aches like crazy now. "You know . . . I think you might have something there, Tony."

"He's gonna come back for you."

"I've been taking precautions . . . putting extra locks on the door and stuff. Hiding all my work tools."

"You should've told someone, June."

Does he have to keep calling me that?

"He frightened me, really put the Indian sign on me."

Tony guffaws, belches, farts, punches my bad arm with his big, bunched-up fist. Can't he see it's in a sling for a reason?

"You fag. . . ." Tony seems to revel in my simpering weakness. His whole body wobbles as he gives me a pitying laugh. He punches my arm again, and I wish he'd stop. It hurts.

"Well, well . . . I knew it had to be someone at the Club."

"You did?"

"Didn't figure on it being Burt, but there you go, you can't be right the whole time."

"So, uh . . . what, uh . . . what do we do now?"

Tony weighs this up for a moment, but I get the impression he has already made up his mind. "I'm gonna lop off his head for you."

"That's, uh . . . that's very decent of you, Tony."

"I don't like people messin' around with the Club, June. One thing guaranteed to make me mad is people fucking my Club over. It took a hell of a lot of hard labor to get the thing this good." He punches my arm again and laughs. "Jesus, you fag. . . ." Tony then turns and unbolts the cubicle door. "This'll be our little secret."

I nod vigorously, despite the agony of it. Tony stops at the open door to the cubicle and turns back to me with what amounts to a philosophical look.

"I always knew this would happen. Put enough killers in

the same room, and sooner or later someone's gonna get a crazy notion. Cops are the same."

Tony slopes out of the cubicle. I sit there for a long time, just gathering myself, taking deep breaths while convincing myself that I am one of the most consummate actors of my generation. I start to get this swell in my heart, and a wave of warm euphoria starts to wash over me until I stand up and realize that I have pissed my pants.

It takes a full twenty minutes to dry my pants under the hot-air hand drier, and when I return to the meeting I discover that the Club is packing up. I see Burt chatting with Betty, making her laugh with a joke he's probably told a hundred times, and then I see Tony pulling on his oilskins, all the time his eyes staring relentlessly at Burt. Chuck Norris is signing seductively to the deaf waitress, and she blushes demurely. Cher squirts a scented spray into her open, cavernous mouth, and James Mason finishes the last of his strong coffee before mumbling something to his dead mother, hearing something in response, and then giggling crazily.

I go over to Tony, and he notices me out of the corner of his eye. He nods imperceptibly to me, attempts to be discreet. "If this turns out to be the real thing, I'll post Burt's head to you."

"Thank you, Tony. Thank you very much."

"I still think it could be a personal thing. You coulda misheard him while you were panicking your balls off."

I need to cover myself fully here. "And, uh . . . what if it is?"

Tony looks at me, gives me a big punch on my now badly bruised and near lifeless arm. "I'll break in and kill you for him. The Club could do with a lift." He gives a big belching laugh and goes, pausing to give the manager and the head-waiter a real mean look and then barging a customer—"Move it, sheep dip"—out of the way as he opens the front door onto the wild and wet night.

Betty's laughter breaks my concentration, and I turn to see Burt bend to kiss the back of her hand and then twirl his wrist and hand like a member of British royalty, bidding her, "Fare thee well, my princess," and I feel so nauseated by the sheer cloying desperation of this that I know for certain the world will be a better place without him.

"Wrap up warm, Mr. Mason, it's a bitch of a night." Cher twists out her cigarette as she passes James's coat to him and then collects her own.

He suddenly looks very lost, very vulnerable. "Is this the end, Cher?"

"Of the Club, you mean?"

"Yeah. I live for these nights. But now it's like some kind of mini Armageddon is taking place."

Cher gives James a hopeless look as she helps him into his anorak. "I know."

"I've got nowhere else to go, Cher."

"None of us has."

James leaves, shuffling off, head bowed. Cher goes to the bar to get some loose change for the cigarette machine, and I make my move on Burt. I give him a big grin and help him on with his coat, despite having only one active arm.

"That was a great story earlier, Burt. So funny. Had me in stitches. Thought I was going to give birth, I was laughing so hard."

"Oh . . . uh, thanks. You liked it, then?"

"It killed me, really killed me." I give a totally superficial laugh to help things along.

Burt nods, pleased. "You know, I did think there was some good material in there."

Now that I've established this great buddy-buddy thing, I

slip an arm around Burt's shoulders. I notice Burt glance at my hand as I squeeze his bicep, but I am determined to ride this out. "Listen, Burt, I was hoping we could talk sometime. . . ."

Burt looks at me, seems a little suspicious. "Yeah?"

I look around and then lower my voice. "It's about Tony."

"Tony Curtis?"

"There's something I think you should know. Only I can't tell you here."

"Why not?"

"I just can't. I don't, uh . . . I don't have the evidence right now."

"What evidence? What's this about?" Burt's nasally little voice is so close, it pings off my ear.

"Wait till I get proof. Are you in the phone book?"

Burt immediately shakes off my arm. "I'm not giving you my number, you little fag."

I look hard at Burt. "It's a matter of life and death." I hold his gaze. "Your death."

Burt's features freeze over, and he looks like a badly chiseled statue. He starts to say something but stops. He looks completely bewildered.

I lean in closer to him, maintaining direct eye contact as I do. "It's a personal thing, you understand. But Tony told me he really doesn't like you, Burt. Not one little bit. Truth is, none of the Club do. It's cuz you fit so many serial-killing agendas. They all want a piece of you. Anyway. Safe journey."

I leave Burt openmouthed and wide-eyed. Like he's just been electrocuted.

HOLDING, NOT FOLDING

I HAVE BEEN DESPERATE to hear news of Burt's demise, but so far nothing has happened. I haven't been able to sleep for two days now and badly need something to happen. It's worse than waiting for Christmas.

I am at the zoo and speaking in hushed tones over the phone to Betty. Agent Wade had been following me, but I managed to give him the slip when I climbed out the back of a temporary latrine and disappeared down a RESTRICTED VEHICLES pathway. My arm is out of the sling, and I can move it a little more freely now.

"Has Tony found out who the killer is yet?"

"If he has, he's not telling anyone."

I really need to know more, and I push Betty. "Why's he not telling anyone? The killer could strike at any moment."

"He just told me to hold tight . . . that he's got a plan."

"What plan, though?"

Betty is getting a little tetchy with me, and I know I have to be careful not to overplay this. "I don't know. As soon as I do, I'll let you know. Okay?"

"Did he, uh . . . you know . . . mention Burt to you?"

"Burt? As in Burt Lancaster?"

"Yeah."

"No."

Dammit!

"Why? What's the deal with Burt?"

"I dunno. The guy gives me the creeps. He's got killer written all over him."

"We all have, Douglas."

Speak for yourself, Betty.

"Just calm down. You're getting paranoid. Now come on, take some deep breaths, Douglas. One, two—breathe. . . . That's right. One, two—are you feeling any better, Douglas? Come on, now—one, two. Breathe, Douglas, you sound like you're hyperventilating."

There's something in the way that Betty pronounces my name that sends a tingle down my spine. The booth I'm in is plastered with calling cards and numbers of call girls and phone-in sex lines. I keep looking at the tawdry ads and imagining Betty as a dominatrix.

"Do you ever take your glasses off?"

"Pardon me?"

I realize what I've said and turn away from the sex ads, trying hard to focus. There's so many things going on, I'm starting to feel like a boxer fighting an invisible opponent. The punches keep on coming, and I don't know how or when to hit back.

"I, uh . . . I meant . . . when you do what you do . . . do you take your glasses off?"

"Uh . . . no . . . I wouldn't be able to see a thing if I did. I wouldn't even know which end of the blowtorch to light." Betty laughs, but it is unconvincing. She is still finding me odd, and I wish I could start this whole conversation again. "Why, uh . . . why do you ask?"

"It's just that sometimes I wear glasses when I . . . you know. . . . Not real ones, fake ones. Just for a change."

"But you haven't killed anyone in years."

This conversation is leading nowhere fast. "It's this horrendous block—it's ruining my life, Betty."

"Breathe, Douglas. One, two . . . in, out . . ."

I breathe for Betty's sake and make myself completely dizzy. "It's just been a really bad time for me. What with the killer and this other punk hounding me."

"Oh, hey. About that guy who's blackmailing you . . . I think I've got a plan."

"You have?"

I decide to listen and maybe grunt a "yeah" or an "uh-huh" every now and then. It's the only safe way for me to get through the conversation. "What you've got to do is find out where he's hiding the photos."

"Uh-huh."

"My guess is it's an if-anything-should-happen-to-me-then-these-pictures-get-sent-to-the-cops-and/or-the-press type of thing."

"Yeah."

"So what you've got to do, Douglas . . ." Cue another tingle. "What you've got to do is find out who would do that for him."

"I see." I can't help myself as I look back at one card in particular that advertises a call girl service. The girl on the card is blond, well endowed, almost a Chesty Morgan, and devastatingly pretty. She is also only a sketch. Her name is Hanna, and she is willing to do "anything and everything, inclusive." I think about taking the card down and giving it to Agent Wade. Then I figure he's probably already got one.

"Now, have you any idea who that someone might be?"

I fall silent, not because I'm thinking, but because I'm not thinking. I don't have anything to offer Betty. She waits a moment.

"Douglas? Are you still there?"

"Uh-huh . . ."

"Well?"

"Uh . . ."

"There must be someone."

"Uh . . ."

"A friend, a girlfriend, maybe?"

Before I know it, I have taken down Hanna's calling card and read aloud from it. "Her name's Hanna and her number's 555-SWEAT."

I can hear Betty pause, surprised by my direct and incisive response.

"Uh . . . 555—what? Hang on, let me get a pen."

I study the picture of Hanna and wonder if it is at all possible that she looks as good as this in real life.

And as I do, I see Agent Wade's face peering in the phone booth. It shocks me rigid.

"Who are you phoning, Dougie?"

"No one—" I immediately hang up.

"Douglas . . . ?" Agent Wade's eyes drill into me.

I reluctantly bring up the picture of Hanna and show him, doing my best to look embarrassed. "You're absolutely right. I do covet women."

It takes another three days for me to shake Agent Wade long enough to manage to speak to Betty again, and we arrange to meet back in the café with the devastatingly pretty waitress and the yes-to-dogs policy. I'm not sure what I'm going to say, so I decide to go with the flow and see what happens. I can always fall back on the hyperventilating ploy if things don't work out.

Betty studies Hanna's calling card, looks at the drawing of the impossibly endowed and fantastically beautiful Hanna smiling hungrily back at her, whip in one hand, hammer-headed vibrator in the other. She seems concerned as she hands the card back to me.

"Are you sure you've got the right person, Douglas?"

"Absolutely. You see, the guy who's blackmailing me is very depraved. He, uh . . . he goes to a lot of strip joints. And also a lot of prostitutes. So my guess is he has become friendly with this Hanna."

Betty sips her cappuccino and then very quickly dabs at her top lip with a napkin when she sees me about to wipe her with my own napkin. She pushes the cappuccino away.

"When I rang the number you gave me, they told me to go to a certain motel room and wait. So I did. About five minutes later two Mexican-looking guys walked in, pointed a gun at me, and then took my purse."

I truly don't know what to say and feel a little flustered.

"So you didn't get to see Hanna, then?"

"I don't think Hanna exists, Douglas."

"But she's got a card . . . that card there. I found it in my, uh . . . I mean, it fell out of the blackmailer's pocket. She must exist. How else would she be able to do a drawing of herself?"

"Douglas, listen to me . . ." Betty is very calm, very rational, and it is only after about a minute that I realize her hand is touching mine. "Listen a moment . . ." I look up and see Betty's near crystal blue eyes. They hypnotize me. "Forget Hanna. That was you being desperate, okay? You were just clinging to something, anything."

"She does exist, Betty. There was probably just some huge misunderstanding at the motel you went to."

Betty tries to talk over me. "We need another plan."

"Maybe I should call her up. Maybe they thought you were from the vice squad or something. Maybe if I went to meet her, it would be different."

Betty withdraws her hand. I make a grab to get it back,

but she is too quick, and I knock the salt cellar over instead. I immediately grab a handful and toss it over my right shoulder.

"For luck."

Then I toss more salt over my left shoulder because I don't know which shoulder is meant to be lucky. I then do them both again, just in case. I'm not sure the customers at the table behind ours are too impressed, and I can guess from the look on her face that Betty isn't, either. I lick my fingers, tasting the salt.

"So . . . how much did they take?"

"Pardon me?"

"These Mexicans, the muggers . . . how much did they take?"

I already have my wallet out, and I have a desire to give Betty all I own in recompense; she can even have my apartment—or at least she could have if I weren't renting.

"Don't be silly, Douglas."

"No, Betty. I insist. How much did they take?"

"I honestly couldn't tell you."

"A hundred? Two hundred?"

"Douglas . . ."

"Five hundred?"

"As if I'd have that much in my purse. . . ."

I fish out all the cash in my wallet. I try to press it into Betty's hand. "There's what? Maybe three fifty there. You take it . . . have it all. . . ."

Betty tries to push the money back into my hands, but I close my fists into balls, tight balls that she could open only if she smashed my knuckles with a hammer.

"I don't want this, Douglas."

Before she can give the money back to me, I quickly snatch my hands away and shove them under the table, fists still in tight balls. "That mugging was my fault. I mean, my God, you could have been killed."

"I wasn't, though."

"But they could have . . . you know . . . raped you . . . or forced you into porn movies. Or even sold you into the white slave trade. Because they do that, you know? These people, they're real opportunists. They drug you, tie you up, and when you wake you find you're suddenly in Africa and guys with bones through their noses are bidding for you."

Betty laughs. She obviously thinks I'm being funny, that I'm making a joke out of something that in truth I happen to find pretty alarming.

"They wouldn't have gotten much for me. I'd be strictly bargain basement."

I stop, amazed that Betty could think so little of herself. I look at her, take in her pulled-back hair, the simple but effective rubber band that holds her ponytail in place, the huge glasses that cover half her face. I see her snow white skin, her dimples, and even though her lips are on the thin side, I know that with the right lipstick or even a massive injection of collagen, they would look eminently kissable. I see the money I tried to give her lying on the table between us. I lift one of my bunched fists from under the table and nudge the money toward her.

"I'd pay through the nose for you." Our eyes meet.

"You're just being kind."

"No, I'm not. I'm being honest."

Betty blushes, but somehow or other she continues to hold my gaze. She nudges the money back toward me. "You don't have to say that."

"But I do. You'd be worth every cent. Honestly, Betty, I'm being honest." I push the money back toward her.

"Please don't say any more, Douglas."

"Why not?"

"I just . . . please, just don't."

I can feel the magic aura we have been experiencing crumbling away. Fast. I find myself picking up the money and slipping it back into my wallet. I realize to my shame that what I thought was $350 amounts to only $38.

Betty gives a vague, empty smile and then lowers her eyes. She looks suddenly vulnerable, and I notice flecks of gray coming through her roots. I make a mental note to send her an anonymous bottle of hair dye.

"I can't get involved with anyone, Douglas." She is still looking down when she says this. I try to stop looking at her roots but can't. "I'm a spider."

This throws me a little, finally breaking my obsession with her hair. "I'm sorry, but did you just say you're a spider?"

Betty gives an almost imperceptible nod. "A black widow."

I lower my head, lean forward, try to get a better look at Betty's face. My chin almost touches the tablecloth in my efforts. "That's no way to talk about yourself." I offer a playful smile.

"Black widow spiders kill their partners after mating with them." Her eyes meet mine, and my playful smile sticks fast, turning into a thin grimace.

I know all about Betty and the six or so men she has killed, but I never once imagined it was because she believed herself to be a rather large arachnid. I thought she burned off genitalia by way of a warped mother fixation.

"I can't seem to help myself . . . I have to kill them, I just have to." Betty looks suddenly vulnerable; her face creases, and her eyes seem much more sunken and tired looking than before. Her words are slow and painful. "As I told the Club, I have sex—mostly with men who aren't successful with women, you know, ugly men, outcasts, social misfits, men that constantly leave the wrong impression wherever they go." I know exactly the type of guy she means, and I hate them as much as Betty does. "And then, as I lie there, watching them drift off to sleep, all I can think is, Why did I let this happen? Why did I let this ugly man, this leather-faced monstrosity, do this to me? Why couldn't it have been a film star or a rock singer, or even just someone remotely desirable?" As I listen, I catch sight of my reflection in the window behind Betty's head and thank the good Lord He didn't turn me into one of these horrors. "All I ever attract is the bottom of the barrel, the dregs, the waste of spaces."

I try to get a few of what I think are key things established here.

"I don't know if this means anything to you, Betty, but I think you're better than that. A lot better. In fact, I'd go as far as to say that we would make a particularly handsome couple." I ease back into my chair and let Betty see my best pouting, brooding James Dean look. "I know I shouldn't say this, but we're a heckuva match."

Betty gives a painfully slow shake of the head. "Try telling my mother that. Jesus . . . you should have heard her. All my life she goes on and on about how I'm nothing, less than nothing. That I'd better not get any fancy ideas about myself. That I'd better just accept that I didn't inherit any of her good looks, or her charisma . . . that I was just no good, no good whatsoever. A piece of plain white trash. That's what she used to call me. Or white bread . . . that's the one I hated the most. White bread. I still don't know what she meant, but it hurt all the same. She used to call me that every single day of my life. Until Tony kicked her to death."

Betty finally looks up, and I have to raise my head abruptly, barely remembering that I had practically been resting my chin on the table. My neck aches a little, and I rotate it, hoping to make it click back into place.

"So please . . . don't, uh . . . don't try and turn this into something, Douglas."

"But Betty . . ." I only just manage to stop myself from saying, "Can't you see how lucky you just got?"

"I'd better go. I'll think some more about your blackmailer."

"But—"

Betty gets up, smiles at me—a thin smile, but one that tries to assume a warmness. I catch a scent of her undeniably strong doggy smell and decide to send her some perfume along with the hair dye.

"I'll see you, Douglas."

Betty leaves. I don't watch her go but do see her again when she passes the café window, head bowed. She glances at me, but only out of politeness. As I watch her, the waitress collects our coffee cups. I look up and see that she is spellbindingly attractive—right up there with Hanna.

"Isn't it great being beautiful? We're privileged. We truly are."

The waitress says nothing. She just collects the coffee cups and walks away. I turn to watch her go, call after her.

"Listen, being mute isn't a problem. I've got a friend who's been to signing classes."

HEADLESS CHICKEN

I

T HAS BEEN five days since I saw Betty, and I had
hoped she might call me after the headway we made
in the café. I have been moping around the house,
sometimes taking in a war movie with Agent Wade, sometimes just sitting in my room and watching the damp creeping higher and higher up the lilac walls. I've never felt this
way about anyone before, and I really want to see her. For
me she sums up the word *woman*. The phone rings, and I
rush through and grab it.

"Yeah?"

"Hi, it's me."

My heart leaps. "Betty. I knew you'd call."

"Tony called me." She sounds scared.

"And?"

"He said he's going to make the Club great again."

"Well, that's just amazing."

"You think?"

"Yeah."

"But what does he mean by that?"

"I dunno. But if Tony says he's going to do something, then
he's sure going to do it."

My mind races. This has got to be a sign that my quite

brilliant plan is working. I glance at the mirror superglued to the wall and smile. Burt is a dead man.

"Can I borrow your car?"

Agent Wade stops typing, looks up at me like I'm crazy. "My car?"

"I want to go out."

"Why?"

"I just do. Is that a problem?"

"And you want my car?"

"What's wrong with that?"

"Maybe I need it tonight."

"Well, you could give me a ride. Where are you going, anyway?"

"That's my business," he snaps at me.

"I was only asking."

"Don't." Agent Wade flashes a threatening look at me, and for the life of me I can't see what the big deal is.

"I'll call a cab. . . ."

"The hell with it—just take the car."

"Not if it's going to put you out."

"Take it, Dougie, okay? I'll make other arrangements. Just make sure you fill her up when you're done."

"I thought you were going to stick close to me?"

"Not tonight. If you want to go out, then you go out. I'm not your jailer." Not yet, I think to myself.

For the first time ever, Agent Wade looks evasive. "Anyway, I've, uh . . . got stuff to do tonight . . . FBI stuff. Hell, I work harder than the president." He adds a little laugh to this, and I can't help but feel he isn't quite telling me the truth. He hands me his car keys.

"Don't scratch it."

As I open the front door a wind crashes in, blowing the pages of his thick report everywhere.

"Damn!"

He quickly shoves me outside and slams the door in my face.

I stand there for a long moment, then step to one side and take a peek inside the living room window. I can see Agent Wade on his hands and knees, grabbing up pages of his precious report and then putting them back in an orderly pile. I then see him stand, scratch his groin, and walk over to my hi-fi. He picks through my small collection of records and CDs and finally finds a CD single that appeals to him. He opens the CD deck and slots the disc in. He pumps up the volume, and even with the howling wind raging around me, I can make out the first few familiar beats of a Murder Rap tune that has just charted at number eight.

Why you do
Why you do
Why you do that thang, Kentucky?
Is you just
Is you just
Is you just a touch unlucky?
Chicken leg
Make them beg
French fry
Make them sigh
Man is gonna come for you
Man is gonna lemon-scent you
Man is gonna box your head
Man is gonna make you dead
Why you do
Why you do

Why you do that thang, Kentucky?
Is you just
Is you just
Is you just a sick fucky?

Agent Wade pops open a bottle of Bud, lets it spurt all over before covering the rim with his mouth, and then cranks the hi-fi up as far as it will go. I can feel the windowpane shudder with the volume, and as I watch him start gyrating to the beat, I can see him mouthing the words off by heart.

I turn away and make for his car; I have to bow my head and hold my oilskins tight around my body as the wind tugs at me, trying hard to blow me off my feet, whipping my hood from my head no matter how many times I pull it back on. I unlock the door and climb in, and as soon as I close the door I feel safe. The wind can blow all it wants, but it won't get me while I'm in Agent Wade's car.

I start the engine, see that the fuel gauge is pointing dangerously close to the empty sign, and realize that yet again I'll have to spend more of my hard-earned money if I want to get over to Burt's boat tonight. It then strikes me that Agent Wade hasn't paid for a thing since I first met him, and I make a mental note to bring that up later. It's not like I'm a rich man.

The car glides away as I drive into the night. I have to pull the seat forward, pump it higher, and adjust the rearview, but eventually I feel comfortable enough to sit back and enjoy the ride. It's nothing out of the ordinary as cars go, but I like pretending that it's mine, and I take a few corners far too fast, tossing the car around like a pro, straightening her up, hitting fourth, and spearing through the rain like one of Agent Wade's boyhood arrows. By the time I have stopped to fill up the car, then driven clean across town and arrived at the small harbor where Burt's boat home is moored, I can just about live with the strong lemon scent that fills the car. Though it was never this strong before and has developed into a very powerful aroma. So much so that when I check out the car, I find about a dozen unopened lemon-scented hand wipes sitting in the glove compartment. All of them from KFC.

The harbor is badly lit, and the white-haired guy who keeps watch from his wooden cabin has fallen asleep with his hands behind his head and his feet up on a small electric heater that probably gives off about one single therm of heat if he's lucky. As I get out of the car, I can hear water lapping—in fact, crashing—against the harbor walls, and I can tell it is not a night to go fishing. I make sure I remember Agent Wade's camera, check that it is loaded, and then set off on foot to find Burt's boat. It isn't easy making out the names of the houseboats moored there, and once or twice I nearly get spotted by an owner as I creep up as close as I can. Burt told me once that a lot of the owners have acquired high-powered rifles as a deterrent for burglars, and the last thing I want is to get my head blown off by some panicky would-be sailor. I use up a good half an hour looking for the *Teacher*—Burt's houseboat—until at last I think I've found it.

Initially I'm drawn to the sound of sawing, which is incongruous, to say the least. I stop, go low, and then inch forward, hoping to get a glimpse of Burt. I suck in deeply as I make out Tony already on board Burt's little boat. The light in the cabin is very low, but I'd know that belching bag of wind's profile anywhere.

The *Teacher* seems to be rocking more severely than the other boats, and that makes it doubly difficult for me to climb aboard. The sawing seems to be getting louder as I manage to get a footing, haul myself onto the gangway, and tiptoe across the rain-lashed and slippery wooden boards. The sawing gets louder still, and Tony adds a massive fart for good measure as I finally sneak level with the cabin and then raise my head very slowly until I can see inside.

It isn't a pretty sight.

Burt may or may not be dead, and Tony has him in a strong grip as he saws through his neck. I can't be sure if Burt is dead from where I'm standing because Tony has probably injected him with a special chemical that causes complete paralysis. According to Tony, your balls don't even swing with this stuff. Tony does this to all his victims, claiming that he has a hole in the heart and can't chase after people like he used to.

Burt has beheaded many people in his killing career, and a lot of it has to do with his failure to make it as a decent human being. Burt used to whine constantly about his upbringing and the pressure brought to bear on him when, after his father had run off with another woman, he was urged by all his relatives to assume the mantle of man of the house. He was only eight at the time and naturally became a little confused. So much so that he started believing he was married to his mother, and in a fit of insane jealousy, he killed his mother's new boyfriend. Because of his tender age, he was incarcerated for five years in a correctional facility. Not nearly long enough, as far as I am concerned. Burt then spent the whole of his twenties proving to the world that he was sane and safe to walk the streets. The ritual beheading of families followed a week after he was given a clean bill of health. Burt's reasoning was put forward in that gratingly unfunny way of his: "If I couldn't be the head of the family, then I decided no one could." Oh, how we laughed at that one.

I steady myself as best I can as the bearlike Tony saws with rough and ready strokes—shaking the whole boat back and forth, such is the strength of the man. I catch him in the camera's viewfinder, and after ensuring that there is no doubt this is most definitely Tony Curtis cutting off Burt Lancaster's head, I start taking photos—only to have Tony immediately stop for a breather. He wipes his forehead and then kicks Burt's lifeless body. "Thick-necked bastard!"

I hold my breath. Wait for a moment. Tony wipes more sweat from his brow, tests his armpits, smells his fingers straight after, grimaces, and then wipes his hands on his trousers. He picks up his saw and is ready to resume decapitating Burt when he hears something and immediately looks my way. I quickly duck down. I hear his lumbering footsteps coming toward the window, and I'm already debating taking my chances in the churning waters when he flings open the window right above my head.

"Neck as thick as a fuckin' tree trunk!" Tony clears his throat and then spits into the night. The wind instantly catches the spit and hurls it straight back into my eyes. Because I dare not move an inch, I have to sit there letting the spit drip down and run into my nose. I want so badly to retch that I hold a hand over my mouth, hoping to God he doesn't hear me forcing the bile back down.

Tony remains there, looking out. "Fucking gonna lose weight doing this." He coughs hard and clears his throat again, but thankfully this time he swallows rather than spitting. "Aerobic neck sawing!" He slams the window shut again, and in a frenzy I claw and tear his saliva from my face.

The sawing starts again, and I am determined to get a shot of this. I peer into the cabin and see Tony kick Burt again—his saw now stuck fast in Burt's neck. Tony kicks hard at him in his rage, puts his foot up against the side of Burt's face, and tugs on the stuck saw with all his might.

I manage to get off a few shots, the click of the camera easily drowned out by the ferociously swirling waters below. I don't take too many, though, because the rocking of the boat is making me feel ill, and besides, I have to turn away when Burt's head snaps clean off under the force of Tony's boot. Even he is momentarily surprised, and he can only stand there looking down at Burt's head rolling back and forth across the cabin floor.

Then I hear him start laughing and know that it's time to get the hell out. I am about to move off when the window is opened again and I am forced to press myself flat as Burt's head comes flying out the window above me—and dammit if it doesn't hit a loose shutter and get batted back into the hood of my oilskins.

"Here, fishy wishies . . ." Tony whistles like he was calling a dog.

I can't hold it in any longer—Burt's nose is pressed into my neck—and I scream at the top of my voice. It is out before I know what I'm doing.

"What the . . . ? Who the fuck's out there?!"

Christ.

I scramble along the side of the boat, leap onto the slippery gangway, lose my footing, and go sprawling headfirst along it.

"Who the fuck's there?" Tony roars above the wind, and I can already hear him charging out of the cabin after me.

I get to my feet and jump the last two yards to dry land. I nearly slip again, but I manage to regain my balance and am ready to sprint off when I catch a glimpse of the camera, which must have spilled from my pocket.

"Police! This is the police! I'm armed!" Tony yells, his bellow louder than the crashing ocean. The slow-moving Tony clambers along the prow of the boat, getting closer and closer.

I grab the camera and tear along the jetty, thanking God for the foulest and darkest night He ever created.

"I said it's the fucking police!" A gunshot rings out as Tony's bulk lands hard on the jetty.

I run faster than a cheetah, pumping my arms and legs, knowing the darkness is my one savior.

And that's when the lights come on.

Fog lights from the houseboats, warning lights, search-lights—you name it, they've got it. People appear from every-where, and I'm suddenly running a gauntlet of angry faces and voices—all of them desperately swinging their lights around, trying to catch me in their beams.

"Who's there?"

"What's going on?"

"I saw someone!"

"Police! Back off, you fucks!" Tony's voice is getting hoarse and breathless from his pursuit.

Some of the lights swing into one another, and the occu-pants of the boats are mutually blinded. They jag around wildly, and one hits the front grille of Agent's Wade car. I've got about fifty yards to go.

A huge gunshot roars out. This is unlike anything I've ever heard, and something screams past me.

"I see him! I see him!"

"Where!?"

"There!"

Another gunshot booms out, and I realize that I'm being shot at by thief-hating boat owners with high-velocity rifles.

"There he is!"

Another bullet crashes through the air, and I'm suddenly in the middle of a gun battle.

"Put those freaking guns down, you pricks!" Tony is still coming after me, but I know I'm making ground on him because only a lunatic would try to run through the salvos that are erupting everywhere around me. Vietnam has come to Chicago.

"Stop freaking shooting or I'll kill you where you stand, you dumb fuck bastards!" Tony lets off a few rounds, smashing some of the fog lights, shattering the glass of cabin windows. "I do the freaking shooting, okay?!"

Tony's voice rises hugely above everything, and as I reach the white-haired man's cabin—ten yards from where I'm parked—the world goes silent. The shooting has stopped, the lights dip down and point away from me, and I am nearly home.

But as I get within Tony's spitting distance of the car, the white-haired man suddenly bursts from his cabin, yelling and screaming for his life, and as I look down I can see that both his feet are on fire. I run smack into him and tumble forward, the flames from his feet scorching my eyebrows as we roll over and over. The white-haired old man yells in blind panic, and I absolutely and unequivocally hate him for going to sleep with his feet on top of a heater. I don't get time to dwell on it because I can hear Tony thundering ever closer.

"Stop that guy! Hey—you with the feet! Stop him!"

I shove the burning man away from me, scramble desperately for Agent Wade's car, and hurl myself behind the wheel. As I gun the engine, I see Tony emerge from the darkness and take aim at the car. I duck right down, slam the car into reverse, and hammer the pedal right to the floor. I don't care where I'm going, all I want to do is get out of there.

Tony's first shot hits the madly hopping white-haired man in the shoulder, sending him spinning off the jetty and into the subzero waters. His second shot takes off a wing mirror, and his third shot misses completely as I reverse straight into a storefront window. As mannequins dressed in knitted fisherman's sweaters fall all over the hood, I grind into first, fail to get any traction, and then skid sideways out of the store. Tony is still coming for me—reloading as he does—but I drag the wheel hard right, hit the main road, and screech down it. I have done all of this with practically only my forehead and above visible. As another couple of shots zing around me, I decide that it might be prudent to drive like this all the way home.

"I'll find out who you are!" Even Tony's great voice is eventually lost in the distance I put between us.

I am not sure how I am going to get the shots I took of Tony developed, but I know of a local photographer's shop across town that I could break into. I could take out a book from Betty's library on how to develop photographs, and it takes my mind off this awful night thinking that I've got a good excuse to go see her. Failing that, I will just bring them to KlippyKlap Snaps, which is currently offering a second set of glossy prints and a free roll of film with every order.

It is only when I park outside my house and let myself in that I realize I still have Burt's head trapped in the hood of my oilskin.

When I take off my oilskins and shake the rain from them, it flops out and lands with a thud at my feet. A damp-looking Agent Wade looks up from toweling his hair dry, sees Burt's head, and then looks toward me. His expression doesn't waver for a second.

"You, uh, bringing your work home now?"

CHER

DEAD RINGER

THE SAME NIGHT that I went out to take the photographs of Tony and Burt, it appears that an illegal immigrant was brutally stabbed to death and had a KFC family-size carton dumped on his head. The Kentucky Killer is in town, and the papers and the television are going crazy. It is hard to tell the difference between them being overfearful or overexcited. It's like a movie star has flown in, and this king of killers is getting more coverage than anyone I ever remember. Proof of God wouldn't generate this much publicity. If it wasn't for the fact that the Kentucky Killer slaughtered countless innocents, I would fully expect him to be there to open the new cinema complex we have just had built. Instead they settle for a movie star whose last three films have flopped and no one bothers to show.

I breathe deeply, trying to take stock of the situation as Agent Wade turns on the news and we settle down to watch the TV reporter trying to interview a Mexican-looking spokesman from the League of Human Rights.

REPORTER: If José knew he was going to die this way, d'you think he would have chosen the Kentucky Killer to do it?

SPOKESMAN: I would rather concentrate on the fact that José was in truth a victim of congressional dehumanization.

REPORTER: Yeah, but think of the positives a second. José's going to get his photo in a best-selling book.

I wonder why the television psychiatrist hasn't made an appearance. So far, he has always refused to be drawn in on the subject of the Kentucky Killer, and I for one would like to hear what's he got to say.

Agent Wade hangs on every word of the news report, then channel hops to another news program and devours every morsel from that one as well. He leans forward, a glint of excitement in his eyes, and I note that sometimes he nods to himself and says, "Uh-huh . . . uh-huh," as the reporters give their on-scene accounts.

Finally the reports end and he looks my way. "He's here. . . ."

I take out and unwrap a candy bar, crunching into it.

Agent Wade is in raptures. "We're so close now, Dougie."

I allow myself to savor the sweet candy, letting it melt in my mouth rather than chewing it. Agent Wade pauses to scratch himself and then speaks without looking up. "He's the one . . . the only one."

Agent Wade then gives me a real sinister smile. He scratches himself again, and to tell the truth, I can't remember him taking a shower since he moved in with me.

That sinister smile stays fixed on his face until eventually he speaks.

"I can smell him."

Later, as Agent Wade dozes in front of a late night horror movie—one that gives me the creeps so bad that I keep imagining there is someone waiting for me in my bedroom—I sneak a look in Agent Wade's jacket, which is hanging on the kitchen door. I gently remove his wallet and his badge and also find some unused napkins from KFC. He has a regulation FBI pen and pad and an unopened pack of gum. I check to make sure he is definitely asleep and then go into the kitchen and lay the stuff out in the not-so-pristine sink.

In the wallet is at least $800, and I can't believe Agent Wade keeps making me pay for everything. I take three twenties for myself just to even things out a little. I then find about sixty receipts for motel lodgings and gas. They are from all over and date back eight months. He is obviously keeping these for his expenses claim. Agent Wade seems to have been all over the Midwest in that time, and I remember the clock on his car reading well over eighty thousand miles. The man has put in a lot of time and distance in his attempts to find me.

I then check his FBI badge, and there is no doubting its authenticity. The napkins seem innocent enough until I note that he has written a number on the back of each one. They are in sequence and read from 286 to 295. Each number is written in red ink.

I can't figure this out at first, but as I unwrap his packet of gum and stuff a stick in my mouth, I start to get this growing shudder running down my spine. Like someone walking on my grave.

I look at the numbers again. I remember the lemon-scented hand wipes, the incessant desire for KFC produce, and realize I need some air. I haven't felt this scared since the night I joined the Club.

A bloodcurdling scream erupts from the living room. I jerk so violently that I spill the wallet. I turn and then realize that the horror film is still playing. I catch my breath, wait to see if Agent Wade has woken, and feel a huge relief when I can't hear him stirring from the sofa. I quickly scoop up the wallet.

"Dougie . . . ?" Agent Wade calls out from the living room. I grab everything and stuff it quickly into my back pocket. I even spit the chewing gum across the kitchen just in case he recognizes that it's his.

Agent Wade appears in the doorway; he looks tired and yawns. "Where's the boot polish?"

"The what?"

"The polish. . . ."

Agent Wade walks toward me, and my heart quickens—and then he reaches past me for the tap. He runs the cold faucet and dips his head under, refreshing himself. When he finishes he looks back at me with a very condemning look.

"This sink is disgusting, Dougie."

I nod, deciding to stay silent in case he hears the tremor in my voice.

"I want to be able to see my face in it."

I nod again.

Agent Wade yawns, stretches, and then does this maneuver that makes his shoulders crack. It is a truly horrible sound and sets my teeth on edge.

"Let's go."

"Where?"

"We've got to keep the pressure on, Dougie."

"Another murder already?"

"Yeah, I'm chomping at the bit here. Ole KK's got me fired up."

"It's late."

"Perfect time to strike. Come on, find me some boot polish. 'Bout time I joined in the fun."

With that, Agent Wade walks out of the kitchen, giving his shoulders another of those hideous cracks.

As soon as he is gone, I turn on the cold faucet and start glugging down as much water as I can. I keep drinking and drinking and drinking. I feel so parched, I don't think the whole of Lake Michigan could quench my thirst. Four words keep doing the can-can in my head. It's a rhythmic beat with trumpets and gongs: Lemon-scented hand wipes. Lemon-scented hand wipes. Lemon-scented hand wipes.

Half an hour later, and we are both wearing black. Agent Wade applies black boot polish to my cheeks, nose, and forehead with a handkerchief. I feel like a marine about to do a midnight raid. Agent Wade finishes, then hands me the boot polish.

"Watch the eyes. I don't want it in my eyes."

I pause, hadn't realized I was meant to do this.

"C'mon, Dougie . . . just watch the eyes, huh?"

I feel uneasy as I dab the handkerchief in the boot polish and start blacking out Agent Wade's face. I finish, and as I step back to admire my handiwork, I see that Agent Wade's blue eyes seem all the more piercing and hypnotic thanks to the black background they stare out from.

"How do I look?"

"Like me."

I pause, and Agent Wade sees that I look concerned.

"What is it?"

"Why are you coming along?"

"Why shouldn't I?"

"What I mean is, you don't need to black up as well, do you?"

"Sure I do."

"Why?"

"It's procedure, Dougie. Procedure." Agent Wade's white teeth grin out at me. "We can't have you grabbing all the glory, can we?"

I don't know how to answer that. I truly don't.

Outside, a car horn beeps. Agent Wade glances at his watch. "That'll be our taxi."

The taxi driver turns out to be a woman who twenty years ago probably possessed the looks and body of a supermodel. The years haven't been kind to her, and I try to make our journey a pleasant reminder of her golden days.

"You know, you could pass for a supermodel's mother." I note that the taxi driver is too shy to respond. "Honestly. You could. And I'm not just saying that."

The taxi driver looks in her rearview at us but still refuses to say anything. I lean forward, give her a warm look, or at least as warm as I can underneath all the boot polish. "Listen, I read about this new science. Everyone's raving about it. Nanotechnology. It's meant to repair all the bad things about yourself. You know, all those duff little molecules inside you. . . . They say it'll be in the high street stores within the next five or six years." I give a big, friendly smile. "So, you know, if you can hold out that long . . . well, who knows, eh? I'll certainly be giving you a call."

The taxi driver doesn't look round, preferring instead to treat my conversation with a silent reverence, which I acknowledge with a knowing smile as I sit back in my seat. Agent Wade glances across at me.

"You can't help it, can you? You're a real stud with the girls."

"Well . . ." I shrug but fail to hide a slight touch of arrogance in my look.

"It's a lesson being with you."

Throughout the journey, the taxi driver keeps glancing back in her rearview, and even though I know she wants to know why we are wearing boot polish, I also know she probably wants my phone number but is too timid to ask. I take the liberty of writing it on the dollar bill I tip her with. And just to make sure she doesn't miss it, I tear the bill in half and give her only the section with the number on it.

"Nano, nano." I grin and wink at her before turning to catch up with Agent Wade as he walks toward Cher's place.

Cher's childhood was basically split into two categories. Category A was before Cher's beloved uncle Ernst was released from prison. Category B was after dear old uncle Ernst rejoined society and was then rounded up and hung by an angry mob for a crime he may or may not have committed. Cher, at the ripe old age of eight—I don't know what that is in Native American years—witnessed the whole thing. Ever since then, she has been on a mission to eradicate the perpetrators. All twenty-six of them and a few of their relatives for good measure. I actually argued that this didn't make her a serial killer, just a rather vengeful person, but the television psychiatrist had sealed the argument with his pronouncement that the "Hanover Hangman" could turn out to be one of the most vicious and unrelenting skillers in modern history.

Agent Wade stops at the foot of her drive and lets out a long, low sigh. I can see that he looks a little troubled.

"What is it?"

"She won an Oscar."

"Who?"

"Cher."

"So?"

"Well . . . she's a star. Can you kill stars?"

I'll admit that I heartily applauded along with the rest of the nation when Cher won an Oscar for her performance in that movie where she plays maybe twenty years younger than her actual age. "But this isn't the real Cher."

I look at Agent Wade's blacked-out face and get the hopeful feeling that he is experiencing some doubts about this.

That he'll just turn on his heel and leave. "I didn't know you were such a fan."

Agent Wade takes a moment, pulls himself together, stands upright, takes a big breath. "Just give me a minute. I'll, uh . . . I'll be all right."

Cher cautiously opens the door wearing a see-through nightgown. It is black, sequined, and flimsy. It's now two in the morning, and she looks great. Under the nightgown she wears a lace teddy, also black. I am in awe of her ability to remain in character whatever the time of day.

As soon as she makes me out, her face contorts into a deep snarl. "You stinking little midget!"

She tries to slam the door on us, but Agent Wade is too fast for her. His arm snakes out and he grips her tight around the throat, pulling her close up to him. She gags, such is the power of his grip.

"Look, uh . . . before Dougie does what he's got to do . . . could I have your autograph? Make it out to Kennet. That's Kenneth without the 'h.' "

By way of an answer, Cher knees Agent Wade hard in the groin. He immediately lets her go and crumples to the ground. I am about to give chase as she races away, but Agent Wade stops me.

"Take this. . . ."

Agent Wade hands me his standard-issue snub-nosed FBI revolver. I take it in my hands and, having never held a gun before, feel slightly in awe of it. It's a lot heavier than I expected.

"Get after her, Doug!"

I feel myself break out in an immediate sweat, lick my top lip, and nearly gag on the taste of the boot polish. I wipe my tongue on the back of my hand and spit black saliva onto Cher's porch.

"I'll go round the back. . . ." Agent Wade climbs unsteadily to his feet and hobbles away.

I try to gather myself, taking deep, calming breaths. The gun makes me feel good, and I grit my teeth and dive into Cher's darkened home. I roll into the large hall, both hands gripping the gun, and come to a kneeling stop, aiming in jerky movements all around me. The place is eerie and silent. I look around and count six closed doors, all leading into downstairs rooms. Why couldn't she have lived in an open-plan? I check the imposing stairway and don't for a minute think Cher could have gotten up it so quickly. I almost lick my lip again but manage to remember not to. I decide the best plan is to test each door as I come to it. The first one is a broom cupboard, but I check it all the same. The second door leads into a kitchen. I take my time edging inside, and I don't take a step until I have checked every angle of possible ambush. There aren't many places to hide, though, and I decide to take a chance and try the door next to the kitchen. This door needs oil as it creaks open. I peer round the door. Here there are many places to hide, and for a moment I toy with the idea of just blasting away in the room, hoping I'll get lucky. I decide this is a ridiculous idea and the sort of thing that only a blindly panicking Chuck Norris would attempt.

Something moves, and I immediately start shooting. I also scream at the top of my voice in accompaniment to the roar of the gun. Bullets fly and crash everywhere. My scream turns into a yell and eventually converts into a single continuous high-pitched Apache war cry as I race around the room, firing indiscriminately.

"Geronimo!"

I hit everything but Cher.

The click of an empty chamber should bring me to a shuddering halt, but I hurl the gun into a glass cabinet and continue to race around, yelling at the top of my voice. I charge out into the hall and kick open the next door. In that room, I pick up anything I can find and hurl it at any place where I think Cher could be hiding.

I have virtually wrecked her entire living room when I suddenly see Cher's face at the window. She's outside!

I look around wildly, grab a small portable television, and attack the window with it. I heave the portable at Cher, and it smashes through the window; amazingly enough, she doesn't even try to get out of the way. Instead, the television clunks into her face and then crashes down beside her. Somehow she remains standing there, upright and unflinching, and I can't believe she never told the Club she was from the planet Krypton. I grab a large speaker that is attached to an expensive-looking sound system, rip it from its moorings, and then turn and hurl it at Cher, who hasn't moved an inch throughout. Her head is angled to one side, and she has what I can only describe as a sultry come-hither look. Which surprises me, considering what I'm trying to do to her. The speaker misses her completely, and as my initial adrenaline rush gives way, I realize that I am weakening by the second. I am exhausted, and my limbs feel like lead weights. But I will not give in. I stagger over to the speaker's twin and prepare to tear it from its bracket when I hear Agent Wade call out.

"Fooled ya."

I turn, and at first I can't see him. Not anywhere. Cher remains standing, staring in at me, and then I hear Agent Wade speak again.

"Over here."

My God! His voice is coming from Cher! I start to back away when Agent Wade's head appears from behind Cher's right shoulder and he grins at me. "Guess who?"

I realize that he must have been holding her dead body upright all the time I was hurling household goods at her, and although he thinks it is a hoot, I am not so convinced. Agent Wade steps away and lets Cher drop to the ground, then starts climbing in through the shattered window. "I bumped into her trying to escape out the back way. She tripped when she saw me—and, uh . . . I think she may have broken her neck as she fell."

I can't seem to close my mouth. I stare wild-eyed at Agent Wade as he looks around at the chaos and mess I have caused.

"That's the boy, Dougie. You just keep that level head of yours."

I still can't close my mouth.

Agent Wade takes a moment to light a cigarette. He looks at me, blows smoke toward the small chandelier swaying back and forth. "Should've heard her neck crack—beautiful, just beautiful. Star quality all the way to the bone."

I don't help Agent Wade drag Cher into the living room because I'm too busy looking for a memento.

"I got you, babe . . ." Agent Wade has a fine voice, but it is nothing compared to Cher's.

I can't seem to decide between taking Cher's entire CD collection or perhaps taking her state-of-the-art automatic bottle opener instead. I give up on these ideas, though, and find myself turning round and reaching for Cher's dark black wig. It seems to be stuck, and I give it a couple of hard tugs until I realize that it isn't a wig but is in fact Cher's real hair. I let her head drop and step away as if I have just received a high-voltage electric shock.

No . . .

Surely not . . .

I look at Agent Wade, who is now taking photos of Cher's prostrate body. He glances over at me and grins. "The boys at the Bureau aren't gonna believe this."

Agent Wade grins and clicks away with his camera, the flash popping on and off, on and off.

KENTUCKY-FRIED CHICAGO

I HAVE TO STAY FOCUSED. I have to stick to my original plan, even though it keeps changing practically every minute. I take a bus to the west side, clutching an eight-by-ten envelope. I've just been to KlippyKlap Snaps and picked up a photograph of Burt Lancaster's final moments on earth, courtesy of Tony Curtis and his rusting saw. The guy who did the developing figured I did special effects work for some film company, and I told him he was absolutely right and that just now I was working on a sequel to *Mary Poppins* where she comes back as a murderess.

Together with the photograph, I also have three letters in my pocket that I have written to Betty. I've got three because I don't know which sounds more appropriate.

> *Dear Betty,*
> *Please find enclosed a photo of your half-brother, Tony. I took it the other night. I can tell you I was as shocked as anyone. What should we do?*
>
> *Yours sincerely,*
> *Douglas Fairbanks Jr.*

Betty,

It's your favorite person ever here. Thought you might be interested in this photograph. It proves beyond all doubt that Tony, your half-brother, is the RAT!!!!!!! I don't think this is the way the Club chairman should behave, do you?

Talk soon,
Doug

My dearest Betty,

I don't know what to say. It's tragic. Truly and hideously tragic. I'm afraid I lied to you about being blackmailed. It's just that I couldn't bring myself to show you what Tony, your half-brother, has been doing. But I can't live with this knowledge or my guilt in lying to you any longer.

WE MUST MEET!!!! I'm going crazy keeping all of this to myself.

Poor Burt . . . I really liked that guy.

Yours with faith (and not a little hope),
Douglas

P.S. I also liked Tallulah, Errol, Richard, Will, Carole, Cher, and all the others Tony must have murdered.

The last letter seems to me to have hit the right note and says all the things I think need to be said.

I had intended to just leave the letter and the envelope at the library for Betty, but as soon as I step inside I get this huge urge to seek her out. I badly want to see her, and I quickly sweep my matted hair into an effective Agent Wade style.

Betty is browsing through *Potted History of Italian Clay Pots* when I eventually find her. The lights are low, and the library is surprisingly warm. She has removed her crocheted shawl, and I note that she is wearing a rust-colored satin-look blouse that shimmers whenever she moves.

"Hi . . ."

"Douglas?"

"Am I disturbing you?"

"No . . . not at all. I was just filing stuff."

"You don't mind my coming here?"

"It's nice to see you."

I warm to this, start to relax. "Well . . . it's nice to see you, too."

I sit at one of the study desks. Betty remains standing, and I find that her bosom is now directly at my eye level, some six inches away. To my consternation, it is extremely hard to look anywhere else.

I feign a big "someone's just walked over my grave" shiver. "Things are really getting spooky, Betty. I needed to talk to someone. Can't quite figure out what's going on."

"Well, I sure can. We're being stalked, Douglas. I know it."

"You think?"

"What else can it be?"

"Heard from Tony?"

"Nothing. He won't answer my calls, is never at his desk. I can't find out anything from him."

I look down at the study desk and notice someone has gouged "Murder Rap Murders Music!" into the wood veneer.

Betty looks so scared and vulnerable that I want to reach out for her and hold her in my arms. Instead my hand slips into my jacket pocket.

"Listen . . . I, uh . . . I think I might have found a reason for Tony lying low."

"Really?"

"Yeah . . . I don't think you're going to like it, though."

"I'm feeling lousy anyway, so what difference will it make?"

"This is major league lousy."

Betty sighs, looks into the distance. "Whatever happened to the good things in life?"

The Club members happened.

"Maybe it'd better wait. This is a bad moment. I'll show you another time."

"Show me what?"

"This." The photograph is out of my pocket before I know it. I thrust it into Betty's hands before I've even had a chance to think it through. She is so shocked by the picture, she stands motionless for several seconds before fishing out her cigarettes and lighting one nervously. And this is despite the NO SMOKING sign plastered to the wall only inches from Betty's head.

"Oh God . . . no . . ."

"When you called I just had this weird feeling. Tony never liked Burt . . . well, no one did, really, but Tony totally hated him."

"He never told me that."

"Tony tells me everything. We're real tight." I twist my first two index fingers in that age-old hand gesture that shows just how compatible two men can be. Though I have to admit, I don't understand how what basically looks like one flesh-colored snake mating with another could ever be truly representative of male bonding.

Betty looks a little vague, unconvinced. "How did you come by this photo, Douglas?"

"I worked on the theory that because Tony told you he smelled a rat, he was very probably smelling himself. So I followed him one night, having the hindsight to take a Kodak camera and special night film with me."

"Foresight."

"What?"

"You had the foresight. You only have hindsight after the event." Betty's voice is weak, troubled. Smoke curls mockingly in front of the NO SMOKING sign.

"Well, whatever—my sight was good enough to get this picture."

I can feel myself reddening, hoping Betty's going to buy this. She glances back at the photograph, and the shock wave hits her for the second time. "Jesus."

"I, uh, I wrote this to go with the picture."

I hand her the letter I wrote. In fact, I hand her all three, and she looks confused, not knowing which one to read first. I realize my mistake, grab the letters back, sift through them, and then hand her the right one.

"Yeah, here it is. This one. I wrote this to you."

Betty reads the letter and looks as though she is going to faint. I pull out the chair next to mine, and she sits down on it, heavily. She holds the photo and the letter limply, stares ahead, wondering what on earth she did to deserve all this. Half a dozen murders at the last count.

"I'd say it was pretty conclusive. Wouldn't you?" I try my best not to ram home the point, but I'm also aware that I need to make sure she gets the gist of it.

"You couldn't get a more complete picture of a rat at work."

"But why's he doing it, Douglas? Why's Tony killing the members? I thought he loved the Club?"

That's a very good point, and one that I truly don't have an answer for. I try to buy myself time by pretending to fall into a sudden and deep thought. "Mmm ... well ... there's all sorts of reasons, I guess. The strongest being that he does seem to enjoy killing people. And to be honest, Tony doesn't really have a set pattern—he just kills anyone that takes his fancy."

"But eventually he'll have no Club left. There'll only be him."

"They say creative people are very destructive."

"Tony's not creative. Show him a work of art and he'd try and eat it." Betty gives me a slightly dismissive look, and I admit it was a weak thought.

"What theories have you got, then?" I decide to put the ball right back in Betty's court. "Why do you think he's doing it? You've read a lot of books."

Betty takes her time, still reeling from the shock of the photographs. "I dunno . . . I really don't. It's not the brother I know."

"Half know—he's a half-brother, remember?"

Betty doesn't bother responding to that, which is a shame because it's a pretty clever play on words. I glance at the photographs, give a big shrug and a loud tut.

"Poor old Burt, huh? I really liked that guy. I was truly fond of him."

"Me too."

I knew it! Boy, am I glad that round-shouldered, wiry-haired freak is dead.

"He made me laugh. I, uh . . . I don't meet a lot of men who can do that."

"You, uh . . . you like to laugh, then?"

"Who doesn't?" She says this wearily, and I step in quickly, ready to lift her spirits.

"Listen, did you ever hear the one about the guy who gets hit by a golf ball? I mean, this guy that hits this golf ball? You heard this? You'll love it—"

"To be honest, I don't think I'm in the mood right now, Douglas."

I give Betty a reassuring grin. "Everyone loves this joke. So this guy hits this golf ball and misses the course completely. The ball sails off onto a nearby highway and bounces through the windshield of a bus. The bus goes out of control, skids across a junction, and causes a major pileup. The golfer—the guy who originally hit the golf ball—eventually finds his ball nestling into the by now dead bus driver's ear, and he turns to his caddie and says, 'My God . . . what do I do now? I mean—my God!' " I grin from ear to ear, proving beyond any doubt that I can make Betty laugh as much as Burt ever did.

Betty doesn't seem to be listening, though. She has drifted off, staring into the aisles, letting her thoughts mingle with the words in the books, letting them become integrated and jumbled until they are meaningless. I know I have to shake her out of her terrible inner torment. I nudge her a couple of times, trying hard to take her mind off her half-brother.

"So the caddie—you'll die, Betty, believe me, you're going to die—the caddie carefully surveys the situation and then looks at the golfer. 'You'll need your eight-iron for this shot.' "

I laugh, slap my thigh, and then notice that Betty still seems distant and pained, looking beyond me. She really must be down, because everyone I tell that joke to normally creases up.

"We'll have to kill him, Douglas. . . ." The words seem to come out of Betty's mouth without her lips moving, a low, guttural murmur.

I pause a moment. "Tony?"

"Yeah."

"Jesus, Betty, that's a tall order. Can't we just run away somewhere?"

"We could . . ." I like the way she says "we." "But that'd be unfair to the others."

"Let's invite them along."

Betty glances back at the incriminating photo and gives a faint shudder. "I can't believe this is happening."

I seize my chance and reach out for Betty. My arm slips around her waist. She doesn't resist—in fact, she leans into me, and we stay like that for a good ten minutes until a fair-haired man appears and asks us to direct him to the canine reference section. It is only when he sees the photographs of Burt's decapitation that he realizes he is asking the wrong people.

Originally, I had intended to jog home from the library because I felt like I needed a good long run to clear my head. But when I get outside, I feel as weak as a kitten, can barely stand up. I feel like someone trapped in the eye of a hurricane; the world is spinning around me, and the air is getting sucked from my lungs. I hail a cab and quickly wind the windows down, not caring that the rain is getting in. I don't know how long I sat with Betty, my arm around her waist, just staring out into nothingness, but it is now very dark out.

As we move through the night traffic, the driver talks constantly, speaking rapidly, punching his words out.

"Fuckin' Kentucky Killer. Fuckin' killed another one today. Some Puerto Rican–Mexican sleaze bag. Fuckin' goin' for the three hundred, you ask me."

I look up and study the grease that sits on top of the driver's hair. It is so thick, it glistens in the glow of the streetlamps we pass under. I have this mad impulse to force him to drive through a car wash keeping the windows down, and if I had a gun with me, I probably would.

"Fuckin' has to come to our fuckin' town, don't he? That's my favorite fuckin' restaurant as well. . . ."

Lemon-scented hand wipes.

The words keep appearing in front of me, even written in the grease of the driver's hair.

Lemon-scented hand wipes.

"Fuckin' murdering scum. Why'd he have to pick KFC? Why not BK or McDonald's? Why's it have to be my fuckin' favorite restaurant in the whole entire world?"

Lemon-scented hand wipes.

"The whole entire universe, in fact. Fuckin' killjoy. I'm gonna take a gun with me next time I eat out."

The world has become a dark and fearful place. I look out at the empty buildings we drive past, see people wandering through the night; most are the dregs of humanity, the offspring of a lost society. I see two teenage prostitutes leaning in the car of a cigar smoker. His hand plays with the blond girl's long hair, twisting it in his fingers, pulling it to his eyelids, and running the golden strands over them. The other girl is a redhead with what can only be called a Vietnam stare, and I have this hopeless thought that maybe she isn't what I think she is.

"I've been with those two. . . ." The taxi driver beeps his horn and waves a cigarette-stained hand at the girls. Neither bothers to look up. "I've been with them both. They do a discount if you take them both together. Two for the price of one and a half."

The driver lets out a low chuckle to himself, and I crane my neck back to try to look at the girls before they fade into the night.

"It's the supermarkets, they're hittin' everybody."

The grease-haired driver doesn't realize that I suddenly want to cry, that I know without question that James Mason was right when he said he thought Armageddon was coming. In truth, it's here already; you just have to look at the faces on those girls to know that.

IT LIVES

A DRIPPING WET Agent Wade sits staring at the television screen, only this time there isn't anything on. The screen is as blank as his expression. He doesn't acknowledge me as I walk in. I'm not sure what to say to him and cross the room in the hope that I can get to my bedroom before either of us has to say a word to each other. My hand is on the door handle when his voice stops me.

"Doesn't it ever stop raining in this city?"

"Never."

I don't want to look at Agent Wade, fearing that if I do, I'll see him for who he truly is.

"Washes away our sins, I guess."

I nod mutely.

"And all evidence that we were ever here."

I force myself to turn and look at Agent Wade and can see that he is actually staring at his reflection in the television screen, that his eyes search out and trace every line of his handsome face.

"You hungry?" I can't think of a single thing to say apart from that.

"I ate out."

"Anywhere nice?"

"Best restaurant in town."

I nod, again mutely.

Agent Wade surprises me by quickly turning and looking at me. He wipes away drops of rain that have run into the light wrinkles under his eyes. "You're sure going to be a hero, Dougie."

I shrug. "Who'll ever know?"

"The victims that will never be because of you."

Agent Wade reaches for a bottle of gin that I hadn't seen and raises it to his lips. The bottle is half-empty, and now I understand why he's suddenly started spouting this dreadful but poetic garbage.

"Want to put some music on?"

"I was going to sit in my room for a bit. Maybe read."

Agent Wade glances to the rain-lashed window. "Ever wonder how many killers are out there? Everyone has a mother, ergo everyone has a need to kill."

"That go for you, too?" The question's out before I can stop myself.

Agent Wade just smiles at this, says nothing.

As I stand there studying him, I start to appreciate fully that I am the only man standing between a peaceful world and years of KFC-oriented murders. I will be the man who killed the man who killed the many.

I walk over to the window as I hear the distant chimes of a church clock striking midnight. I look outside and see a prostitute, or a girl who's trying to look like one, getting frog-marched into the back of a cop car by a burly Popeye-armed cop. The cop's partner, a female cop whom I would love to have dinner with one night if I weren't seeing Betty, is kicking in the car headlights of the girl's bemused-looking pimp. I open the window and call out to them.

"Excellent work, Officers. Excellent work."

The cops look over at me, and I give them a big grin and a wave. They say nothing as they climb into their car and drive off, windshield wipers on fast speed.

I turn and look back at Agent Wade, peering down at him, and know that I'm not afraid. That cometh the hour, cometh Demon Dougie.

JAMES
MASON

A SLIGHTLY SMALLER
MEETING

THE WORLD HAS BECOME a rain-eroded Roman amphitheater. There are Christians and there are lions and in between there is me. That's the only way I can think to describe what is happening. I'm four kills away from Doomsday. I note that there is only one member of the nerdy quiz team left, and both the manager and headwaiter of the bar and grill have been replaced by new personnel who seem keen on tearing down the wooden veneer of the bar and grill and replacing it with shiny black-and-white ceramic tiles. When the workmen eventually finish, it will be like eating in an elegant washroom.

I should be happy that this is nearly over. All I've got to do is kill James Mason, Tony Curtis, Chuck Norris, and then . . . I can't bring myself to think about it. I glance at Betty.

God, no.

Smoke rises steadily from five cigarettes, rising high enough to stain the new tiles. James dunks teabags into a cup of hot water and seems concerned that he can't make the tea strong enough. "It's weak, Mother—it's weak. Just look at it. It's like water, I tell you."

Betty looks very pale and very drawn. She keeps glancing dolefully at Tony as he gnaws at an extra-large piece of sweet corn. I want to take her in my arms and hold her tight, whisper to her that everything is okay, that somehow or other her man is going to come through for her. She won't look my way, though, and I try to get her attention by kicking at her under the table. But she has kept her eyes fixed firmly on anything but me. I resort to kicking her just for the hell of it until Chuck leans over and eyeballs me.

"Kick me again, you ugly little midget, and I'll bite your fucking toes off."

I fall silent, strategically withdrawing my foot, though still having the presence of mind to vow secretly to kick Chuck to death one day. Soon.

Tony bangs the table to get everyone's attention. He seems pleased with himself. "Just want you all to know that from now on things are getting back to normal."

I smile inwardly, start to look forward to one of the few Club nights I have left. I hope someone has a good story to tell.

"Normal? So where's Burt and Cher?" Betty tries to look bravely at Tony, like she is demanding an answer.

My breath catches in my fast-drying throat. I got so wrapped up in things that it only now dawns on me that Cher was killed after Burt, so he couldn't possibly be the Club rat I made him out to be. I try to swallow, but my Adam's apple won't budge.

Tony considers for a moment, eyes everyone deliberately.

"Neither of them will be coming."

There is a lingering silence as no one dares speak. We all wait for Tony to reveal more. He looks at us with a heavy heart.

"I was called to a burglary, and it turned out to be Cher's

place. Bastards had ransacked the place. We found Cher with her neck broken."

The lingering silence becomes oppressive as the Club takes in the news of the tragedy. Tony looks really cut up.

Chuck isn't buying it, though. "A burglary?"

"That's right." Tony nods.

"And you believe that?"

"Seen enough in my time to know."

"Some cop you are," Chuck sneers, and then immediately regrets it when he sees Tony's eyes burn with a sudden and intense rage.

"It was a burglary. Got that?"

Chuck is hesitant, so much less of a man than I originally thought. He nervously scratches what looks like a spreading rash on the side of his neck. "So what about Burt?"

"Burt turned out to be a bad fucker. And believe me when I say we're all better off without him."

I glance at Betty, and I can tell that she isn't buying Tony's story.

"Did you do something to him, Tony?"

"Let's just say I had the Club's interests at heart."

"You killed him?" Chuck is again hesitant.

Tony shrugs. "Someone had to do something."

"That's it! I'm outta here. I'm quitting the Club before I'm next."

Tony calmly takes a thin slice of ham from Chuck's plate, rolls it into a tube shape, and then pops it into his mouth like it was a cigar. "No one's gonna be next. I've seen to that."

"Sure you have." Chuck has lost all his old sparkle, and I am deeply disappointed to see him fold so easily. "Nice knowing you all, but I'm hightailing it. . . ."

Chuck rises as Tony sucks the ham tube into his mouth and swallows it without chewing. He then grabs Chuck's wrist, stopping him dead in his tracks. "You can't leave, Chuck."

"Try and stop me." Chuck is trying to sound tough, but it's not very convincing when we all now know he's a pantywaist.

"We need you, Chucky-boy. Who else is gonna provide the funny stuff?"

"Get Dougie to do it—he's a riot."

I start nodding to myself, feeling good that Chuck thinks of me in this way.

Tony belches. "Dougie's a shit stick, Chuck. He's only funny if you laugh at him."

I glance at Betty and hope she might tell Tony different— that if I wanted to, I could bring the house down with my golf joke.

Chuck won't be moved. "Let go of my arm, Tony. I don't want to cause any trouble."

"Chuck, I want you to understand something, okay? I want you to forget all about the others. I've seen to that little problem. Okay? There's gonna be no more people going missing. Big Tony's seen to that. So let's just sit back and enjoy the company."

"What's left of it." Betty says this with an acerbic edge, and Tony glances at her, narrowing his eyes.

"You got a problem as well, Bets?"

It isn't easy for the nervous Betty to look Tony in the eye, but she just about manages it. "I want an unconditional guarantee that nothing is going to happen to any of us."

"From me?"

"From you."

Tony pauses, shrugs—then laughs again. "Look, the Club is my life, okay? The Club means everything—more than everything. So I'm going to promise you that things are going to improve a hundredfold from now on. There's going to be no more sudden disappearances." Tony suddenly looks at me. "Ain't that right, Dougie?" He catches me unawares, and all I can do is stammer a response.

"Whatever you say, Tone."

"There you go—straight from the horse's ass. If Dougie says it's gonna be okay, then it's gonna be okay."

Tony grabs his jacket and pulls out a rolled copy of the evening edition. He unrolls it, licks his finger, and then thumbs through to the "Lonely Hearts" page. "Anyways, things just got a whole lot better."

After finding what he has been looking for, he lays the newspaper out flat, irons it with his hand, and then turns it round for Chuck to read first. "I've got a little treat for you all."

Chuck looks down and reads the newspaper. I strain over, trying my best to read it with Chuck, and he selfishly snatches it away. "Get your big nose out."

I sit back down as Chuck reads the item, then starts to laugh to himself. "Oh, Jesus . . ." It's a nervous laugh, but there is an undeniable excitement in there as well. "Fuck."

"What is it?" Betty's eyes are suddenly alert; she looks from Chuck to Tony and then back to Chuck. "Chuck?"

James suddenly slaps the air in front of him. "Shuttup, Mother, I wanna hear Chuck." He slaps the air again for good measure. "One day you're just going to have to learn to hold your tongue." He "slaps" his mother again. "Goddamn can't hear a thing."

"You fuckin' finished?" Tony glares at James, who looks at him, rubbing his now "sore" palm and then blowing on it as he nods. "I think she got the message."

"Good. Now shut the fuck up." I can see in Tony's eyes that he badly wants to waste James.

"Chuck?" Betty is really keen to know what has made

Chuck start shaking his head in amazement. He lets out a low, appreciative whistle as he reads the paper again, this time reciting what he is reading.

T.C., I'm hungry. Know a good diner? The King.

A hush descends over the table. Tony sits there grinning like a cat, watching our faces as we take in the news.

"KK?" Betty's voice is soft, lilting, innocent.

Tony keeps grinning.

"He's coming?"

Tony nods.

"Jesus H." Chuck is stunned, looks a little on the pale side.

"Not Jesus, Chuck—the Kentucky Killer." Tony is wringing every last drop of enjoyment from this.

I don't know whether to laugh or cry. Agent Wade is going to join the Club? Does that mean he'll put himself on his own list? And will he still expect me to finish the job? So many thoughts crowd my mind, and I start to drift away in this wretched mangle of impossible thoughts.

"I thought you didn't want him joining?" Betty is much more animated now as she shows a touch of her half-brother's steelier side. "You said you didn't want him at the Club, not ever."

"Changed my mind." Tony rolls another slice of ham into a funnel shape and wedges it into the corner of his mouth.

"Why the sudden switch, Tony? You've been against it forever." Chuck scratches his neck again but seems to be gathering himself.

"Whasammatter, scratchy? You not like the idea?"

"'Course I do. I'm nervous as hell, but I've gotta say I'm up for it. Only a fool wouldn't be."

For some reason, they both turn instinctively and look at

me. But all I can do is shrug; my head might be on my shoulders, but my mind is in another state.

"Mother wants me to take her home." James gulps down his strong cup of tea as fast as he can.

"You ain't going nowhere, Jimmy."

"She has a slight headache."

Tony gives James a derisory look, then leans forward and lights one of the table candles. He waits for the candle to start dripping wax, and then he pulls it out of its holder, stretches over, and fixes it firmly and squarely in the middle of James's dinner plate. His eyes meet James's.

"Imagine this candle is your dick, Jimmy . . . okay? Just imagine it. It's on fire, it's melting, and it's going to burn like this for at least another six hours. Imagine what that's going to feel like. . . ." I have never seen Tony so cold or so calculating. James swallows nervously. "No one leaves the Club. No one."

Tony leans across and suddenly blows James's candle out. The suddenness of it makes all of us jump, and I admit that I am genuinely impressed by this unsettling display. I also try my best to memorize Tony's speech about the candle.

James gives a meek shrug. "In that case, we'll stay."

"I think this calls for a celebration. Your round, Dougie." Chuck sucks hard on a cigarette, eyes squinting through the smoke, as he tries to get the party mood going again.

"I'm always buying the drinks." These must be the first words I've said in an age. I find them reassuring, and they help my confidence. "I must've bought more drinks than everyone else combined."

"Why break a habit?" Chuck gives an ironic laugh, and I can see he is getting back to his old self. I signal to the deaf waitress, who is busy at another table.

Betty pushes back her seat, and the grating noise it

makes draws everyone's attention. "I've got to go to the powder room."

"Gonna make yourself pretty for KK?" Tony laughs, but Betty says nothing as she gets up and leaves the table. As she passes me, she inadvertently puts a hand on my shoulder and squeezes it. I understand instinctively what she means by that and look up, catching her eye as I do. She then bends and whispers in my ear, "I want to see you. . . ."

I didn't think I could get any more excited, and my skin stretches as tight as it can go trying to hold everything in. Betty moves past me, and I drink in that sweet canine odor.

The deaf waitress appears, and I pick up a glass, point to it, and then splay my fingers wide apart, indicating that I want five of the same. The waitress nods, then turns to Chuck, who gives her an encouraging look. She nods to him and walks to the bar to get the drinks.

Tony leans over and grabs my wrist suddenly, and for one horrible moment I think my sweat bands are going to be wrenched off, revealing Tallulah's ink dots. "Headless chicken."

He gives me a big grin and a sly wink. He looks round and makes sure no one is listening as he leans up close to me, our faces barely inches apart. "Chop chop." He pronounces the words like they're some kind of code, and at first I don't get it.

"What?"

Tony scowls, tries again. "I *saw* Burt off."

Finally I get what he's saying and instantly break into a big smile and start nodding my head enthusiastically. "Oh yeah—I kinda realized that when he didn't show tonight. Great gag, though. Saw him off. That's funny, Tony. Great joke."

Tony beams at me, and just to make sure I truly do understand, he draws a line across his throat and make a nauseous guttural sound from the back of his throat as he does.

I feel like tossing him one of the photos I have of him and saying, "No need to labor the point."

"That's a weight off my mind, I can tell you, Tony. I've been barricading myself in every night, I've been so scared."

Betty returns from the powder room, sees me talking and laughing with Tony, and I immediately sit back and try to make like I'm just playing along with him. She stops again and bends to me.

"Can you do tonight?"

I give a slow nod. "No problem."

"We'll go somewhere quiet."

"I know a place."

Betty takes her seat as the deaf waitress returns with the drinks and starts putting them down in front of us.

Chuck watches her for a moment and then stands. "Listen up, everyone, I've kinda got this announcement to make. I wasn't going to say cuz of me wanting to quit and all, but now that it seems like I'm staying put—well . . ."

We all turn to Chuck, who now reaches for the waitress's hand and grips it tight. She stands beside him, smiling demurely at all of us, and I can't help but think they make a lovely couple. While the waitress signs, Chuck translates slowly for the rest of us.

"Hi, everyone. I know this is a little out of the blue, but I would very much like to join your Club. So far, I've only killed seven. The manager, the headwaiter, and five guys who made up a quiz team. I poisoned them all."

I glare wild-eyed at the cow pie that sits in front of me with two big bites out of it. Even Tony looks alarmed as he starts spitting out a mouthful of food all over the table and hacking up as much debris as he can.

"It's okay . . . I'm very careful. . . ."

My heart starts to slow.

Tony drags a hanky down his rough tongue, cleaning every last scrap of chewed food from it. "Fuck!"

"I would like to be known as Raquel Welch."

Tony immediately holds up his hand. "Whoa there. We've already had one of those."

"And believe me, one was enough." I laugh on autopilot, not realizing that no one else is joining in. I get a look from Betty that tells me to calm it a little.

"What does it matter?" Chuck seems surprised.

"I can't allow it, Chuck—sorry."

Chuck seems disappointed and rapidly signs to the deaf waitress, and she too looks really crestfallen.

Tony shrugs to her. "Rules is rules."

The deaf waitress looks lost for a moment and then gets very animated, signing faster than Chuck can speak.

"Myrna Loy? You had one of them?"

Tony pauses to think it over for a moment, glances at James. "Have we?"

"Can't remember one."

"Myrna it is." Tony grins at Myrna and Chuck. "Well, this is sure turning into a night to remember. Everything is rosy in the garden again. Welcome aboard, Myrn."

As he speaks, Chuck signs to Myrna, who offers a fey smile.

Then, like the gentleman I am, I pull out a chair for Myrna. "You can have Cher's chair. Probably still warm."

I watch Myrna take a seat and begin to wonder how many goddamn killers are out there. Seems I can't kill one without another one springing up. I could spend the rest of my life doing this.

SEX TIME

BECAUSE WE CAN'T BE SEEN leaving Grillers together, I arrange to meet Betty at the same motel room that Tallulah Bankhead was killed in. I phone ahead, using Agent Wade's name, and it gives me a slight thrill to pose as someone new—the excitement of pretending to be a loser like Grandson-of-Barney for nearly four years is starting to lose its allure. The woman who checks me in is at the very least in her nineties, and I figure she must have been incredibly attractive seventy years ago. Her straight chin and high cheekbones have kept her skin taut and almost wrinkle-free, and even today she is what I would call a handsome woman.

"Kenneth Wade?"

"Kennet. Kennet Wade. There's no 'h.' "

The woman nods and scrawls the name into her check-in book with a shaky hand.

"I'll be expecting company, so if you could—"

"Company?"

"My, uh . . . my girl's calling round. Very pretty, big glasses, lovely smile. So if you could just direct her to my room . . ."

"I'll have to charge you double."

I study the woman, giving her a very stern look. It seems

everywhere I turn someone is trying to make a fast buck, and I'm getting just a bit sick of it. I give the woman a solemn, unforgiving shake of the head, letting her know exactly how I feel.

The woman hands me the same keys that Agent Wade dropped in the rain all those weeks ago now. "Room eight. Better warn you that some girl died in there a while back. . . ."

I give a good impression of looking really surprised. "Wow. No kidding?"

"They told me ink poisoning did her in."

I make a good joke here. "Listen, I promise not to take any fountain pens in there with me." I open my jacket wide and, grinning, let the woman see that I have absolutely no pens in my inside pockets. "See? I'm unarmed."

The joke causes the woman to start coughing and hacking, and I pat her bony little hand. "No more jokes. I promise."

After watching late night television in room eight for about half an hour, I hear a timid knock at the door. I have switched on the lamp, and the red hue from the new bulb they screwed in gives the room a powerful, near mystical aura. I flick the remote and kill the sound on the television.

"Yeah?"

"Douglas? It's Betty."

I get up from the bed, walk to the door, and open it. Betty is dressed in a cream-and-tan patchwork blouse, and her beige skirt stops just above the knee. I realize that she must have gone home and changed, just for me.

I step aside to let her into the burning scarlet light of the room. She seems reticent as she scans the room, and I note that she grips her purse tightly to her.

"It's okay, there's no Mexican muggers in this room. I've checked all over." Betty nods as I pick up the remote and gesture to the television. "Are you interested in bats? The Nature Channel is devoting an entire evening to them."

Betty gives a small shake of the head, and I turn off the television. I go to the cabinet at the side of the double bed. There are two glasses there and a bottle of Scotch. I start pouring two healthy measures.

"Incredible creatures. They use sonar to see in the dark."

"I know, I've read a few books on them."

I tut to myself, I should have guessed.

"Water?" I show the glass of Scotch to Betty, and she nods.

"Just a splash."

I cross to the stained sink in the corner of the room, and after a big struggle with the rusty faucet, I manage to turn it on. Betty gets more than a splash, and I hope she doesn't notice. I return to her, hand her the Scotch and water, and then collect my own glass of neat Scotch from the cabinet.

"Well . . ."

Betty gives a tiny smile. "Well."

"Here's to, uh . . . well . . . here's to Cher. Wherever she is." I clink my glass against Betty's and take a small mouthful of the Scotch.

"To Cher . . . I'm going to miss her . . ."

Betty's voice suddenly trails off. She freezes, her mouth falls open, and she looks utterly stunned and bewildered. "Oh my . . ."

"What? What is it?"

"Uh . . ." Betty looks at me, tries to calm down. "Uh . . ."

"Sorry, I didn't realize you and Cher were so close."

Betty takes a big mouthful of her Scotch, and I must have got the mix just right, because she immediately takes another stiff drink and empties her glass. I take the tumbler from her and fix her another drink.

"So . . . what made you want to meet me?"

Betty still seems a little bewildered, and I can see this is going to be tough for her. "Uh . . . I was going to talk to you about Tony. You see . . . I can't kill him, Douglas."

"No?"

Betty's voice is tiny, distant, caught in the back of her throat. Her chin trembles, and I know that despite her best intentions, she really cares for Tony. "No . . ." She swallows hard. "I just can't."

She finishes her drink and hands me the empty glass. As I fix her a third Scotch and water, I hear the springs of the bed as she sits down, and when I turn she is staring hard at me. She takes the drink from me without a word. I try to put her at ease. "If you're not up to it, then I'm sure I can manage it on my own."

Betty sips at her drink, gripping the glass tightly in both hands.

"I'll make it as painless as I can."

"Hold me."

I stop, look at Betty, don't know what to say. She looks up at me with those big, appealing, watery blue eyes. "Hold me, Douglas. Please. . . ."

I look around for somewhere to put my glass.

"I need to be held."

My heart rate is increasing tenfold. My mind is going blank, but somehow I manage to drain the neat Scotch, and despite the horrendous burning sensation in the back of my throat, I put down the glass and then sit beside Betty. She turns to me, and I get a blast of whiskey from her breath.

"You know what I do to men, don't you?"

"This'll be different, I know it."

"I have to sleep with them first, Douglas."

"Won't hear me complaining. . . ." I smile gamely, not believing my luck.

Betty drains her glass, and I get up to retrieve the bottle

of Scotch when I feel her hand on my thigh as she pushes me back down, keeping me close by her. "I need that hug."

My heart is going like a jackhammer. I raise an arm and then pause. I'm not sure how to do this right. Her bosom seems to be everywhere, and I have difficulty in sliding my arms around her without touching it. Eventually I manage it, and I feel her nestle into me, her arms wrapped around my waist, the top of her head resting just under my chin. We stay like that for maybe ten minutes, and her hair tickles my nostrils so much that I sneeze. Twice. Betty pulls away, but I won't let her go, not now, and I grab her back to me.

"I'm holding you, Betty. I'm holding you. . . ."

One of my wristbands slips as I clamp an arm under Betty's chin. Her eyes are drawn to the strange tattooed dots that are now revealed to her. She frowns.

"How'd you do that?"

I look down at my arm and remember the savage struggle I had with Tallulah Bankhead. I gently let Betty's head go, and she sits upright again.

"It's an army thing."

"You were in the army?" Betty is genuinely surprised. In fact, we both are.

"Uh, yeah. I, uh . . . I did a few years. Marines, mostly."

Betty looks at me as if she doesn't know whether I'm joking or not. "You got into the marines? What were you, their mascot?"

I laugh heartily but completely falsely at this.

Betty seems reticent, is becoming more withdrawn by the second. "So what do those dots mean?"

"There's, uh . . . there's one for every kill."

Betty is curious. "What war was this?"

"I dunno. I forget the name they gave it. It was on TV, though."

Betty looks up at me, searches deep in my eyes, and then before I can react her mouth finds mine and crushes it with her lips. She kisses me long and hard, and I feel like I'm in heaven. She finally breaks away and looks hungrily at me—the lioness in her coming to the fore, and I swear she's going to growl at any moment.

"I want you, Douglas."

"You've got me, Betty."

"My place. Sunday."

"What's wrong with now?"

"I, uh, need to do things first."

I shrug. I guess I can just about hold off for six days. It'll give me time to buy some new underwear and body spray. "I'll be there."

Betty pauses, glances down at my wrists again. "That letter you gave me last week—with the photo of Tony and Burt. You said you really missed Cher."

"I do, God knows I do. She was something, wasn't she?"

"Yeah . . . she was." Betty gives me another ferocious kiss and meows like a wildcat at me. "I'm gonna make you so hot."

Betty grabs her bag and strides out of the motel room. I sit there in amazement. I knew I had a lot going for me, but this is unbelievable. One minute Betty's this meek and mild-mannered librarian and the next I've turned her into this sex-starved slut. I shake my head and blow out my cheeks, really unable to take it all in. God, I feel like a million dollars.

I lie back on the bed and let it all sink in. I glance at my watch and wonder if I should maybe wear a suit for the occasion. First thing tomorrow I'm going to find the best mustard-colored garment money can rent.

I reach for the bedside phone and cradle it to my ear. I fish around in my wallet for the card of the suit rental company but find Hanna's calling card instead. I study it for a moment, think, What the hell, and start dialing. Boy, I'm on a high right now. My thumb covers one of Hanna's breasts, and as I listen to the phone ringing at the other end, I swear I can feel Hanna's cartoon nipple hardening under my thumb.

"Yo, wha' you want?" The voice on the other end of the line surprises me. It is deep, manlike, and I can't really be certain what sex I am talking to. I blame the bad connection.

"Uh . . . Hanna? Is that you?"

"Wha' you want?"

"It's Douglas, Dougie . . . Just thought I'd say hello, you know. . . ."

"Wha' you want?!" The voice hardens, is impatient.

"So . . . how are things with you?"

"Wha' you want, fukka?"

I feel all-powerful, completely omnipotent, thanks to Betty.

"Listen to me a minute, Hanna. Just listen, okay? You tell those two Mexican guys, those muggers, that I'm going to light a candle for them. You understand what I'm saying here? That's one candle each. You tell them that, okay? You tell them I'm leaning over and lighting those candles. Right as we speak." Hanna hangs up on me. I debate pressing redial, but I know I've made my point.

I put down the phone and then make a fist, curling my arm and making my bicep bulge. I run a hand over the bicep, feel it, press it, admire its sinewy hardness. Hercules, if he were alive today, would be impressed.

I tear Hanna's calling card into little pieces and toss them into the air above my head. They sprinkle down like winter snowflakes, and I can't help grinning from ear to ear. Christmas is coming.

THE LAST LIST

~~TALLULAH BANKHEAD~~

~~RICHARD BURTON~~

~~CHER~~

TONY CURTIS

DOUGLAS FAIRBANKS Jr.

BETTY GRABLE

~~WILLIAM HOLDEN~~

~~BURT LANCASTER~~

JAMES MASON

CHUCK NORRIS

MYRNA LOY

A GENT WADE studies the list and isn't at all happy.

"Where the hell did she come from?"

"She works at Grillers."

"This puts everything out!"

"I didn't invite her."

"I hadn't allowed for this, Dougie. We're just going to have to double up. You take James Mason, I'll take Betsy."

I need to think—and fast.

"What's the big rush? KK's going to turn up to a Club with no members."

Agent Wade pauses, glances at me, and for the first time I think I may have said something that has gotten through to him. He grins. "Hanging around me must be rubbing off on you."

I am so relieved. "So what do we do?"

"We've definitely got to kill one of them. Betsy gets my vote."

My breath catches in my throat. "Thinking about it, James is actually two killers. It's him and his mom. That, uh . . . that might make more sense. To kill him first, I mean. He's easily the more dangerous."

"His mom?"

"She's imaginary."

Agent Wade lets out a long sigh, shakes his head. "These people, Dougie . . . sheesh."

"Maybe I should do him."

"Maybe we both should. He sounds like a nutcase."

I'm starting to calm a little now—I've bought us some time. Betty and I are going to get out of this, I swear it.

Agent Wade glances at the list again. I'm beyond trying to tell him that I shouldn't be on it. He produces his silver cigarette lighter, snaps on the flame, and holds it below the list. I watch as the flames eat up the list, and Agent Wade holds it until his fingers are nearly burned before dropping it to the floor. Specks of black ash mingle with a ring of smoke, and he blows hard, sending the smoke and ash all around my living room.

Agent Wade looks me straight in the eye, and I swear there's something disturbing hiding behind his bright blue stare. He rises to his full height, looming over me, threateningly turns up the flame on his lighter until it must be about six inches high. He lets me see the flame, then suddenly snaps it out. I don't know what this means, but it is obviously meant to serve as some sort of dire threat.

"Let the fires of hell claim them all!"

I study Agent Wade intently and start to get this sudden and golden vision. In it I see him lying facedown in the crocodile house. Being eaten.

It's the only answer.

COLD CHAMOMILE

JAMES MASON is one of those gaunt, bony, long-limbed guys who should be arrested on sight. His eyes bulge, his skin is taut and sallow, and he has pockmarks on his face and neck. Sometimes he has a boil on the back of his neck to go with the pockmarks, and I know for certain that he pays someone to squeeze it, probably a prostitute. He has huge, and I mean murderously huge, hands, and his nose is broken in maybe twelve places. He once showed me a photo of his mother, and to be honest, you couldn't tell the two of them apart.

I like him.

His stories are delivered in a very dry tone, which sounds sarcastic but probably isn't meant to be. He hardly ever touches his food and only drinks herbal tea. He carries herbal tea bags in his wallet and gets the deaf waitress—or should I say Myrna—to bring him cups of hot water, into which he dunks his herbal tea bag. Usually rose leaf or chamomile. Once, when he wasn't looking, I saw Chuck empty half a salt cellar into James's teacup, and to my amazement, James never seemed to notice and drank it all without batting an eye.

James lives in a modern-looking apartment in Dallas

and has recently been decorating it in "Mom's favorite corn-flower blue." I pay cash for my flight and head for the terminal carrying a length of lead piping in my bag. It immediately sets off the airport metal detector and I spend a good thirty minutes being interrogated by an obese security guard. It seems they automatically question anyone carrying this much lead. The delay causes me to miss all my connections and I arrive in Texas six hours later than planned. A Texan security guard then spends two hours threatening to hit me with the lead piping, unless I tell him why I'm carrying it around with me. Eventually his boss walks in and tells him to let me go. He's been through every page of the airport's guidelines and apparently lead isn't mentioned anywhere and they have to let me go.

The outrageously expensive cab I take to James's place pulls up half an hour later. The driver is a short-jawed chocolate eater who listens to a medical phone-in over the radio. I study the driver and know that he probably wanted to be a doctor once but gave it all up when he realized he had the IQ of a water buffalo. I get out, grudgingly pay my fare—no tip—cross the street to a diner, and spend two hours sipping expensive coffee and watching a cable movie about a woman who donates her bone marrow to save her daughter's life, only to have a dog run off with the marrow and eat it. The dog turns out to be possessed by the devil or something. Either that or it was just hungry. I don't really concentrate on the movie because I keep thinking about my date with Betty on Sunday. I've decided that we can hide out on Burt's houseboat—maybe even sail it somewhere warm and dry. I don't want to hang around any longer, and I'm hoping that James and his mom will be my last kills for the foreseeable future. Agent Wade, aka the Kentucky Killer, can join the Club by all means, but me and Betty are getting out. Only when I'm good and ready will I come back and finally rid the world of all known skillers—federal agent Kennet Wade included.

Evening closes in, and as I pay my tab I can see James pull up, having a huge argument with his mother about her irritating penchant for backseat driving. After opening the passenger door for his invisible mom to get out, he gets back in the car and takes the ramp down into the underground car park under his apartment block.

I wait twenty minutes and then cross the street to James's apartment.

James's killing career could have been sponsored by Waddington's, the brilliant minds behind the ingenious board game Clue, because to date he has used a dagger, a length of rope, a candlestick, a revolver, and a wrench to murder his victims. James told us that when he was eight, his mother, an alcoholic, used to beat him regularly with empty bottles of Waddington's brown ale, beer she used to get from visiting English sailors in return for sex. He had originally intended to kill drunken English sailors but found that murdering jurors who concluded against him was much more satisfying.

As I approach James's apartment, I pull out the length of lead piping, feel it heavy in my hands, and ring his doorbell. I quickly tape over the eyehole so that he can't see who is out there on the landing and then bring up the lead piping like a baseball bat, ready to swing it as soon as James opens the door.

I wait five minutes before trying the doorbell again, regripping the lead piping as I do.

Still no one answers.

I check the number to make sure I've got the right apartment—the last thing I want to do is cave in some innocent person's head—but I'm at the right door, and he should be answering.

I try a third time, finding that the lead piping is becoming increasingly heavy in my hands.

I can't believe James isn't answering. I check around to make sure no one has seen me, then I try the door.

It's open.

I take a moment, pushing the door gently. "Pizza boy."

I press my nose and my right eye into the crack between door and jamb and try to see if I can detect any sign of movement inside. It all seems very still, and I push the door open a few more inches.

"Hawaiian with extra pineapple?" My whole head is inside the door now as I crane my neck, eyes screwed up, peering into the darkened apartment.

Nothing.

Absolutely nothing.

I grip the lead piping tight as I step in and close the door gently behind me. My eyes are getting used to the shadowy room, and I can smell the cornflower paint and see white dust sheets covering every possible item of furniture. I can feel my pulse racing as I take a few silent steps farther into the apartment. Something is telling me to get out of here, but equally I seem compelled to keep edging farther inside, my eyes darting everywhere, waiting for something, anything, to happen.

"Garlic bread supreme for two?" There's a quiver in my voice now, and I realize that unless pizzas are delivered in a lead piping shape, no one watching me is going to believe a word of it. I opt for silence as I ease open a door and realize I'm staring into James's bedroom. The thing that draws my attention the most is a huge double bed with a skeleton lying on it. Not a real skeleton—one of those fake things tutors wheel out in biology class and then make "my, that's some diet you're on" type of jokes about. It's wearing women's silk underwear and a pair of zip-up thigh-length boots, and I have to confess that James is even more messed up than I thought. I don't know whether to laugh or puke.

I move on from the bedroom, find a small but stylish kitchen, can see steam rising from an avant-garde kettle; two mugs with teabags on strings stand waiting beside it, and there's a loaf of bread freshly opened. All the signs of life, but I'm damned if there's anyone in.

I check out a store cupboard, a bathroom, and a spare bedroom but can't find a thing. James is nowhere to be seen. I look at the length of lead piping that I'm still clutching and start to feel pretty stupid as I come back into the living room, unable to fathom how and why James isn't here. My eyes are used to the darkness by now, and I can make out pots of cornflower paint sitting on the rungs of a stepladder. A roller lies in a tray awaiting paint, and after I switch on a side lamp, I can see that all told he's done a pretty good job so far. I might take a leaf out of his book and do my place up the same. The white sheets covering the furniture have several splashes of blue on them, and as I look up I can see where James has been painting over a splash of red on the ceiling. I decide to leave; this is turning into a waste of time. . . . I stop suddenly.

I quickly look back at the splash of red on the ceiling, watching it drip onto the white dust sheet below. I walk over, peer up at the splash, and immediately know what I'm looking at.

I glance around wildly, heart thumping so hard that my ribs are going to end up bruised. I check again, desperately making sure there's no one else in the room, and then reach forward and pull away the bloodstained dust sheet. It's like being hit by a train when I see what is sitting on the sofa. A man, tall, thin, bony—and currently stabbed to death, hence the arterial spray on the ceiling—sits very upright with a carton over his head. A KFC family-size bucket, to be more precise. I can tell just from looking at the body's huge hands that it is James, but I have to make completely sure. Using the tip of the lead piping, I gingerly push up the KFC bucket until I can see James's gaping dead mouth crammed with lemon-scented hand wipes. I raise the bucket farther and find a typed sheet stapled to James's forehead. I lean closer still.

Hi, Dougie.

My soul kicks savagely at my insides, scratching and tearing to get out of my frozen body. That old familiar mantra of four years ago, from when I first joined the Club, returns.

Get the hell out, Dougie! Get out, get out, get out!

And this time I heed it. I turn and flee from the apartment, thundering onto the landing and taking the emergency stairs, somehow having the presence of mind to make sure no one sees me as I head down into the car lot built underneath the apartment block. Thanks to the lead piping, I easily smash open the side window of a white Cadillac and jump in behind the wheel. I don't care that the car alarm is now screeching as I hot-wire the engine, slam it into drive, and roar away. It takes me a good fifty miles before I find out how to turn off the damn alarm, and by this time I'm driving along an empty freeway to God knows where. Rearing up before me is a nameless world, and I break the speed limit trying to escape the eerie, cemeterylike landscape. I grab the mobile phone and punch in the number for Betty. I don't know what time it is in Chicago, and in truth I don't really care. Her answering machine kicks in, tells me the number of her mobile, and I call that, punching the keys so hard that I break a nail.

"Douglas?"

"Jesus . . . Betty . . . God . . . help me . . ."

"What is it, what's wrong?" Betty's voice crackles, is hard to make out—it sounds like she's standing in a wind tunnel.

"I love you."

"Douglas . . . ?"

"I do, Betty. I love you and love you and love you."

"Start breathing, Douglas. One . . . two . . ."

"Betty, I mean it. I want to go away with you. On a boat, Burt's boat. We'll sail to Mexico together. You, me, and your dog."

"What dog?"

"Please say yes, Betty. . . ."

"Look, we'll talk when you come over Sunday."

"I can't wait that long."

"You have to."

"Don't make me beg you, Betty."

"Douglas . . . I'm going to help you. Are you listening? I'm going to help you. Everything's going to be just fine. You won't have to worry anymore."

"I love you more than anything in the whole world, Betty."

"And I love you, too, Douglas. Now go back to sleep."

"Sleep? I'm driving, for chrissakes!"

"Driving? Where exactly are you?"

"Texas."

"What are you doing down there?"

"I, uh . . . I dunno. I guess I took the wrong turn."

"What about the meeting tonight? Will you be back in time for that?"

"I didn't know there was one."

"It's an emergency meet. KK's posted an ad. He's coming tonight."

I'm so insensible that I can't take this on board and seem capable only of declaring my undying love for Betty, as if this single feeling can combat everything bad that's happening to me. "Betty . . . I . . . I really, really—"

"I know, Douglas. I know."

Betty hangs up, and I grip the phone hard in my hand, wishing I could somehow squeeze Betty out of it so that she'd be there with me. When she doesn't appear, I toss the phone away and instead notice the odometer. I gaze intently at the dial as the miles roll hypnotically past, going from the tens to the hundreds, and on and on and up to the thousand mark and beyond.

When I get back to Chicago, I don't truly know where to go. I definitely can't face Agent Wade, and I'm not sure I can face the Club, either. I arrive at the harbor to find that the waters are still and the sun has broken through for the first time in what must be a decade.

There is a definite buzz in the air, and as I pass the security guard's hut, I can smell warm bagels. It could also be his burned feet, I guess, but I don't bother looking.

Burt's houseboat, the *Teacher,* is empty, creaking gently in the quiet tide. I drag my weary self aboard, find his bunk, and crash facedown on it. I am in hell, and I don't know the way back.

SON OF SUDDENLY

I WAKE TO THE SOUND of a familiar voice. Burt's small portable television is on, and as I open my eyes, trying to establish where exactly I am, I look around to see the face of the television psychiatrist staring back at me. From the tiny black-and-white screen, I hasten to add.

His face disappears, to be replaced by a drawing of someone sitting on a sofa with a KFC bucket placed over their head. The television psychiatrist comes back on screen and slowly, gravely, shakes his head.

"Victim number three hundred and one." A shot of James's skeleton lover complete with underwear and thigh-length boots is flashed up, with the psychiatrist's voice-over. "Is this what America is coming to?"

The psychiatrist shakes his head solemnly. "Let's concentrate on the victim for a change. Put to the back of your minds that he was killed by the Kentucky Killer, and instead, think hard about what sort of man—a lawyer, no less—dresses up a skeleton and takes it to bed with him. And then think that perhaps this man deserved to die, that our fine friends in forensics have established this man as a notorious serial killer—"

A hand reaches over and flicks off the screen. I sit up suddenly at the sight of Agent Wade offering me a cup of chamomile tea.

"Figured you'd be here."

My heart break-dances inside my chest, and I can hardly hold the cup of tea without spilling it all over myself.

"Tried the zoo first, then thought to myself, Now where would I go if I were Dougie?" Agent Wade chews on a nail, bites it, and then spits it out. "I see you've got a sense of humor."

"I'm sorry?"

"Dumping the KFC box on James's head. Very funny."

"I didn't."

"Dougie . . ."

"He was like that when I found him." I'm not sure why Agent Wade is playing these games with me. "He was, I swear."

Agent Wade looks at me as if he's waiting for me to break into an uncontrollable smile, like I'm joking and it's only a matter of time before I own up.

"There was even a typed message stapled to him. 'Hi, Dougie.' I wouldn't have put that there."

"Wasn't mentioned in the news report."

"Maybe they forgot."

"A message like that would make headlines: 'Anyone Out There Know a Dougie?'"

"Someone else killed him." I try hard to get my point across as I set down the cup of chamomile tea. Chamomile? I glance at the cup like it's got a snake in there or something. Where the hell did Agent Wade get the teabag from? He had to have been in James Mason's apartment.

Agent Wade sits at the bottom of the bunk—close to my feet—and I find I really don't like being this close to him. He produces a newspaper and tosses it over to me. I pick it up and see that it is folded open at the personals. On the top half there is nothing but lonely guys looking for even lonelier girls. Some lonely guys seem to be happy to ask for either—a lonely girl or a lonely guy, or even both at the same time. One ad asks for "any color, creed, sex, or religion, just please, please write to me," and I know from experience that that sort of pathetic begging will get him nowhere. I invert the page, read the bottom half, and trawl through more ads from society's misfits, and then finally I see it.

It's Club night and the King is in the mood to party.

I remember the phone call to Betty and glance at my watch. It's seven in the evening; I haven't been asleep as long as I thought.

Agent Wade grabs my sports bag from the floor and unzips it, showing me what's inside. "I brought a change of clothes for you. How about having a shower and a shave, and after you're dressed I'll drive you over to the Club."

"I'm not going."

"Don't start that again."

I fix my eyes on Agent Wade, not about to budge. "I'm not going."

"You've got to—KK's going to be there. I want that guy, Dougie."

"You go, then. Take a seat somewhere, the next table, even, wait for the meeting to wrap, and then take him out after he leaves."

"That's your job."

"Seems to me I'm getting a lot of help lately, so what does it matter?"

"I can put you in the electric chair, Dougie." Agent Wade snaps his fingers. "Like that."

"Not before I tell the world who you really are."

Agent Wade looks up sharply, and I enjoy this.

"Oh yeah, I know your little secret."

"What are you talking about?" Agent Wade seems confused.

"Really want me to spell it out for you?"

"Gonna have to."

"You killed James Mason. You got there before me, didn't you. You stopped off at KFC, drove into the underground car park, went up the emergency stairway, and stabbed him to death. What did you do with the chicken? Just eat it on the way there? Toss the bones out the window? I've never seen anyone eat as much fried chicken as you do. Plus your car smells like a lemon grove."

Agent Wade frowns deeply, looks pretty lost, but I know he knows how to act and don't buy it for a second. "Are you trying to tell me I'm the Kentucky Killer?"

I give him a slow and deliberate hand clap. "That FBI training you've been given—boy, it made you bright."

Agent Wade's lips curl up at the edges, and his perfect teeth are revealed as a grin illuminates his face. "Did I make that tea too strong or something?"

"C'mon, just admit it. There's only me and you on this boat. So c'mon. Tell me it's true."

Agent Wade picks up my teacup, sniffs it, and takes a sip. He places it back down and snorts out some laughter. "Dougie . . ."

"What?"

His voice hardens abruptly. "Go shower. We've wasted enough time already."

I don't move a muscle. Agent Wade is getting angrier by the second, looks like he might start beating me around the head. "You've got three seconds, Dougie."

"I'm not going."

Agent Wade's regulation FBI revolver is out of its holster before I can take a breath. The tip of the barrel is squeezed hard against my nose, and his finger eases back the trigger. "Shower for me."

KENTUCKY DEBUT

AGENT WADE pulls away from Grillers, beeps his horn a couple of times, and then disappears onto the interstate.

I stand looking at the bar and grill and find that I can't move. I'm wearing a badly crushed velvet jacket and jeans. The jacket is the most expensive item of clothing I possess, and it's the first time I've been able to wear it without fear of the rain ruining it. Agent Wade said I had to wear it because I had to look my very best for KK. The moon is full tonight, and the dark blue sky is cloudless. A forecaster on Agent Wade's car radio claimed that this dry spell was going to last a week or more.

I can see Chuck's low-slung Pontiac Firebird sitting in the car park. Betty's silver Datsun—nearly two hundred thousand miles on the clock and still going strong—sits next to it, but apart from that the car park is empty. There was a time when it was full, and I reflect on that for a moment. Remembering that the sight of all those parked cars filled me with an unadulterated happiness as I jinked toward the main entrance to meet up with people I came to call my friends.

I sit down without saying anything and take in Chuck and Myrna, who sit close together—and then Betty, who sits opposite me. I note that she has put on a lot of makeup—heaped it on would be more appropriate—and she looks like one of those women who sell beauty products in department stores, bulging dark-rimmed eyes, bright red cheeks like a clown, and a fake mole. I can only presume she wants KK to notice her.

Chuck, who has donned his best snakeskin jacket, looks ill at ease tonight and is obviously glad that Myrna is holding his hand under the table. He can barely bring himself to look at Tony.

"Thought you said things were going to be okay, Tony?"

Tony, who hasn't done anything more than comb his hair for the big moment, fidgets in his seat. "Guess you're talking about James."

"And the small fact that KK killed him. The same KK who's s'posed to be coming here tonight. Nice work, Tony, really can't wait for him to show." Chuck's irony is fast turning into a simpering whine.

Tony muses for a moment and to be honest doesn't look that confident. "So what are you doing here, Chuck, all dressed up and looking your fancy best?"

"Same thing you are. Safety in numbers. He comes in, we take him down. Hard and fast."

The entrance door to Grillers suddenly swings open, and the Club turns as one—eyes trained on the door—waiting with bated breath. A boy, maybe twelve at most, looks in, casting his eyes around Grillers until he sees us. The boy stares at us a second as he finishes off a fried chicken wing and tosses the bone out into the car park.

The boy starts walking toward us. He has very dark hair and even darker eyes, and he possesses that air of confident indifference that the youth of today seem to believe makes them cool. He ambles over, dressed in jeans that are baggy and a nylon jacket with a beer slogan stitched into it.

"That can't be him. Can't be." Tony is mesmerized by the kid.

"How young did he start? Musta been in the cradle." Chuck is equally bewildered.

"Could just be a mad dwarf like Dougie there." I don't bother to respond to Tony, my eyes fixed on the kid as he stops at our table and gives us a lingering, attitude-based look.

"You the killuhs?"

No one says anything.

"You the killuhs?" The kid is already getting impatient with us, but I'm damned if anyone has the nerve to respond to him. My voice is trapped way in the back of my throat, that's for sure.

"Last time, gooks. You the killuhs?"

"Who wants to know?" Thank God, Tony has finally pulled himself together.

"Ansa question . . . you killuhs or not?"

"Sure—that's us. What do you want?" Tony glowers at the kid.

"Message for you."

"Who from?"

The kid isn't in the least scared of Tony. "Message is man ain't showin'. Message is man gon' kill killuhs."

I look up at Betty and see her staring back at me, questioning me: Is this really happening? Even her pale complexion looks drained.

"Who told you this, you little punk?" Tony grabs the kid by the scruff of the neck, pulling him toward him.

Still the kid remains unfazed. "Man tol' me."

"What man?"

"Didn't see. Planted a letter and dough in my pocket when I wasn't looking."

"Lemme see that letter!" I blurt this out, glad that Tony still has the kid well gripped.

The kid looks at me, big proud, tough face. "You pay first, killuh."

"How much?" Chuck has turned pale as he yanks out his billfold and starts peeling off notes. "Twenty, thirty?"

The kid snatches $40 from Chuck and then hands over the letter. Tony lets the kid go, grabs the letter, and unfolds it. It is typed and unsigned.

Go to Grillers
Give to killers
No need to show
No need to go
Seen them now
Know them now
Watch them cry
Watch them die.

Tony looks up at us and then glances to the kid. "You still here?"

"You real killuhs?"

"Wanna find out, punk?" Chuck stares hard at the little kid.

"You're nuthin'." The kid makes this street sign with his hands that presumably means "Fuck you," turns on his heel, and swaggers off in a rolling-hipped, loose-limbed stroll. "Nuthin', nuthin', nuthin'."

"Jesus . . ." I have never seen Tony this unsettled. He takes in a great gulp of air, sucking it down into his huge lungs.

"Me and Myrna want at least a coupla guns each, Tony. Can you arrange that?"

"Yeah, sure. What about you, Betty?"

Betty sits there, looking silent and shaken. She nods. "Make it a forty-four."

"I'll see what I can do. Hoo boy."

I look at Tony, can't believe he's forgotten about me. "Uh, Tony . . ."

Tony shakes his head, wrapped in thought. "Why's KK doing this? What's he got against us?"

"Tony . . ."

Tony finally looks my way, deeply irritated. "What?!"

"You didn't ask me if I wanted a gun."

Tony shrugs halfheartedly. "Get your own."

I sit there stunned, unbelieving. I've given some of the best years of my life to this Club, and this is how I'm repaid? I sink back in my seat, notice Betty looking across at me, almost in pity. If it weren't for her, I'd leave the Club, the city, even the entire country. But someone has to protect her from Agent Wade. The others, they can go to hell. But me and Betty, we're going to find our way to heaven.

HOMO SAPIENS ALONE

WHEN I GET HOME I find that my apartment looks like it's been burglarized. So much for my pristine living conditions. Agent Wade's clothes are strewn everywhere, there are dirty plates and cutlery scattered around, my sofa is now home to a soiled duvet, and my CD player is stuck. The line "Chicken leg, make them beg" plays over and over until I give the player a big kick and watch the tray shoot open, bringing the incessant noise to a close. I take out the CD, look for a possible scratch, and then place it back in its plastic case. I scan the living room and wonder where Agent Wade is.

The phone rings in my bedroom, and I walk through—only to pull up short when I see that the words *Hi, Dougie* have been painted in huge cornflower blue letters all over my bedroom wall. Christ!

I almost forget the ringing phone as I stand there in a state of complete mental breakdown. A window is open, and the blinds rattle in the breeze. The phone keeps ringing, and I finally, weakly, reach for it.

"Yeah?"

"Douglas."

"Betty . . . hi . . ."

"You okay?"

"I dunno. . . ."

"That makes two of us."

"Hi, Dougie" must have been painted fifty times all around my wall; the words are everywhere I look. I let myself slump onto the bed, closing my eyes tight.

"I don't understand what's happening, Douglas. First Tony's killing the members, now KK is. And then I thought that you . . . uh . . . you were, uh . . ."

"I was what?"

"It doesn't matter." Betty takes a moment to compose herself. "The reason I called . . . Is that offer still on? About taking Burt's houseboat and sailing away together?"

My heart leaps. They are the sweetest words I've heard in a long time. "God, is it ever."

"Have to warn you, I'm not a great sailor."

"Don't worry. You've got that old sea dog Captain Dougie to look after you." Assuming I don't get violently seasick like I usually do when I'm on a boat.

"When shall we leave?"

"Anytime's good for me."

"Tomorrow? After lunch?"

"That's perfect. You know where the houseboat is?"

"Better give me directions."

"Okay. The boat's called the *Teacher,* by the way."

"The *Teacher?*"

"We can paint over it."

As soon as I hang up, I start opening my drawers, ready to pack. Only there aren't any clothes in there. I yank open the wardrobe and find that it is empty as well. I can't believe this and go straight into the bathroom and snatch the lid off my laundry basket. It too is completely empty.

Someone doesn't want me to leave.

But let's see them try to stop me, because clothes are the last thing I'll require. I'll probably be naked and in bed with Betty for most of the trip anyway. All I need is my wallet and maybe a crate of sick bags. I start to feel more positive, knowing I'm less than twenty-four hours from a brave new world.

The front door opens.

I fall silent, listening hard. I close the bathroom door.

Someone steps inside and gently closes the door behind them. Their footsteps are made gingerly, silently, and I listen with a lump swelling in my throat as the extremely light footfalls first enter the living room. There is a pause, but then they're on the move again, quicker this time, taking less trouble not to be heard. The intruder enters the bedroom, maybe expecting to take me by surprise in there.

Again the footsteps stop.

Everything goes silent.

Even my breath seems barely audible, mainly because I have stopped breathing.

The intruder is probably taking in the graffiti on my bedroom wall. It buys me time to look for a weapon, but the best I can come up with is a fake porcelain lavatory brush.

The silence is becoming unbearably loud now. It is attacking my eardrums with its nothingness and booming around inside my head.

What was that?!

Something moved—right outside the bathroom door!

How did the intruder get there without making a sound?

I grip the lavatory brush so hard that my knuckles lose all their natural color.

The thunderous silence returns.

Christ.

Quarterback builder, quarterback builder . . .

The door is pushed gently open.

This is it.

Judgment Day.

The door opens wider.

Quarterback builder, quarterback builder . . .

Wider still.

Qb, qb, qb . . . Do I have to abbreviate everything?

Wider and wider.

I was so close to becoming a hero.

Agent Wade stands tall, imposing, and evil, framed in the bathroom doorway, his blue eyes a piercing evil cobalt.

"Hi, Dougie."

It's as though someone has injected me with a paralysis-inducing drug. The kind Tony uses on his victims.

"You finished in there?"

I still can't seem to speak.

"Saw you decorated your bedroom."

It is then that I notice that Agent Wade is wearing William Holden's false eyebrows. The same ones I took from his glove compartment.

"It's different, I'll give you that."

I glance to my left and see that my left arm is working independently of me, raising the toilet brush into the air, fingers still clenched around the handle.

"I didn't see anyone turn up at Grillers. Apart from some kid. . . . Guess KK didn't show, huh?"

My arm stops in midair, the lavatory brush raised like a weapon, and I hear myself growl. A low, guttural sound.

Agent Wade looks pretty pissed off. "What have we got to do to get that guy? I really thought we had him."

He closes the bathroom door and walks softly into the living room. He feeds in a sheet of clean paper and starts typing. I hear him give a loud and impromptu belch and can easily make out the familiar sound of a lid being unscrewed from a gin bottle. The gin is poured into a tumbler—a seriously healthy measure—and the bottle is banged down hard on the coffee table. Agent Wade lifts the tumbler to his lips.

"Geronimo."

I listen as he takes a big gulp. Using my right hand, I have to physically unclench the fingers of my left hand from the toilet brush and watch as it drops at my feet. I stay there, listening to the end of the world begin.

After spending most of the next twenty minutes typing furiously, Agent Wade suddenly erupts in a flash of rage. "Christ. All I do all day is type! Type, type, type! It's all paperwork, this job. Pure freaking paperwork. I didn't join up to sit behind a desk all day."

I had yet to see Agent Wade sitting anywhere but on my sofa, and his outburst breathes life into my limbs. I emerge in time to see the typewriter nearly hit me full in the face as Agent Wade hurls it at the wall a couple of inches to the right of me.

"Why didn't he show, Dougie? Why the hell didn't he show?!" Agent Wade is already drunk, and his blue eyes have turned watery gray. It's like the gin has risen up his torso, gone on past his neck, and now laps behind his eyes. He stinks of the stuff.

"What did you do with my clothes?"

"Huh?" Agent Wade lurches drunkenly toward the sofa and lets himself fall facedown onto it.

"Where are they?"

"Where is he? Where's KK?" His speech is badly slurred.

"You're KK, you stupid ass."

"Where is he, Dougie? I've spent three years on the road, driving everywhere, I've been in more KFCs than anyone on the damn planet. I'm hooked on the stuff . . . I'm a chicken wing junkie."

"Listen to me, you drunk—you're the Kentucky Killer. You found him years ago. Just look in the mirror."

Agent Wade raises his bleary-eyed head, and I can almost hear the gin sloshing around inside him. "Is it you? Are you him? Are you? Tell me, Dougie . . . are you KK?"

As I look at Agent Wade, I know without question that it's time for him to die. I don't care how I do it, but this is the end of the road for the Kentucky Killer.

I roll up my sleeves, revealing my sinewy Douglas Fairbanks Jr. wrists, and I study my hands as I bring them up and can the feel raw power surging into them. These fingers could strangle a lion. I take a step toward Agent Wade, who has let his head flop back down. I take another step as he grunts and slobbers over the sofa, nestling into it, making himself comfortable as he moans. "Where the hell is he?"

I get closer and closer. Agent Wade snorts, can't get his breath, and then coughs. I freeze, wait for him to nestle down again. I get within a foot of him, bring my hands up, find that I'm talking to myself over and over. "Die, die, die, die . . ."

Agent Wade starts snoring, long inhalations, his back rising and falling with each snore. From this angle I can't really strangle him, but I could snap his neck. That'll make up for Cher.

I go for his throat, but before I can lay a finger on him, Agent Wade has his gun out and the barrel is wedged hard against my left eyeball. His gin-ridden breath clouds over me as his eyes bore into me.

"Try and stick to the plan, Dougie. Huh?"

CHUCK
NORRIS,
MYRNA
LOY

LOBSTER ON MY MIND

I STILL CAN'T BELIEVE that the sun is shining and take it as a good omen. It streams into my room, and as I lie in bed, feeling this bright new dawn burning away the last traces of dark cloud, I stretch and yawn, casting off last night's hell. I went to bed in my clothes and don't have to bother doing anything other than slipping on my loafers. I go to the bedroom door, open it a fraction, and peek through at Agent Wade, who lies unconscious, still facedown in the sofa. I'm not even going to attempt to sneak past him—the guy's quicker than a cobra—and instead go to my bedroom window, slide it open, and climb out into a fine spring day.

I jimmy the lock on Agent Wade's car door, jump in behind the wheel, and pray that the engine catches the first time after I hot-wire it. After five attempts it starts, and I'm already halfway down the road when Agent Wade charges out of my house, waving his gun around and yelling, "Come back, you little freak . . . come back here now!"

I nestle back into the leather-look seat, take the first left onto the highway, and press the pedal to the metal, as they say. Nothing's going to stop me now. Not even the fact that I have no earthly idea how to drive a boat. Though I hope to have mastered it by the time Betty and I reach the Gulf of

Mexico. I've decided we can sell the boat when we dock and use the money to set up a roadside caravan diner. Once we get that up and running, we can think about expanding. Within two or three years, we could even be rivaling KFC.

I get within a mile of the harbor in time for breakfast, which I grab at a drive-in Hannibal Hanimal joint and eat greedily at the wheel of Agent Wade's car. I scatter the debris of the meal all over his seats, even opening the salt packet and shaking it into his in-car radio system. I decide that he should know what it feels like to have something you love desecrated, and this simple little act helps make up for the mess Agent Wade has made of my house. And my life.

I leave the car about half a mile from the harbor and walk the rest of the way. It is so good to be out without oilskins, and I even nod to a few passersby, who look as happy as I do that the sun has finally broken through.

The harbor itself is a hive of happy, whistling sailors, as they clean their boats, run guylines here and there, crank up the engines, replace the shattered glass of their fog lights, and paint sections of faded woodwork. The security guard whirrs along the wooden jetty in a motorized wheelchair, his feet still heavily bandaged, and even he has time to pull up beside me and shoot the breeze.

"Hell of a day."

"Hell of a day."

"Perfect sailing weather."

"Perfect."

"Still as a mill pond."

"You said it. Mill pond still."

I can't wait to become a sailor. I really can't, and I make a mental note to get a captain's hat as soon as I can—and maybe even a pipe.

I walk on down the same jetty that I thundered along not

so many nights ago now, running for my very life. I suppose in a way I'm still running—or at least chugging—but today I know for certain that I'm going to get away.

The *Teacher* floats proudly near the end of the jetty. The car tires that are nailed all along its side rub up against the peer, squeezing in and out as if the boat itself is breathing. I board the boat like an admiral, marching onto it with an air of belonging. I look and feel like I was born to sail the seven seas.

It takes me all of five seconds to find Chuck Norris sitting in the captain's chair, and as I turn and scramble for my life, I slip and fall down a hatch into the living quarters below. I land hard, coming face-to-face with Myrna, who lies out on the same bunk I had slept in. I say face-to-face merely as a figure of speech, because her head is obscured by a KFC bargain bucket—just the way Chuck's was.

I crawl away on all fours, scurrying like a rat as far away from Myrna as I can get. I sit up, wedged against the wooden wall of the living quarters, believing that I can't have woken up yet, that I'm still in my bed, tossing and turning from a terrible nightmare.

The boat bats against the jetty, the sunlight arrows in as the sun climbs higher, and Chuck and Myrna are as dead as the dodos Chuck once made that really crass joke about.

Sure, this is a nightmare, but I'm not dreaming it.

I have to find a phone, I have to call Betty, tell her the plan has changed.

Oh God . . .

What if Agent Wade's got to Betty as well?

Mayday, Mayday, Mayday.

A boat passes, sending a big ripple thudding into the side of the *Teacher*. It also sends Myrna skidding off the bunk and onto the wooden floor. The family bargain bucket rolls off

Myrna's head, and there is a typed note stapled to her forehead. I crawl slowly toward the note, reach out, and snatch it from Myrna's head before scrambling back to the sanctuary of the living quarters wall.

End

I stare at the note, my eyes blurring, unable to focus until I wipe them with the bottom of my black velvet jacket. I try hard to keep a level head as the houseboat bobs up and down. I can hear normal life outside as sailors stop to chat, gulls squawk, and engines *phut-phut* on their way out to sea.

I take a big breath, determined to be a part of the real world and not be dragged any further into this serial-killing madness. I edge low past Myrna, find some steps, and crawl up them into the steering cabin. Chuck is still there, tied to the captain's chair, and I force myself to shove my hand underneath the KFC bargain bucket and grope around for the note that is stapled there. I tear it off and then duck down as another boat chugs past, the captain waving to Chuck, and then double taking when he realizes that Chuck is modeling some very fancy headgear. The captain sails on past, probably wondering where he can buy a cool hat like that.

The

I put the two typed notes together and realize that I was meant to read Chuck's note first. That's so typical of me.

It is all I can do to keep from haring along the jetty, screaming at the top of my lungs, but somehow I manage to walk in an orderly fashion, nodding to smiling sailors and trying to smile back as much as I can. The security guard in the wheelchair whirrs over to me when he sees me and offers a broad weather-beaten grin.

"Perfect day for it."

"Fuck you."

I don't bother to even glance at the security guard's stunned face as I march onward, walking faster and faster, until after a quarter of a mile I can bear it no longer and break into a jog. The jog develops into a sprint, and my arms and legs are like nuclear-powered pistons as I career toward Agent Wade's car. I've got to get to Betty.

I start the car at the third attempt, rev the engine hard, and then hear someone speak as though they are about to belch.

"June, June, June . . ." Tony tuts like a monkey. "You sorry little fuck."

I can smell strawberries on Tony's breath as he leans forward from the rear seat and figure he must have gone somewhere upmarket for breakfast. The shattered wing mirror lands on the passenger seat beside me—the same one that Tony shot on the night he lopped off Burt's head. He belch-talks again.

"I picked this up, sent it to forensics, and they ran a check for me. Clever guys, these forensic gents. Got me a license number. Seems you're running around in a government-owned car. Should be executed for that, June. That's as close to treason as it gets."

"Look, uh . . . I know what you're thinking, Tony, but believe me, you are badly mistaken."

Tony isn't listening. "You any idea what the Club meant to me?"

"You've got to listen to me. Betty's in trouble, Tony—"

"You took it from me. Snatched it clean away."

"Please—"

"They were my friends!"

I get a heavy-handed cuff round the back of my head, and my nose smashes against the steering wheel as I jerk forward, the horn sounding briefly.

"KK ain't comin'. He ain't even in town, is he? That was just you smoke-screening everything."

"Betty is in—"

I get another clump around the head, smash into the steering wheel, and sound the horn again.

"There ain't much of you, but you'll do for a between meal snack."

I get another smack round the head, and the horn beeps once more. I'm attracting the attention of several people, most of whom think I'm some sort of pal of theirs. They smile and wave in case I'm someone they know.

"Tony, you've got it all wrong, you've—"

I feel this sharp, piercing jab in my shoulder, and I wince in agony only to find that three seconds later I can't feel a thing. My body starts to numb up so bad that I can't even move my eyes. I stare straight ahead as Tony gets out of the back of the car, opens the driver's door, and shoves me over to the passenger seat. I don't feel any of it as Tony props me up against the passenger door, drags a seat belt around me, clips it in, and starts driving. He opens the glove compartment and stuffs an empty hypodermic needle in among the masses of lemon-scented hand wipes. When he sees the hand wipes, he shakes his great ugly head.

"Really livin' the part, weren'tcha?"

I really wish I'd had my eyes closed when Tony injected me with his paralyzing drug because I'm not sure I want to see what is going to happen to me.

Tony starts whistling to himself—"You Are My Sunshine," it sounds like. He whistles for a good half hour, and by the time we pull up round the back of a large diner in an industrial site, I am humming along to the tune. Well, in my head I am. He had driven round and round, looking for the perfect place to do whatever he is going to do, and I hoped for a moment that he was going to give up altogether when he remembered this diner on the east side.

Tony leaves me in the car while he locates the rear door to the diner, and after selecting from a set of police regulation skeleton keys, he opens the padlock on the door, unlocks the diner door itself, and walks in.

I try to move, God knows I do, but I can't even get my eyes to blink.

Tony appears again, checks around him that no one's watching, and opens the passenger door, looking at me with absolute distaste.

"I loved that Club."

He slaps me across the face—or at least I think he does because I don't actually feel him make contact or anything, I just see his big arm lash out and jerk across my view.

"Loved it more than life itself."

Okay, okay—you've made your point.

He takes a handful of my hair and drags me from the car. I land in the dust, which clouds up around me, and am dragged by the hair all the way toward the diner. I can see my feet trailing out behind me, leaving two gouged tracks—perhaps the last sign that I was ever here on earth.

The drug I've been injected with hasn't deadened my sense of smell, and I catch the distinctive aroma of boiling cooking oil. The floor of the diner is pristine clean, and the steel tiles shine, throwing my own reflection back at me. I am dragged past industrial-size freezers, steel cabinets filled with utensils and food supplies, ovens and dishwashers that stand tall and spectacularly germ-free. Tony stops at the source of the hot oil, and I can just about see that I'm now lying at the foot of a huge deep-fat fryer. Trust Tony to like greasy food.

Tony turns the switch of the deep fryer to high, and after a few seconds the fat starts to sizzle and spark.

"This place don't open till twelve on weekdays. Gives us nearly two hours."

From my ground view I see a mouse peek out from under a steel container, raise its nose in the air, and twitch it, taking in the smell of the boiling hot oil. It disappears with a start when it hears Tony slit open a huge bag of frozen French fries and dump them into the flaring oil.

"Mustn't forget the side portion."

I am trying hard to be scared, but I think the drug inside me is numbing my emotions. In fact, I have never felt this calm and rational at any time in my life. There is no panic, no gut-churning terror, only a serenely relaxed state. I guess I'm high in some way, which suits me just fine. Okay, I'm not going to walk out into the sea and let Neptune claim me, but really this isn't such a bad way to go. Dipped in boiling hot oil and then eaten. That's not so bad.

Boy, I must be close to an overdose.

Tony bends, his huge knees cracking loudly, and starts tugging at my pants. He should have removed my loafers first because the pants get caught in the shoes, and no matter how hard he tugs he now can't get either off. Shoes or pants.

"Freakin' dumb-ass."

Tony pulls my pants back on and slips my shoes off. He whips off my pants, pauses to hold them up against his legs, and cackles. "Where'd you shop? The toy store?"

He tosses the pants across the kitchen and reaches for my black velvet jacket. He gets my right arm trapped and nearly twists it off trying to remove the jacket. I know he does this because I can just about feel my tendons straining in protest.

Tony wrestles with the jacket some more until he gives up, grabs a kitchen knife, and hacks it free of me. My beloved jacket lies in shreds in front of me.

I blink.

Tony stands up straight, panting hard, and decides to have a cigarette to help him get his breath back.

I blink again.

My arm hurts where he twisted it.

I think I can feel my toes.

Tony breathes out smoke rings. "Maybe I can start again. Maybe me and Betty can get the Club back on its feet. It's not like there's gonna be no more serial killers. There's gotta be— it's a fact of life. Gotta be someone out there thinkin' it over, debatin' it. Should I, shouldn't I? Do I really wanna be a no- body all my life, or do I really wanna be somebody and have books and movies made about me?"

The feeling is coming back to my fingers. My face glows from where Tony slapped me in the car.

"Yeah, we'll start again. Only with more rules. IDs are a given. No one gets in without an official ID."

Keep talking, Tony, just keep rabbiting about your pa- thetic little Club. My knees and elbows now throb from where I've been dragged around.

More smoke rings are blown into the air. "Swearing an al- legiance ain't a bad idea. An oath of honor. 'Thou shalt not fuck my Club over.' "

I can feel blood spreading through me, energizing my limbs, pushing the numbness away.

Tony's cigarette lands close to my face, and his big boot crunches out the smoking red ember. He bends toward me. "All this talk has made me hungry."

Tony raises me into a sitting position, unties my tie, and starts unbuttoning my shirt. He looks me in the eye, and I try my damnedest not to blink. "I'm one of those guys who live to eat. I ever tell you that, June?"

My shirt is slipped over my still-numb shoulders. The feeling is coming back to me, but not nearly quickly enough. In fact, it'll probably only be when I'm hoisted into the deep-fat fryer that I'll be at my sensate peak. Which just about sums up the luck I'm having today.

My boxer shorts are the last item of clothing to be removed, and Tony does this with a certain amount of awkwardness. "I'm no faggot, but this has to be done. Last thing I want is your crotch material getting stuck between my teeth."

Only the tops of my thighs, my chest, and my shoulders remain frozen as I am lifted into the air by the hugely strong Tony. The smell of boiling oil attacks my nostrils, and I know I am going to scream.

"Lobster time." Tony grunts hard as he heaves me up and tosses me toward the oil.

Only I don't let go of him. I grab on tight with my feet and hands and hang there while he registers what's happening. "Hey! What the—"

I sink my teeth into Tony's shoulder, feeling his dark, sweaty body hair entering my mouth but not caring as I grip him with everything I can think of. Tony yells out, drops my legs, and starts hammering desperately at my head.

"I do the freakin' eating!"

My feet feel the cold steel tiles underneath them, get some traction.

"Stop biting me, you freak!"

My head is spinning from Tony's pummeling, and it's now or never. I get more purchase on the cold floor. I'm at one with terra firma again and, bracing myself, I let go with my teeth, bend a little at the knees, and shove Tony as hard as I can.

"Hey!"

Tony's worn shoes slip and slide on the highly polished flooring, and he stops batting my head as he feels himself shunted backward toward the deep-fat fryer. His hands flail and grasp at anything within reach, utensils fly everywhere, crashing down, my hands now coming free from gripping his back, my fingers reaching up and finding his great jowls and grasping them so tight that my fingernails break his skin.

I shove so hard, I almost go over into the deep-fat fryer with Tony. At the last moment, I let go of him and watch as his voluminous body backflips into the boiling oil; his head goes in first, and his screams are instantly muted to a gurgling, bubbling hiss.

I leave him there, the lower half of his giant body sticking out of the deep-fat fryer, his legs still shaking in violent spasm, as French fries turn black around him. I'm still heavy limbed from the paralyzing drug, and it takes all I've got left to collect my clothes and get dressed. After nearly stepping on the inquisitive mouse, I stagger out into the warm day. By the time the diner opens for business, Tony should just about be done.

JETTY MINUS BETTY

I MAKE IT TO THE LIBRARY Betty works at in just over thirty minutes, the whole journey spent praying to God that Agent Wade hasn't got to her. I'm chancing all on the hope that Betty was planning on joining me on Burt's houseboat only after she had finished her morning shift, because I think she's the diligent type who lives by strict moral codes. I still don't know how Agent Wade managed to go out last night, kill Chuck and Myrna in his gin-doused state, and make it back without my hearing a thing. The guy is frighteningly capable. I don't even want to know how he knew I was planning on getting away with Betty on Burt's boat—though knowing him, I figure he probably read my mind or some equally chilling FBI thing.

I take the steps leading to the library two at a time, running in past a geriatric couple, beating them to the revolving door, and pushing so hard that I almost get spun out into a librarian carrying a stack of books. I glare at the librarian.

"Betty! Where's Betty?"

"Who?"

I don't bother to get into a debate with the woman and take off, looking all around the library for Betty. I glance down aisles, I push browsers out of the way, and I generally make as much noise as possible in the hope that I will attract her attention.

"Betty! Where the hell are you? Betty—for chrissakes!!"

I get some severe looks from a group of silent readers at the study desks, but I don't acknowledge them as I charge down aisles, covering every inch of this bookworm's maze.

"Betty!! Betty!!"

Someone shushes me and points to a SILENCE sign, and I feel like tearing down the sign and making them swallow it.

I turn a corner, almost collide with a librarian who has a trolley filled with books, shove the trolley out of the way, and grab the librarian—pushing him hard up against the romance section.

"Where is she? Betty! Where is she?"

The librarian stammers weakly, "Wh-who's Betty?"

"Betty's Betty."

"I don't know any Betty."

Out of the corner of my eye, I see a burly security guard march past the romance aisle, stop, turn, and then start heading for me.

I glower at the librarian, suddenly realizing he can't possibly know who Betty is—he'll know her only by her real name. "The girl with the big pink-rimmed glasses. Watery blue eyes, thin lips . . . likes humorous guys. Lank hair."

"You mean the temp?"

"The who?"

"The temp. . . . Can't remember her name. I, uh, think her contract's up with us."

The burly security guard is hurrying toward me, and I know I have to get out of here. I give the librarian one last plaintive look. "She's not working today?"

He shrugs and shakes his head, and as the security guard

catches up with me, I drag the book trolley across the aisle and dart into the geology section.

I thunder past readers, knocking books everywhere as the guard does his level best to catch me. Eventually I lose him by stopping at the paranormal section, grabbing hardbacks and hurling them at him. Books can be pretty deadly in the right hands, and a copy of *Strange but True* winds him long enough for me to charge out the revolving doors, leap the ten or so steps to the sidewalk, climb into Agent Wade's car, and roar away.

Betty's rented apartment is within walking distance of the library, and I get there in next to no time. I hit the stairs running, and not caring that my exhausted legs are starting to die on me, I skid out onto her landing and head for her door.

Which is swinging wide open.

No . . . please . . . no . . .

I hardly dare look as I edge along the landing and peer around the doorjamb. The apartment has a still quality to it, an almost unearthly inertia. No breeze puffs the net curtain, no draft ruffles the papers sitting on her telephone table. It's as silent as a morgue.

I have to force myself to step into the hallway. I can smell that familiar doggy odor, and I nearly start crying there and then, thinking that I'll never get that close to Betty again.

I creep past a large acetylene tank with a welder's mask hanging round the taps. On the floor beside the tank is a connection for a blowtorch, and it looks though Betty were preparing for a kill, as she had taken the precaution of covering most of the hallway with sheets of what looks like asbestos.

I carry on into the main living room and find myself in a bright sunlit room, dust particles dancing in the rays like glitter. They are the only things that move. I check out Betty's bedroom, see that she has a double bed in there, and for a fleeting second I picture Betty and me writhing in raw, naked ecstasy. I feel so choked by this image that I back out of the bedroom and close the door as a mark of respect. Searching the rest of the apartment bears little fruit. Betty is not there, and I wonder if she is indeed anywhere other than heaven now.

A soul-searching drive back to the harbor only adds to my heartbreak. Cop cars are parked haphazardly, sailors have formed a small crowd around a police barrier, and the wheelchair-bound security guard whirrs frantically back and forth, trying to see what is going on. Burt's houseboat is crawling with police and forensics experts wearing white nylon overalls. A stretcher containing a body is manhandled off the boat, rocking so badly that someone loses his footing and Chuck's body slips off and splashes into the water. Immediately three cops dive in after him, almost as if they think he's trying to execute a daring escape. The news reporter I'd previously seen interviewing the League of Human Rights guy is now making a report direct to a camera crew. I can't hear what he is saying, but he is obviously very excited as he demonstrates, using a KFC bargain bucket, exactly how KK slips the bucket onto his victims. The reporter doesn't realize that he finishes his report with half a French fry mashed into his hair.

I turn away. The boat was my last hope.

It's nearing lunchtime, and I thought that just maybe Betty might have made it, that for just once in my lousy life something went as planned.

I can feel tears welling in my eyes, and it makes it difficult to drive as the road and approaching vehicles keep blurring. I feel like letting my eyes fill up and simultaneously putting my foot right down—a crude attempt to join Betty—but even though my despair is all-consuming, I know I still have one last job to finish.

Agent Wade Is Dead.

BETSY
GRABLE

FAMILY-SIZE MEAL

HALF AN HOUR after making the necessary phone call, I walk up to the counter at KFC. There is a foreign-looking girl serving. She looks up expectantly, a bright smile and happy, laughing eyes. I am convinced that she must be a model in her spare time, or at the very least an actress.

"A family meal, please."

The girl just looks at me, dumbly smiling away.

"I want a family meal." I have to stress this. Underline in spaced-out words exactly what I want. "Fa-mi-ly me-al. *Comprende?*"

The girl keeps smiling, her sparkling eyes boring into my brain until it hurts.

I speak once more, as slowly and as deliberately as I can. "One family-size meal—please."

A shadow falls over me, and I experience a slight chill. I turn around and see Agent Wade standing there looking at me. I hold his look, no longer scared of anything. "I figured we could share."

Agent Wade nods as I turn back to the foreign girl. "Family-size meal." I snatch up a flyer describing the said meal and she suddenly nods, smiles her bright smile, and takes the money for it. I turn back to Agent Wade and shrug. "Seems the best place to finish this, don't you think?"

Agent Wade still says nothing, and I'm glad because I don't want to hear his voice—not ever again.

We take a seat by the window. Agent Wade slides in first, and I sit opposite him. I open the family meal bucket and start dishing out equal measures. Agent Wade watches me intently until I'm finished. When I look down at my portion, I suddenly realize that I'm not hungry. Agent Wade looks much the same way, because he doesn't touch the food. I pat the family bucket knowingly.

"Guess this is all we really need."

"And these." Agent Wade pushes four sachets of lemon-scented hand wipes my way.

I nod, collect them, and pop them in my pocket. "I'm doing this for Betty—you know that, don't you?" I offer this as earnestly as I can.

"Figured you must have some sort of reason."

"I loved her."

"That's a big love, Dougie."

"We'd made plans. Were going to sail to Mexico and set up a fast-food chain."

Agent Wade shrugs. "Can never have enough fast food." His eyes are bloodshot, and he looks mighty weary, almost as if his soul—that's assuming he ever had one—has checked out. He's aged at least ten years since I first met him.

"Now it's down to you and me."

"Mano a mano."

"You got it." I nod, not having a clue what Agent Wade just said or even what language he spoke it in.

I glance at the bargain bucket, look at the smiling face of that white-haired ex–army colonel depicted on the side—the face that says, "Come and dine with me, and I'll tell you all I know about war."

"Dougie?" Agent Wade's voice interrupts my reverie.

"Yeah?"

"I've got a gun pointed at your groin."

Agent Wade makes me drive across town, all the way back to my apartment. We park, and with the gun in his jacket pocket, aimed at the small of my back, he makes me walk inside. I'm still not scared, though, and know I can get out of this—just as soon as I come up with a decent plan. Which for the moment seems to be eluding me.

The front door shuts behind me.

"Take a seat."

I go toward the sofa but feel myself pushed toward one of the wooden chairs that sits at my dining table.

"Sofa's mine."

I allow myself to be shoved forward, watch Agent Wade drag the chair out with his foot, and I sit down. The bargain bucket is dumped unceremoniously on the table in front of me. Agent Wade crosses to the sofa and slumps down, the gun aimed at me the whole time.

He reaches for his briefcase, searches around, and then produces a tiny handheld tape recorder—one of those things businessmen recite into while they sit at their desks trying to look important enough to keep their jobs. Agent Wade sets the recorder on the coffee table, presses "record," and glances up at me. "I'll type it up later."

"Type what up?"

"Your confession."

I'm not altogether sure that I understand. Agent Wade sees this and spells it out, his words pronounced slowly and definitely. They hit home, as if he were jabbing me in the chest with them.

"I want to hear it all. Every little thing. Don't leave a word out. Just tell me—in your own time—how and why you became the Kentucky Killer."

I have met many crazy people over the last four years, but Agent Wade beats them all hands down.

"What!?" I almost laugh, this is so ridiculous.

"In your own time, Dougie."

My mind starts to clear, and I suddenly see it all. "Oh . . . I get it now. You're running interference. Pinning it on me to give you some breathing space. Well, I'm not saying a word."

The gun is raised, the trigger eased back. "Dougie . . ."

"Uh-uh." I shake my head, meaning what I say. "Uh-uh."

"I'll shoot your balls off. One at a time."

I instantly stop shaking my head. "What do you want me to say?"

"Just start from the beginning."

"You'd better tell me when that is, then."

Agent Wade reaches across, angrily swipes the recorder from the coffee table, switches off the record button, rewinds, and starts all over again. "For chrissakes, Dougie!"

"What?"

"Just tell the damn story!"

"You want me to make it up, is that it?"

"I want you to tell me what happened. How it started, why it started, how come you've stayed free for so long. A guy like you can barely tie his shoelaces, so how the hell you managed it I really don't know."

I think I'm missing something. There's a piece of the jigsaw that disintegrated before I could even get the box open. "You're making a big mistake here. I'm not the Kentucky Killer."

Agent Wade's eyes blaze with exasperation. "Dougie, you killed James Mason and stuck a carton over his head. You killed Myrna Loy and Chuck Norris and stuck cartons over their heads. You killed two Mexicans and stuck cartons on them as well. You posted ads in the paper, and you turned up at the Club the night KK said he would. Only no one knew it was you. I should have guessed when you got so wound up about not contacting KK. Should have known I was getting too close for comfort. You pretend to be this dumb-ass jerk-off, but I know better. It took me some time to cut through that low-rent personality of yours, but I got there in the end. So come on, Dougie, just share it with me, huh?"

"You've got the wrong guy."

"Why'd you kill the members? Is it because you want to be the only one? Or is it that they mess it up for you, detract from your glorious crusade? Maybe they were just plain stupid and irritated you—a brilliant killer like you lumbered with trash like that."

I'm not a psychiatrist, but anyone could see what's wrong with Agent Wade. "It's a split personality thing, right?"

"Huh?" Agent Wade loses focus for a second.

"Schizophrenia. That's what it is. You're schizoid, yeah?"

Agent Wade looks at me with a deep frown. "We're talking about you here, not me."

"But are we, really?" I say in my best psychiatrist manner.

"Dougie, this gun is loaded." Agent Wade has heard enough, aims straight at my groin, but I'm on a roll now.

"Maybe it's the chicken, maybe they put something in the secret recipe that you're allergic to. You should have tests."

Agent Wade wearily snatches the recorder, rewinds the tape, and starts again. He sets down the recorder with a loud bang and glares at me, teeth gritted. "Last chance, Dougie. You can do it with balls or without. It's your call."

I try my best to put myself in the shoes of the Kentucky Killer for a moment. I scratch around inside my brain, trying to pinpoint the things I know about him so that I can reel it off and then be done with it all. The bargain bucket sits there, Colonel Sanders's grinning face mocking me. I stare hard at the face—so hard, in fact, that he turns into Santa Claus and I hear the thud of his body as he jumps down my chimney and lands hard in the grate.

"It was Mom. She made me do it."

The voice doesn't belong to me. I know this because I'm not a woman, and this particularly sardonic voice definitely belongs to someone of the opposite sex.

"Mommy, Mommy, Mommy . . . ," the voice sneers in contempt.

I turn.

Betty stands in my bedroom doorway, looking more beautiful then ever. A vision.

I smile broadly, knowing I'm looking at an angel, understanding that there is life after death, and certainly after this amount of death, heaven has to be teeming with life.

"Betty . . ."

"Hi, Dougie."

She floats toward me, moving with grace and elegance, skipping past the prostrate body of Agent Wade as he lies on the floor, a pool of blood spreading like the Dark Angel's crimson wings around him. Betty removes a glinting silver rod of truth from his back and brings it up, wiping a liar's stain from it.

"One bargain bucket and two heads. Not a good equation."

Even in death she retains that strong canine aroma, and it wafts around me, seasoning my very existence.

"I tried to save you, Betty. I did, I swear it."

"And I saved you, Dougie. Till last."

I look up to find that Betty's eyes are now hazel, her hair is much shorter, and she wears very little makeup. She looks like she has been under a tanning bed too long, as she is now as brown as a cup of milky coffee. I figure heaven must be closer to the sun, which actually makes a lot of sense.

"You did me proud, Dougie. Wading through those pieces of garbage like a guilt-free lumberjack in a rain forest." Betty lights a cigarette, inhales deeply. "Like what I did to your bedroom, by the way?"

I'm fascinated, because Betty has cotton wool wedged into her mouth to make her cheeks look plumper. Maybe she's been eating lumps of cloud.

"I heard about the Club from Tony. He loved it so much, he was busting a gut to tell me how great it was. I had to join. But there was that weird thing about KK. No Kentucky Killer, thank you very much. I kept asking him how come KK couldn't join, but he said it just wouldn't work out. I figured he was scared KK would make him look small time, maybe even take over the chairmanship. So I invented this new killer—little prim and proper Betty."

Agent Wade groans, tries to raise his head. Betty glances at him, tuts to herself. "That was something I hadn't counted on. A federal agent, of all people. You never told me about him, Dougie."

"I was too embarrassed. Imagine what the Club would've said."

"That fucking Club. How dare they not invite me! There you all are, having this great time together, and there I am, lonely as hell, wishing there was someone I could talk to, someone who would understand me and appreciate my efforts. All I wanted was to be one of the gang."

Betty's cigarette smoke swirls around me, hypnotizing me, tendrils dancing like snakes.

"But then I thought, If the Club doesn't want me, then I don't want the Club. And boy, was I gonna make them pay. Course, soon as I realized what you were doing, I figured what the hell, let midget britches do it for me." Betty's voice has a rancorous edge that I'd never detected before. "I tried my best to keep you out of the shit. Jumping in every chance I got to stop you from shooting yourself in the foot. Though I thought long and hard about letting them get you after what you put me through in that motel with those Mexicans. I soon got my own back on them, though."

I look again at Betty, staring harder at her, seeing her pale flesh, watching her chest rise and fall with her breath. There's something almost human about her.

"Have to admit, killing Jimmy and the sign language love-birds was unavoidable. Couldn't let you have all the fun."

Finally it sinks in.

Betty's not dead!

She's alive, and she's standing here, right in front of me, so close I could reach out and touch her.

"He didn't get you! Agent Wade didn't kill you."

My hand reaches for Betty, and my fingertips brush the soft skin of her face. She's warm.

"Tony's dead, Betty." I say this gently, brushing a strand of hair from Betty's eye. "He's not coming back."

"Saved me a job, I guess."

"Dougie . . ." Agent Wade starts to crawl toward me, pulling himself onto his elbows, doing his level best to get to me.

Betty fishes a sheet of paper and a small staple gun out of her jacket pocket. "Real handy you had a typewriter."

"Dougie . . ." Agent Wade miraculously raises himself higher, only to get a savage boot in the face from Betty that sends him onto his side, his neck jerking back so hard that for a minute I think she's broken it.

"I'm talking here!"

Betty positions the typed note against my forehead, lines it up so that it sits squarely, and reaches for the staple gun.

"Don't move now, Dougie. . . ."

The staple gun is pressed against my forehead, awaiting Betty's downward pressure.

"Know why I kill like this?"

I offer a faint shrug, careful not to move my head for fear of ruining Betty's carefully positioned note. "Your mom?"

"Clever boy, Dougie. You got a brain in there after all."

"To be honest, it's always the mom."

Betty is about to staple the sheet to my forehead when she suddenly has her feet dragged from under her. She slides down, smashes her chin on the edge of the table, and falls toward Agent Wade, who grips her ankles with all his might.

"The gun, Dougie! It fell under the sofa," Agent Wade screams at me before Betty turns and kicks hard at him. But he hangs on for grim death, and at long last I get the chance to do something right for once in my life. I take a run and dive for Agent Wade's gun, skidding along the carpet, my arm snaking under the bolted-down sofa, my hand closing on the fallen revolver, fingers reaching for it, stretching, grasping, knowing that if I was just a couple of inches taller, I'd have it.

Betty kicks hard at Agent Wade, manages finally to get free of his grip.

But I am tall, I know I am. I'm bigger than everyone thinks, I know it.

My fingers inch along under the sofa, my arm is almost out of its socket as I stretch as far as I can.

Betty grabs her knife and comes for me. "Bye, Dougie."

I'm bigger than anyone. I tower over people; my shadow blots out skyscrapers. They've had me wrong all these years.

I Am Someone.

Betty's knife flashes through the air, its razor tip driving toward my heart. The bullets get home first, though—blowing Betty to kingdom come in the process.

AMERICAN HERO

T HE TYPED NOTE READS:

Number 303.

Betty couldn't even come up with a secret recipe for me. Just a stupid number, making like I was a statistic instead of the hero I am.

I wanted to bury Agent Wade, but there was no real way of doing it without attracting a lot of attention. Instead I laid him on the sofa, switched on the television—some Randolph Scott movie, where he aims his weapon at seminaked Indians—and cupped his arm around the empty KFC bucket. Couch potato heaven. Betty I dragged into the washroom and dumped there. I don't really know why, but I just didn't want her sharing the same room as Agent Wade. She didn't deserve to.

I have finally found the security camera still, the photo of me killing Errol Flynn. It was wedged under the loose tiles in my kitchen, the same tiles that I myself had tried to uproot in my desire to escape Agent Wade all of two months ago now. As I look at the photo again, I realize it is nearly impossible to make out anything at all—it looks more like a picture of E.T. poking his long red finger into a sack with a bra wrapped round it—but just for good measure I tear the photo into tiny pieces and dump them into the waste disposal. I feel like a free man.

A new man.

GERONIMO

EPILOGUE:
FEDERAL AGENT

So there you have it. My story. At least the story so far. Chicago's just one of many places I intend to visit. I drive Agent's Wade car everywhere now, flash his shield, and get free parking practically anywhere I want to. Even in spaces reserved for the disabled. In fact, I often lie in wait as they approach their allotted parking spaces, only to floor the accelerator and dart in right in front of them. Waving the FBI badge in their angry, righteous faces has become one of my all-time favorite gags.

I have changed my name again. Douglas Fairbanks Jr. is no more. I am now called something else, and I think it is perfectly suited to my new mission in life.

Only yesterday I knocked on the door of someone I thought could develop into a serial killer, given time. The woman, easily well into her sixties—you're never too old, is my motto—and lame, peered at me with a real look of what could only be called guilt. I flashed the FBI badge at her. "Hi, I just thought it fair to warn you that I know what you are planning to do. Your murderous intentions have been noted, so take heed. Because I am watching you."

"Whassat you say? You'll have to speak up. . . ."

"Make one wrong move and I will be in your face faster than you can say Elizabeth Taylor."

The woman tried her best, but there was no way I was going to let her fool me, and I think she knows that now. When you've spent the amount of time with skillers that I have, spotting one is like second nature.

I have decided to pay a visit to every single would-be serial killer I can find. I am going to warn them all that I am on their case. Sitting in the trunk is Agent Wade's typewriter, and every month I make out a report and send it to FBI headquarters at Quantico, just to let them know that I'm out there keeping this country safe. I was born for this life.

I switch off Agent Wade's mini tape recorder. All this talking has made me thirsty, and I take a long, refreshing sip of Bud. I sit back in the two-man booth where—in what feels like another life—Roger and Rock sat. I glance over to the corner of the room where the Club first met.

I can almost see cigarette smoke rising in clouds to the ceiling. Familiar faces appear, laughter erupts, there's a scuffle, hand gestures to a waitress, someone does a magic trick. I catch snatches of dialogue from voices I will probably never forget.

"I kill, therefore I am."

"Hey, Larry's got a new tie. Someone's birthday, by any chance?"

"Sweet Jesus, that bitch was askin' for it. Beggin' me, 'Do it, do it, do it.'"

"It's in his kiss, that's what it is."

"I turn people to stone. Not literally, you understand, but I kinda replace their blood with plaster of paris. My wife thinks I'm at pottery class."

"Hey, Dougie . . ."

"Yo, Dougie . . . big man. Hey, good to see you."

"Dougie, over here . . . saved you a seat."

"Dougie . . . this Club would be nothing without you."

"Dougie . . ."

"Yo there, Doug . . ."

"Dougie's here! Hey, everyone! Dougie's here! The fun starts now, folks."

"Dougie, you are hilarious. . . . You kill me, you really do."

A waitress steps into my view and breaks my concentration. The voices and faces fade away, and the grin on my lips slowly shrinks. I let my eyes rise the length of the waitress's body and meet her jade green eyes. She smiles and awaits my order, pad and pen ready. I glance at the menu, trying to find something remotely appetizing. I eventually close the menu and hand it back to the green-eyed waitress.

"I, uh . . . I guess I'm not hungry."

"Nothing there takes your fancy?"

"I'm a fast-food guy at heart."

"Suit yourself."

The waitress shrugs, collects the menu from me, and turns to go, but I suddenly catch her arm, taking her by surprise. I swear to God, there's something about her.

"Hey—hands off!"

Jesus Christ, they're everywhere.

Green-Eyes glares at me as I flip out my ID and shove it under her nose. "Federal agent Kennet Wade. Got something you want to tell me?"

I go for my gun.

ACKNOWLEDGMENTS

First and foremost, huge thanks to Barbara J. Zitwer and Valerie Hoskins. Their matchless determination and belief made this book possible. To my great dad, Brian, and my lovely mum, Beryl, who made me possible. To my equally lovely sister, Mandy, and brother, Tim, who always thought this was possible. And to Rachel, Alexa, Naomi, and Milo—who are the best kids possible. Also to Karen Kosztolnyik for her insight and creativity and to Rebecca Watson for being Rebecca Watson.